For Chris

Chapter One

WAITING TO UNFURL

• WILL •

It was her shoulders I missed most. Lame. I know. Even when we were together, it had been months since she'd worn those little tops girls have with no sleeves. But when I thought of Sam 'til I could almost feel the ache of her not beside me, I remembered her shoulders. Not hidden and winter-pale. 'Cause in my memory, in my dreams just before I woke up six thousand miles too far away, I saw Sam's shoulders. Brown in the sun, arms pumping hard. And I'd see those bones—shoulder blades—and they'd look like tiny wing-buds. Nested, just waiting to unfurl.

Man, I missed her.

1

Chapter Two

CONTINENTAL DRIFT

• SAM •

Just before midnight, I slipped outside. The house had grown intolerably hot. Plus I didn't think I could face having to fake-smile with my sparkling apple cider flute raised high for the New Year's count-down.

I wanted Will.

I wanted his kiss as the clock turned to midnight. I didn't want him six-thousand miles away. Did the continents, I wondered, feel lonely for each other as they drifted apart eons ago? My heart hurt to imagine it.

I tried to think what Will would be doing now. Probably sitting down for breakfast: croissants and coffee thick as mud. I pulled my sweater tighter around my shoulders and tried to find constellations while the count down to the New Year began. *Ten, nine*—was that

Cassiopeia? *Eight, seven, six*—that one had to be Orion. *Five, four, three*—could Will see Orion in France, or were the stars different there? *Two*—the tears began. *One.*

Happy New Year.

I miss you, Will.

Chapter Three

GROUND HOG'S EVE

• SAM •

After watching me mope around for the month of January, Sylvia insisted we throw a party.

"Chrétien needs this," she said, sitting on the edge of my bed. "You said he was having a hard time making friends."

"*Christian*," I reminded her. "Gwyn says *Chrétien* sounded like 'cretin.'"

"Right, right." Sylvia nodded. "Let's throw *Christian* a party, so everyone can get to know him."

I knew why Syl wanted a party. She hoped to snap me out of my morose state.

"You want to help him fit in, right?" she asked.

Boy, did I ever. It wasn't like I could tell the truth about his sometimes-odd behavior. "*This is Christian, he's from the seventeenth-century, where they had different manners than we have."*

We'd told everyone he was a French exchange student. I couldn't go around sharing that he was my personal bodyguard assigned to me by a six-hundred-year-old Frenchman. That his job was to assist in protecting me from Girard Helmann, head of Geneses Corporation. That Helmann was a Neo-Nazi who wanted to kidnap me because I could turn invisible.

Sylvia smiled at me and reached over to tuck a stray hair behind my ear. "Plus, Sammy, honestly, you need to make a little more of an effort here, sweetie. Your dad's getting worried."

I reached over to hug my step-mom. "I just miss Will," I said, letting a few tears squeeze out. "But I'll be fine."

She was right, though, about me making an effort. My dad was the reason I'd come back from France instead of disappearing with Will. Dad had lost enough when Mom died.

"Okay, then," said Syl, releasing me. "We're having a Ground Hog's Eve party next weekend."

"Ground Hog's 'Eve'?" I laughed as I said it.

"See? You're laughing," she said. "My evil plan is working!"

We stuffed the kitchen fridge and the fridge in the garage and still had to ask Bridget to store the items

Sylvia ordered from the Las Abuelitas Bakery Café. Good thing, too.

Everyone was turning up for our Ground Hog's Eve party.

Gwyn arrived early with her long-suffering mother, Bridget Li, and the bakery goodies. "Next Ground Hog's Eve, *I'm* throwing the party for you, Christian. And it'll be *private*."

As she edged beside him, he flushed.

"Give me some sugar, sugar," she said, aiming her cheek toward his lips. "It's how you say hi in France, right?"

"Gwyn," I murmured.

"What?" she said, collecting her kisses. "Christian doesn't mind."

"Uh-oh," said Sylvia. "I said 'Welcome, *Chrétien*' when I called in the cake!"

Gwyn smiled. "Already taken care of."

Bridget Li nodded in agreement.

As Sylvia changed the banner to read "Christian" instead of "Chrétien," he whispered to me, "I have forgotten. What is your quaint form of '*Je suis ravi de faire votre connaissance*'?" (I'm ravished to make your acquaintance.)

I sighed. "It's 'hello,'" I replied. "Or 'hey,' if you're feeling less formal."

Like that would ever happen. I'd given up trying to cure his habit of bowing in the direction of anyone to whom he received an introduction. At least he'd stopped taking women's hands to kiss the air an inch above them.

"I shall remember to perform only the most abbreviated form of obeisance," he said, eyes sad, like it caused him physical pain to give up his deep bows.

Gwyn was the one who thought to teach Christian a dance step just before guests arrived.

"Let's see you dance," she'd said, arms folded.

"What manner of dancing?" he asked.

"Uh, something simple. Peasant-y," replied Gwyn.

"A *contra-dance*," he said, nodding. "Country-dance, you say in English."

He launched into something that looked like it came out of a ballet Sylvia had taken us to see in Fresno.

"No, no, no, no," moaned Gwyn. "Please! You don't want to look like that." She switched her voice to a low murmur. "Although it would certainly cut down on the female competition if you did."

Gwyn showed him something called The Serpent which she said had been big in LA a year ago. "No one will have heard of it here—they'll think it's from France." She never lost a chance to poke fun at our small town even though she loved Las Abs.

"Start here," Gwyn said, indicating her ankles, "And snake up a slow roll through your calves, hips, waist, chest—good! That's really good." She turned to me. "You better have a fire extinguisher handy, 'cause that boy is hot."

Before anyone else arrived, Gwyn had him doing The Serpent like he'd known it all his life. I stared. It was like he'd turned into rock-star-Christian sending seductive messages with every wave of his body. Which was annoying, because I was growing to care for him, but not in *that* way. I blinked and shook my head and thankfully, he turned back into just-Christian. I walked away to help Sylvia set drinks outside in coolers, somewhat redundant in February in the central California foothills.

As people started arriving, introductions became my job although I would have preferred to disappear. The things I do for love of my step-mom. "This is Christian. He's a cousin of Will and Mickie Baker and while we were in France, our two families cooked up a student-exchange."

Smile. Make an effort, I reminded myself, knowing my dad would be watching. I didn't want him to worry.

The party was a success. The weather was mild for February, meaning it hovered just *above* instead of just *below* freezing. Most of my classmates crowded out on the deck to dance. From inside, I watched my French bodyguard snake-dancing for all he was worth with four or five girls trying to grab a piece of his beef-cake.

I wiggled fingers at Christian, a tiny wave. He smiled back. Leaning my face against the sliding glass door, I thought of the missing boy I loved. A tear traced the curve of my cheek and I turned aside.

Gwyn had grabbed the karaoke microphone to do a New Year's-style countdown to midnight for Ground Hog's Day. Too late, she realized this prevented her from actually *kissing* Christian once the clock ticked down. On the stroke of midnight, one of the cheerleaders captured Christian in a lip-lock that looked deadly. Gwyn glared at them, her arms crossed, murderous intent written into her tight, hard mouth.

I smiled and shook my head. No way was Christian ever going to go out with her, because that would involve him leaving my side. Something he refused to do.

By two in the morning, everyone had gone home. Dad said clean-up could wait 'til the sun rose. I fell into bed but I didn't feel tired. Between the ache that was Will's absence and the change in time zones from France to California, I hadn't been sleeping well for a month.

Plus, Christian's duties included standing guard over me by night (invisibly) which I seriously dare anyone to be all "whatever" about. It felt weird having him there even if I couldn't see him. Officially, he slept downstairs in the spare room. He wouldn't take the guest room on the second floor.

"It would be unseemly for me to occupy the same floor of the *maison* as your virgin daughter," he'd said to my dad.

Sylvia had pretended to sneeze into her napkin to hide a fit of giggles. My dad had kept a straight face and nodded his agreement. I'd fixed my eyes on a spot on the kitchen ceiling, internally considering my dad's response should he find out the truth—that Christian spent every night *chez moi*—in my room.

Often, as I drifted to sleep after hours of staring out my window, I thought I heard echoes of a song: sad, and in French; or of chanting, in Latin. I hadn't asked Christian about the sad song, but when I mentioned the chanting, he admitted it was him.

"I celebrate the hours, after the fashion of a priest," he said.

Meaning he prayed seven times a day, including the middle of the night, using a scripted set of Psalms and prayers in Latin. I remembered Sir Walter saying Christian's ability to hear thoughts exceeded even his own. Maybe it was the same with his ability to "broadcast" his thoughts.

Christian and I had discussed this ability a few times.

"You carry the blood of the de Rochefort's in your veins," Christian had told me. "As do I. You and I will most likely hear one another's thoughts from time to time, especially when invisible."

"Great," I'd said.

"Your ability will strengthen, the more it is exercised," said Christian.

I'd nodded, not sure I wanted to grow this particular muscle any bigger. It made for very noisy nights.

I sighed, rolling over in bed so that I faced my wall instead of the space I knew Christian inhabited invisibly. Maybe I wouldn't "hear" him as well if I turned away. But every time my mind relaxed, I caught echoes of his song.

I flipped back around, my legs tangling in covers, and read 4:06 AM on my clock. I considered asking him to maybe keep it down when I felt something icy pass over me. My eyes opened in time for me to see a light-haired man materializing beside me.

It wasn't Christian.

As I drew breath to scream for help, the stranger slapped one hand over my open mouth and jabbed a needle in me with the other hand.

Excerpted from the personal diary of Girard L'Inferne.

Circa 1985

The error, I begin to see, lay not so much in the aims I set for my children in the 1930's, but rather in the methodology which I employed to gain those ends. Half a century ago, I set my mind to the creation of soldiers who could endure deprivation, who were capable of survival, of self-denial, even. And I thought to ensure their loyalty to me by utilizing methods shown effective. Their loyalty I had—for a time. For an exceptionally long time, by any merely human standards.

But I see now, as the twentieth century draws to a close, that I merely postponed the time when they would begin to turn against me to gain their own selfish ends. I saw self-serving behavior as a desirable goal. I preserved the lives of those who showed themselves capable of such behavior. And now I reap the bitter fruit as, one by one, they turn from serving me to serving their own desires.

They even believe me blind to this. But children, your Father sees everything. Have you forgotten this most essential lesson?

Chapter Four

SALAAM

• WILL •

Putting everything down on paper was Mick's idea. I think she just got sick of watching me stare off into space all the time.

"Will, hon," said my sister, "You're doing it again."

I turned to see what Mick wanted. "What? I'm not doing anything."

"Duh. And you need to stop. Now." She shifted her voice from demanding to pleading. "Get up and exercise, okay?"

"Someone made running a felony," I reminded her. She'd been extra cautious the last couple weeks in Paris.

"Fine. So read a book or a newspaper or something."

I rose from the couch and crossed to the table by the window where stacks of books awaited. It wasn't the first or last time I tried distracting myself with a book. Sir Walter provided me with plenty. But before long, my eyes wouldn't be on the pages anymore 'cause I couldn't stop thinking about Sam.

Leaning my forehead against a cold pane of glass, I thought about our phone conversation, early this morning.

Sam had sounded so close. Like she was next door.

We'd talked a few minutes in a stilted "code," passing information back and forth. *No, Sir Walter hadn't made any new 'friends'*—code for forming alliances against Helmann. *No, we still didn't know when 'winter' might arrive*—code for Helmann's apocalyptic slaughter of humanity.

No, I didn't know how I was going to survive on two phone calls a month with the girl who'd taken my heart with her when she left.

"How's school going?" I'd asked next, trying to sound caring. When all I really felt was abandoned.

"It's okay," she said. "We're throwing Christian a party tonight, to help him fit in."

"Fitting in's good," I said.

"Yeah," she said. "Will? I miss you so bad. It's like a part of me got left back in France."

I could hear her sniffling, maybe crying.

"The best part of me," she said in a whisper.

I closed my eyes and it was like I could feel her breath all warm on my face, the way it would feel if she were really here, whispering to me.

"Close your eyes," I said. "You're here with me." And I described how Paris looked that morning. How the sky went all pink around the edges. How the soaring buildings cast these chocolate-brown shadows along the avenue below me. How the birds were trying to convince spring to show up.

We were both silent for a minute, listening to one another's breaths.

"Thanks," she said at last, in a voice so sad it cracked my heart into tiny pieces.

We'd hung up feeling sadder and emptier than ever.

I pushed back from the pane of glass, sighing deeply.

"Will," said my sister.

"I'm fine." A complete lie. "Totally fine."

She looked at me from under furrowed brows. "I think I know fine when I see it. Fine involves a healthy appetite. And an interest in basketball stats. And telling your sister you're going to do dangerous things."

I dragged my sneaker across the floor, listening to the low squeak it made on the polished wood.

"How 'bout you open the book in your hands?" asked my sister.

I shoved my copy of *Chanson de Roland* her direction. "You read it. That way you can't watch me."

"It's in French, dweeb."

"Oh. Right." I reached for the stack of books in English. Ones I'd already tried. Ones that couldn't hold my interest either these days. I handed her the one on top. "English. Knock yourself out."

She pushed the book back across the table towards me. "I'm not the one who needs to snap out of it." She lowered her voice and muttered. "Plus I don't *need* a history book living with the History Channel incarnate."

I wasn't sure if she meant me—for my love of history—or Sir Walter—for his ancient years. But the lowered voice probably indicated she meant him. If she wanted to insult me, she usually spoke louder, so I'd catch it.

Outside, the midday sky was trying to decide if it wanted to rain or not.

"That's it," Mick said, rising and shoving her arms through jacket sleeves. "Come on. We're going shopping."

I gave her a tired look that said *you-don't-really-expect-me-to-come-along.*

"You're coming. Get off your lazy *derrière*, little brother. I can't speak the language here. I need you."

"*Derrière*'s French," I said, not moving.

She growled. "Get up and put on your jacket or I start kicking your *derrière* out the door." She waited for me to make a move, which I didn't. "Please?"

I grunted and rose, pulling my jacket on just as Sir Walter materialized on our side of the front door.

Immediately, I sank back into the chair by the window. "Sir Walter, Mick wants to pick something up at the store. Would you mind going and translating for her? I was hoping to catch up on my reading here." I waved my copy of *Chanson de Roland*.

Our grey-haired friend smiled at me. "But of course. I should be glad of the fresh air, having spent the entire morning apart from my flesh. *Mademoiselle?*" He opened the door, gallantly indicating with a raised arm that she precede him.

She shot me a sad glance and sighed. Then she left with Sir Walter.

I returned to staring out the window, thinking about Sam.

Mickie re-opened the door and stuck her head in. "You'd better not be sitting there like that when I get back." The door slammed shut.

Sometime later, my stomach growled at me, a rendition of *feed me now*. It had probably been a couple hours since lunch. Hard to say, though, since I didn't have a cell on me anymore. "Too dangerous, too easy to trace," according to Sir Walter.

The door of our Parisian apartment flew open. Mickie laughed at something Sir Walter had said. I loved how he could put her in a better mood. Well, when she wasn't arguing with him.

I grabbed *Chanson de Roland* and pretended to read.

"I *knew* it!" shouted my sister. "Don't bother with the pretending. You've been staring out the window the past two hours, haven't you?" She didn't wait for my answer. "Well, those days are *over*, Mister."

Her boots clomped across the shiny wood floor. She pulled something blue out of a bag and thumped it in front of me, grinning.

"Another book?" I asked.

"No, idiot-boy. It's *blank*." She crossed her arms as if in triumph.

"You bought us a blank book?"

She shook her head and sighed. "Brain-damaged. That's the only explanation. I bought *you* a blank book so you can write down all your depressing thoughts instead of thinking the same thing over and over." She mussed my hair and reached into her bag, pulling out a stupid-looking pen that was maybe supposed to be a quill. "Look! I found you an authentic feather pen!" She smiled, clearly delighted with herself.

I handed the pen back to her. "It's just a ball-point pen glued to a feather, Mick."

Her face fell. "I thought you'd like it. It's historical."

A tsunami of guilt washed over me. "It's . . . amazing. The whole idea is . . . brilliant, Mick. Really."

A tiny smile tugged at one corner of her mouth. "You'll use it?"

"Of course I will," I promised. "There's a fine tradition of chameleons keeping journals. I should have thought of it myself."

She frowned. "Oh. Yuck. I didn't think of Helmann and his journals."

The tsunami struck again, with double force. "Hey, I was joking. You're the best sister ever. This is exactly what I need to stop staring at the sky all day." Which was a total lie. What I needed was Sam.

Something in my guts knotted at the thought of her name. I ignored it. Shoved it down to my toes. "I'll use it every day. Promise."

Idiot, said a voice inside.

But my sister smiled and hugged me, and the waters of guilt receded.

Sir Walter had busied himself perusing *Chanson de Roland*. He turned a page, the expression on his face one of intense interest.

"So what's on the menu today?" asked Mickie.

"Hummus, I think. And perhaps falafel," said Sir Walter, tapping the cover of *Chanson de Roland*. "I'm feeling inspired by this tale of valorous Arabs."

"I didn't mean *literally*," said Mick. "I just meant, like, what are we going to do today to make Helmann's life more difficult than it was yesterday?"

Sir Walter did his little thing of ignoring an immediate question in favor of moving ahead with his own agenda. "Do you know, if not for Monsieur Roland, we would all perhaps dine daily upon such delicacies of the Middle East."

Mick covered her eyes with one hand and murmured, "Here-we-go-again-with-the-history."

"Will," said Sir Walter. "I believe you need exercise."

Mick dropped her hand from her eyes and flicked a glance my way. "Badly."

"We shall set forth in search of dinner: a dinner in honor of the Mohammedans who fought the noble *chevalier* Roland," said Sir Walter.

"I think I'll just nap on the couch 'til you get back," said Mickie.

I winked at her—she wasn't up for a walk with me and Sir Walter discussing the finer points of a battle fought nine centuries ago.

"Let's go," I said.

We stepped out and down a set of stairs. Outside, the weather threatened rain, but couldn't quite work itself up to it. Instead, it felt like the sky was spitting on us.

"We shall need to leave the elegance of Paris' eighth *arrondissement* to find hummus worth eating," said Sir Walter. Our French friend had set us up in some really sweet digs.

"So where do you get good hummus?" I asked, heading automatically for the Métro.

"We journey to the *banlieues* today. To Clichy-sous-Bois which is not reachable by Métro or RER train." Sir Walter held out an arm to stop me from taking the stairs to the subway. "And considering we have promised your sister an evening meal, I believe we should travel more swiftly than would be possible by city transportation."

Sir Walter veered us into an alley that led into a windowless courtyard. He extended a hand so we could keep track of each other while we rippled. "To be honest, young Will, I seek more than just hummus. And it lies within the troubled *ville* we visit today."

As we prepared to ripple, I eyed Sir Walter out of the corner of my peripheral vision.

"Will?" he said.

"Yeah?"

"You are standing in a pose that puts me in mind of one who prepares for a race."

I felt the blood rushing to my cheeks. I'd been doing this little tally with me and Sir Walter. Who could ripple fastest. He always won.

"Yeah, okay. Maybe I'm racing you," I said.

"Are you indeed? And to what end?"

I tapped my shoe along a crack in the cement. "Something's been bugging me. Ever since a couple weeks ago when you dodged Helga's bullet. You know, in the cave? And I *didn't.*" I had the scar to prove her bullet had been faster than me. "So I've been trying to speed up. I mean, I was always way faster than Sam, but you make me look like I'm standing still."

"I see," said my bearded friend.

"I *should* have been able to grab her when those dudes showed up at the Well of Juno with guns. But I was freaked that a speeding bullet would beat me. Which it did. And it bugs the crap out of me."

Sir Walter nodded solemnly.

"And I noticed you sent your son Chrétien to protect Sam, so I'm guessing he's like some speed-demon, too, or you would have let me go, right?"

"Your sister would not have consented to your leaving," interrupted Sir Walter. "Nor would you have hurt her by leaving without her consent."

"Hmmph." I knew he was right, and it totally irked me that I cared so much about Mick. Right then, I missed Sam so much it hurt to breathe. "You didn't answer my question. Is speed the reason you sent Chrétien and not me?"

"Of course not," said Sir Walter. "You are foolish to frustrate yourself with these comparisons."

I dropped my eyes and my voice. "I should have saved her. I should have been able to and I couldn't."

Sir Walter pulled his hand from mine and placed it instead upon my shoulder. "My dear young man, you are not the only one who failed to carry Sam to safety at that moment. Hear me when I say this: I judged it too close to call, whether or not I could reach her—and safety—prior to one of us being shot. My dear Will, I chose to stand my ground just as you did. Do not doubt your choice.

"In truth, Will, you are very nearly as fast as either Chrétien or myself. And perhaps, if you apply yourself, you can match our ability in changing form swiftly."

He gave me two pointers on getting away fast: don't hold any tension in your body and imagine you're an arrow in flight. The arrow thing just messed me up worse. But the suggestion to relax was useful. I imagined tension as something pouring out of my body, and twice, I beat Sir Walter.

"And now, my swift young friend," said Sir Walter, "I believe your sister awaits her dinner."

My stomach gurgled like a broken garbage-disposal. "She's not alone," I said as we grasped arms and rippled.

I beat him that time.

Sir Walter pretty much knew Paris like I knew the layout of Las Abs High. Locker over here, track that way, Mr. Polwen's six-period biology over there. So the old guy just *zoomed* through town with me in tow getting us to Clichy-sous-Bois. I won't lie, it wasn't as pretty as the part of town he kept an apartment in. Maybe it used to look better. Or maybe not. I mean, the buildings appeared pretty modern, but they looked so *old* somehow. Run down. There were a handful of restaurants, small hole-in-the-walls like you'd see anywhere in Paris, but featuring cuisines like *Turque* or *d'Afrique*. I saw some graffiti written in flowing lines not from the alphabet I knew.

What do you see? asked Sir Walter from inside my head.

I wrote back on an imagined yellow note-pad. *Teeny restaurants. Like the Latin Quarter. And a bunch of freaking tall buildings.*

One of those tall buildings is today my concern, he said.

I'd tried the talking-in-your-head thing, but I couldn't get it. Sir Walter never heard a single thing I said, so I'd given up and gone back to writing my thoughts using a yellow note-pad and pencil, like I'd done with Sam.

Okay, I wrote. *Which one?*

Sir Walter hummed under his breath (yeah, I could hear that in my head, too) and began moving ahead and to our right. We approached what looked like a crop of tall buildings, all smooshed in close to one another. The one Sir Walter wanted sat in the middle. It looked totally abandoned; the doors all sealed shut—some with wrought-iron gates to drive the point home.

Invisibly, we slipped inside.

Let us rise to the première étage, said Sir Walter—the first floor, which in France is on the second floor for some weird reason. Like no one in France noticed they already had a floor *one*.

Sir Walter made us practice—well, he made *me* practice—walking up through the air to get to the second floor. He didn't need any practice as he'd been doing this for centuries. Sam and I had only just learned it was possible. To be honest, it kind of freaked me out, looking down and seeing all that air beneath my feet. But I held off writing him about it. He'd already admitted he had a thing with heights, so it might have been a little cruel to carry on a conversation about how my stomach twisted all funny when I looked down. We wriggled our way up through the ceiling like we were made of vapor.

What does your sense of smell tell you? asked Sir Walter.

Maybe he had me confused with Sam. She could smell anything she passed through. *Nothing.* I wrote back. Chalk that up as one more thing I'd have to work on.

I catch the odors of abandon, said my friend. *The building has remained empty for some time, but the decay has not yet completed. Believe me, to lack the ability to detect scent: it can be a mercy.*

I could believe that easy enough. Some of the places Mick and I lived right after Mom died totally reeked from leftover trash.

We cruised through each of the rooms on this level. Moving slowly, with our free hands extended, we zig-zagged along each floor, passing through the walls dividing the levels into apartment or office-size rooms. It was a bit like being in the world's longest queue to ride an attraction at Disneyland. Only without the ride at the end.

I didn't know what we were looking for, exactly, and I'm not clear Sir Walter did either. I just felt glad Geneses had picked the smallest, shortest building on the block, 'cause this was pretty much the most boring thing I'd done in a really boring week.

There's nothing here, I wrote as we looped back and forth along the third floor.

Nothing yet, agreed Sir Walter.

Unless you count moldy carpets, I wrote. *Maybe he's developing some super-germ to take over the world.*

Sir Walter didn't reply. Man, I was going out of my mind with boredom. After a tour of the fourth and final floor, he spoke again.

Perhaps we have arrived too early. This building is among the most recent of my cousin's numerous acquisitions. We should have begun our investigations with a building he has controlled for a longer period of time, said Sir Walter.

I can hardly wait, I wrote back.

Truly? said Sir Walter. *Myself, I find this most tedious.*

I guess sarcasm didn't translate so well on the written page.

He spoke again. *It is time to come solid and find some of the remarkable food which we promised to your sister.*

After drifting back down through the floors, we exited and found a location blocked from view on all sides to ripple solid. Hunger ripped through my stomach as soon as my body solidified. A few streets over, Sir Walter bought five orders of hummus, pita bread, and falafel. Before leaving, he did one of his little bows except with his hand on his forehead saying, "*Salaam,*" to the owner instead of "*Au Revoir.*"

I begged a couple of bites off him before we rippled to travel back to the apartment. When we arrived at our apartment building, we passed through the front door and came solid in front of Mick. She didn't even startle. She never does, she's so used to me rippling around the house all the time. I can't imagine what I'd have to do to spook my big sister, which is kind of a sad waste of the ability to rematerialize, if you ask me.

"Smells good," she said, looking up from typing on a tablet computer.

Mick had been keeping up on various forums and chat sites covering news of the central valley in California. Sir Walter had given Mick the job when she demanded something *useful* to do.

"Wait 'til you taste it," I said, unfolding the top of the largest bag.

"This is French?" she asked, grabbing a falafel.

Apparently she hadn't been paying attention to what Sir Walter said about *food of the noble Mohammedans*.

"In a manner of speaking, yes," replied Sir Walter. He explained how, following the second World War, and again after Algerian independence, many North Africans had relocated to France where their children and grandchildren still struggled for recognition as full citizens.

After he finished, I asked if we could talk about the building.

"What building?" asked my sister.

Sir Walter frowned, which made his eyebrows bush into a serious uni-brow. "You are aware that I desired to use the first black book, the one Pfeffer stole, to convince certain personages that Helmann is not to be trusted?"

We nodded. He'd been real quiet about his activities the last ten days.

"I am afraid I did not succeed in that effort," he said. "Geneses Corporation has been, in the last several years, quietly acquiring real estate properties across Europe."

Sir Walter then rattled off a list of locations across France, Spain, Italy and North Africa. "In each of these places, Geneses has purchased property. They are, all of them, located within areas inhabited primarily by a population Jewish, Muslim, or Indian in composition."

"Uh-oh," whispered Mick.

I felt a sick knot in my stomach. "Knowing Helmann, he's not buying up these buildings to hold bake sales for the locals."

"Sales of baked goods?" Sir Walter looked confused.

"A charitable activity," explained Mick. "As in, we all know Helmann feels anything but charitable towards the people groups you just mentioned."

"*Precisement*," said Sir Walter. "I had hoped to persuade officials in the government of France to look with a critical eye at these purchases, to perhaps raise an inquiry. I allowed certain officials to look inside a copy of the black book, so as to demonstrate that the origins, and therefore the aims, of Geneses deserved a closer look."

Mickie rolled her eyes. "I could have told you that would crash and burn." She shook her head. "No one's going to object to Geneses buying buildings based on

29

what Helmann did seventy years ago." She sighed. "You guys are the history buffs. Think for a minute about Carnegie, Rockefeller, Margaret Sanger: they *all* supported the Eugenics movement. Would you expect the government to shut down their present day organizations for what they did in the last century? No one cares anymore."

"Except you," I said.

My sister gave me a sad half-smile.

Sir Walter nodded thoughtfully. "I should have consulted you, *Mademoiselle*. Your observation that 'no one cares' might then saved me a great deal of wasted effort."

My sister's smile grew a little bigger. She used to look just like that when Pfeffer praised her for a really good insight.

I turned to Sir Walter. "So obviously you're worried about this real estate buying spree. What do you think he's up to?"

"I know not."

"Did you snoop around inside?" asked Mickie.

Sir Walter dabbed his lips with a small paper napkin from the food bags.

"The building was empty," I said, popping a tenth, and sadly the last, falafel into my mouth. "There's no telling what he wants it for."

"Ugh, please, swallow before you speak!" said my sister. "It's like you were raised in the wild by animals."

"You rai*th*ed me," I said, winking at her, my mouth still full.

Sir Walter finished his after-meal tidying. "I believe it is time for us to pay an investigational visit to one of Helmann's European headquarters. Rome is quite lovely this time of year."

Excerpted from the personal diary of Girard L'Inferne.

Circa 1987

I have, with much labor and consideration, devised an education which I believe will forestall or even eliminate the undesirable behaviors I now observe among the very best of my first children.

The traits I shall keep—the ability to deny the demands of the flesh, fearlessness in the face of danger, loyalty to me alone—to these shall be added the ability to act selflessly. In effect, to act for the good of another before acting for one's personal good. I observe that this ability guided many of the great leaders of the past to victories denied their contemporaries. Caesar's armies, intensely personally loyal to him, also fought for Rome. For Rome, that is, for her citizens who would never take up a sword, Caesar's armies gladly laid down their lives when Caesar asked it of them.

Self-sacrifice, in acts great and small, I shall teach and reward. When this is added to loyalty and self-denial, I believe I shall at last possess the army I require. They will follow me as Caesar's Romans followed him.

Chapter Five

DECENT SOURDOUGH

• SAM •

I was cold as snow and immobilized.

And someone was rippling while holding on to me. My eyes flew wide as I saw Christian—across the room—move from invisibility to solidity, launching himself at me and my assailant.

Before I could call out Christian's name, I'd vanished in the stranger's arms. I could feel motion. My other senses hovered just beyond my reach, which was slightly terrifying. Maybe this was a side-effect of whatever drug I'd been injected with. But I felt certain I moved. And that meant it could be very dangerous for me to try rippling solid.

I thought of how I'd seen Christian come solid in my room. How he'd failed to reach me in time. But was he following me somehow? Could I find this out?

I hesitated to write out a message to Christian. I didn't know if he'd "see" it, and I feared my abductor might. In fact, my experience of "hearing" Sir Walter, and lately Christian, in my mind had made me wonder if most ripplers except me and Will took this type of communication for granted.

Fearful that the person kidnapping me could access my mind, I visualized a number-line, and started counting: one, two, three . . . I could keep this up all day. Or until we solidified and I discovered who'd taken me and why.

Before we stopped, I reached the eleven-thousands. I felt myself thrown roughly onto something. A couch. Hard. Slippery. Cold. The room was dark, but I felt the sensation of my flesh returning.

Then a bright light came on, and my eyes attempted to compensate; they couldn't dilate properly, and the light made them ache. With agonizing effort, I succeeded in closing my eyes. I tried speaking, but my mouth wouldn't cooperate. I'd been drugged with something that kept me mostly immobile. But excepting movement, my regular senses had returned with my solid form.

"Welcome," said a pleasant voice from behind me.

I couldn't turn my neck to get a good look at the man who'd spoken.

"Ah, how impolite of me," said the man's voice.

I recognized that voice.

Hans.

Hearing him circling in front of me, I forced my eyes open.

"Hmm, the relaxant seems to be affecting your speech. Inconvenient, that. I must ask Fritz if something can be done to target the drug's effects more quickly away from the vocal chords and mouth." He jotted a quick note on a pad and replaced it inside his jacket. Elegantly dressed, hair an unnatural blond, eyes piercing blue—he looked just as I remembered him from last fall.

I might be paralyzed, but seeing him again made my skin crawl.

"So, I am imagining your first question, had you the use of your tongue, would be something along the lines of what it is that I wish with you, yes?" His eyebrows raised a centimeter. "Try blinking once for 'yes.'"

Apparently it didn't occur to him that I might wish to answer in the negative. I refused to blink.

He looked annoyed, but it passed quickly, his face returning to a smooth and calm mask. "Very well, my dear," he said. "Let's give you a few minutes to recover, shall we?" And with that he exited the room.

My face wanted to frown in anger. My legs wanted to jump up and off the couch so that I could bang my fists upon the closed door. But I was stuck immobile on a white couch in a white-painted room with an impossibly clean white floor.

Well, I wasn't exactly stuck. Hans apparently didn't know I could ripple. My mouth tried to smile, even though the muscles wouldn't respond correctly. I calmed myself sufficiently and imagined Will's arms around me.

Nothing.

I imagined the clear-flowing stream of Illilouette Creek.

Still nothing.

It wasn't that I couldn't calm enough to ripple. I was laughably calm considering my circumstances— locked away in an unknown location by a known enemy. Whatever Hans had shot inside me, it prevented rippling.

But why hadn't Christian prevented my kidnapping? The one and only reason I'd agreed to allow Christian to spend every night in my room, every day by my side, was that *he* was my back-up plan in case I needed to escape and couldn't ripple to safety on my own.

So where was he and why hadn't he prevented Operation Sam-Snatch?

"Christian?" I spoke his name aloud. Then immediately I began second-guessing the wisdom of calling his name out loud. What if the room was bugged? Besides, if Christian had managed to follow along, wouldn't he have grabbed me and taken me back home by now? The truth ran along my spine like an icy finger: I was alone.

I wrote his name on a paper in my mind's eye, the method Will and I had used for communication while rippled. *Christian?* Then I called out with my thoughts in case he could hear them.

Christian? Are you there?

The room remained silent.

I was alone.

But where? And why? I should have let Hans tell me something. Anything.

Hans had indicated that the drug would start wearing off. Maybe then I could ripple. I began to test my muscles—tried blinking my eyes, attempted wriggling my fingers. My eyes could open and close better now, but my fingers felt like dead things splayed upon the couch. I gave up on my extremities and tried to move parts of my face.

Eyebrows. Mouth. After some time had passed— perhaps half an hour—I thought I might be able to speak. My version of "*Hans, you bastard,*" came out sounding like "Ha-ans, suu buhs-thurt."

The door opened suddenly.

37

A young man, maybe college age, walked inside. Unkempt brown hair. Bringing a funny smell with him. Nothing gross, just . . . odd, like the smell and the clinical room didn't match. His shoes trailed dark granules, dirt maybe.

"I'll be caring for your dining needs. Simply let me know anything you'd like to eat or drink," he said. "Still trouble with speech?" Swiftly, he injected me with something.

"Augh," I grunted. The needles were getting old, fast.

"You should be able to speak in a moment or two," he said. "Any type of food you'd like, just ask. Sky's the limit."

I felt warm prickles run from my neck and along my spine, down into my arms, legs. I tried wriggling my fingers. Mobility had returned.

I tested my voice: "Any food at all?" I asked, an idea forming.

"Yes," he replied. "Whatever you feel like."

"Sourdough bread." The effort required to speak faded entirely.

"Sourdough bread?" he asked. "No problem. You want butter? Cheese?"

I didn't answer, thinking hard.

"Just bread, then," he said. "Okay, anything else? Coffee?"

"What time is it? And where am I?"

The blue eyes dropped to his feet. He wore Brooks running shoes. A very expensive pair. "I can't tell you that."

I scowled. "How am I supposed to know if I want coffee when I don't know what time it is?"

He gave no answer.

"Can you get hot chocolate for me?" I asked.

"Certainly."

"I only like Ghirardelli," I said.

"Not a problem."

"I want chocolate-syllaberry," I added, hoping my request sounded innocent. "And some butter and jam." I held my breath, waiting to see if anything I'd asked for struck him as odd. Apparently it didn't. "I'm very hungry," I said. "How long will you be? Or is that a question you can't answer?"

He frowned, looking at the list he'd written. "Shouldn't take long at all."

I sighed with relief as the door closed upon the odd smell I'd managed to place.

Kelp—he smelled of seaweed.

The black trail of sand left by his shoes confirmed I'd identified the odor correctly. Mr. Room Service had been running recently. With spendy Brooks like those, he had to be a very dedicated runner. One who ran daily and appreciated the challenge of running on sand. I looked at the tiny grains leading to the door. Black and grey. I knew of only two places with black sand beaches. Hawaii and San Francisco.

This was what made me ask for chocolate-syllaberry cocoa and sourdough bread. Although you could get decent sourdough anywhere in the state of California, the stuff baked in the San Francisco Bay Area had a unique tang. One I hoped I'd be able to identify. And the cocoa? You could buy Ghirardelli hot cocoa at any major grocery store. We even had it in Las Abs. But you could only get special flavors from a Ghirardelli Chocolate Store, and only three of those carried my dad's syllaberry syrup. The stuff was obscenely expensive and made in very small batches.

If Room Service brought back what I asked for, it would mean we were within easy distance of three possible locations, all in Ghirardelli Square, San Francisco. If only I could tell Christian where to find me!

I quieted my mind. Until the man trailing black sand returned, I determined to silently call for Christian. I repeated his name over and over in my mind. I even risked speaking it aloud. But it was useless. No one could hear me. I was alone. At least until the guy in Brooks returned.

But in the end, he wasn't the one who brought my meal. Hans delivered it.

Chapter Six

BACK FROM THE DEAD

• WILL •

We took a train from Paris to Rome because, according to our French friend, "Only mad-men drive in Rome." But also because Sir Walter's Citroën lay under the rubble of his ancestors' castle. My sister buried her nose in one of the journals we'd recovered from Helga's car, currently under the same rubble. The only time Mick looked up was when we passed through Nice, France.

"If I ever get the chance, I'm coming back here to see the Marc Chagall Museum," she said.

Sir Walter smiled. "It is well worth the visit, *Mademoiselle.*"

They had to explain Chagall to me, and they showed me pictures on Sir Walter's tablet computer. I couldn't believe someone who'd lived through the attempted-destruction of his entire race could produce works of such playfulness and beauty.

"His work gave hope to many generations," said Sir Walter, "But especially, I think, to those who had survived the Holocaust. Such bright colors, such elegant representations of angels, men, and beasts, of the joy of an ordinary life."

After that, Sir Walter did some checking on his list of properties Helmann had acquired.

"I like this not," he said. "Geneses owns a building quite close to the *Musée Chagall*. What can he be up to, my cousin? What evil does he now devise?"

Whatever it was, we were on our way to Rome to find out.

From *Roma Termini*, the Eternal City's massive train station, we taxied to yet another luxury apartment Sir Walter rented with cash. On our way, we'd driven right past the Coliseum and the Forum Romanum, and I'm not exaggerating when I say it just about killed me to stay in the taxi. But then I thought of Sam, of how the sooner we wiped Helmann's ugly face off the planet, the sooner Sam and I could be together. It helped some.

We ate dinner at a restaurant called a *Trattoria*. Mick stuck with pizza, but I took Sir Walter's advice and ordered this potato dumpling—*gnocchi*—that was absolutely the best thing I've ever eaten. Like a combo of tater-tots and cheese ravioli only a hundred times better. And the velvet-y white sauce? I'm not ashamed to say I shined my plate clean using a hunk of crusty bread.

"I'm never leaving Rome," I said as the waiter took my plate away.

Mickie smiled and coughed a single word into her napkin. "*Girlfriend*."

Which kind of took me down a few notches. Mick must've felt bad, 'cause next thing you know she's offering to buy us all Italian ice cream. But *gelato cioccolato* didn't taste anywhere near as good as Sam's lips crushed against mine. I let Mick finish my ice cream.

Sir Walter and I dropped my sister off back in the apartment and then rippled so we could check out Geneses' Roman headquarters. Sir Walter said things slowed down at night in Helmann's other offices, so you could maybe have a shot at coming solid if anything interesting was lying around that needed to be borrowed for an indefinite period.

The headquarters building itself was plain, hardly even marked. A tiny brass sign by the front door said *Geneses Internationale*. Sir Walter and I slipped through the warm bubble of a solid-glass door.

Glass rules, I wrote.

I heard Sir Walter's soft chuckle, which I figured meant roughly, *Fist-bump, dude!*

What are we looking for first? I wrote.

Anything useful, came the answer.

Which, honestly, was not a useful answer *at all* if you ask me. I wished I had eyes to roll for times like this. I let Sir Walter take the lead. He found an office marked *Signore Pepe, Vice Presidente,* and we passed through the door. It was this dark old wood, all polished like Bridget Li's counters back in Las Abs. I tried to smell it or taste it, but I wasn't Sam, and to me it pretty much seemed like wood.

Sir Walter aimed us for a set of file drawers; there was no computer on the desk. Rippling solid, he flicked a key card in front of the lock, and the file drawer swung open.

Coming solid myself, I murmured, "Nice."

Sir Walter turned to me with his forefinger pressed to his lips. Universal sign for *shut up, already.* I looked over my friend's shoulder. Everything was in Italian, which I couldn't read, so after awhile I started getting bored and also sleepy from being solid at night. I fumbled around in my pockets for something to write on. Finding a flattened empty gum pack, I grabbed a pen off the desk and wrote:

I'm rippling. I'll stick to yr right side, close.

Sir Walter looked up and nodded.

I felt a lot more alert once I rippled out of my tired body. Seriously, I needed to get back to running just so

I could get back some energy. Sir Walter sighed heavily enough that I wrote him, *Quiet, remember?*

He gave a sad little half-smile and a nod my direction and then rippled invisible.

I find nothing apropos of the recent purchasing by our friend, he said, apparently using the term "friend" a bit more loosely than I would have done. Then he muttered, *Mon Dieu, c'est impossible*, which I understood just fine even if I didn't see any impossible things in the locale of this office.

What's impossible? I scribbled on my notepad.

Listen, do you not hear something?

He was right; I heard voices. *I hear talking*, I wrote.

I hear the signature of one whose thoughts are most familiar, said Sir Walter.

Helmann? I wrote.

No, no, he said, his voice with an eager edge. *Do you not recognize this man's thoughts?*

Dude, I wrote, *basically 'deaf' in that department. You're the only person whose thoughts I've ever heard.*

Quite, quite, said Sir Walter. *But I thought perhaps the thoughts of your sister's advisor might come through to you.*

My sister's WHAT? I wrote, so fast the letters looked like scrawl.

It is Monsieur Professeur Pfeffer whose voice you hear approaching us even now.

45

Excerpted from the personal diary of Girard L'Inferne.

Circa 1990

A Corps of one thousand chameleons. This is what I shall require. Thankfully, I need not couple with a thousand mothers this time to produce the offspring I have need of. Technology is a most excellent servant.

Fritz has no lack of racially-pure volunteer surrogates from countries newly free of Soviet domination. Hunger, for food and gold, are our allies at this time. Most propitious, this falling away of the walls separating East from West in Europe.

My one thousand chameleons shall do more than Hitler's hundreds of thousands. He cleansed only millions of humanity's dregs. My purging of humanity shall be numbered in billions.

Chapter Seven

CALL IT PENANCE

• SAM •

Hans entered the room pushing a little trolley like you get in a hotel room. My cocoa had been poured into a ceramic mug, but I could smell the spicy scent of syllaberries rising with the steam.

I knew where I was, at least.

"I thought we might breakfast together, as we have much to discuss," said Hans, smiling as he removed the covers from plates containing thick, sliced sourdough with butter and jam for me and brown rolls with deli meats and cheeses for him. "I really find it impossible to keep up with the myriad beverages young people today consume. I visited a coffee shop last weekend only to discover my simple coffee with a splash of cream had at least fifteen words to its description. And then I had to specify the temperature at which I preferred to drink." Hans smiled at me as he offered a crisp cloth napkin across the trolley after draping one upon his own lap.

"So it's morning now?" I asked.

"Ah, yes, I believe it is," he said, briefly consulting a cell phone. He held it a second longer that necessary, like he wanted me to notice it.

"That's my phone," I said, accusation in my voice.

Hans sipped his coffee and arranged cheese upon one of the rolls. "May I assume that you would prefer your parents not worry as to your whereabouts or state of, ah, health at the moment?"

"Of course I don't want them to worry," I snapped. "Take me home and that'll be a non-issue."

Hans smiled. "I have already ensured it will be a 'non-issue' by sending them a message."

"You texted my parents?" I asked, feeling my face growing hot. "What, like a ransom note?"

Hans looked taken aback. "Of course not, my dear young woman. I merely indicated your intentions to spend the day in Fresno with your, ah, *Asian* friend." He pronounced it "A-zee-un."

"They'll figure that out as soon as they call Gwyn," I said. Instantly I regretted revealing her name.

"Gwyn Li and her mother Bridget are even now driving to meet you at Shibuki Spa for a day of luxury and relaxation in the Japanese tradition," said Hans.

So he knew their names already.

"They're Chinese, not Japanese. There's a big difference," I said angrily.

"Yes, yes," said Hans, brushing his fingers through the air in a dismissive gesture. "That is neither here nor there. You indicated that you would prefer your parents not worry as to your disappearance. I have gone to great pains to ensure they will not." His own voice carried an impatient edge.

"So why am I here?" I demanded.

Hans' face smoothed back into implacable good humor. "You are a very important young woman, my dear Samantha."

The hairs on the back of my neck bristled when he used the epithet 'dear,' but I let it go.

Hans continued. "And your devotion to your family is admirable. Most admirable." From inside his jacket pocket, my phone jingled. He checked the text. "Ah, here we are. Your father David Ruiz wishes you a pleasant day with your friend."

I wondered if that was an accurate rendering of my dad's text. It didn't sound like any text my dad would send. "Give me my phone," I said.

Hans continued as if I hadn't spoken. "Family loyalty should always come above loyalty to anyone or anything else."

I thought of the siblings he'd tormented in long-ago Germany.

"I wonder if it would surprise you, Samantha, to learn that you and I are distant relations?" Here he paused.

I hadn't thought it through before, maybe in subconscious self-defense. Hans was Helmann's son. I was the great-times-a-bazillion grand-daughter of Helmann's wife. We were some strange form of in-laws. At least we weren't blood-related.

Hans' mouth moved into a small sort of smile. "You will understand that I have no wish to harm you, or indeed to detain you longer than necessary, seeing as we are *family*."

"So I'll ask again: why am I here?"

"You have something that I would very much like to possess." Here he leaned closer. "Of course, I could simply take what I want, but that would be bad manners on my part. And I believe you might be made to see how a free gift from you would benefit many, not least yourself."

He wants my blood. Or my genes. Or whatever Helga wanted. "I'm listening," I said, my voice sounding a million times calmer than I actually felt.

"Samantha, I wonder, have you ever done something which later you found that you very much regretted?"

"Of course," I muttered, wondering where he was going with this.

He looked contemplative for a moment, running a finger along his chin. "I have, myself, many regrets. And I have vowed, as a result, that moving forward I shall do all in my power to benefit mankind. Call it penance, if you will. I wonder, young as you are, how much you know of the suffering of humanity?" His head cocked to one side and he sighed heavily. "Alas, of personal suffering you have known much."

I crossed my arms, forcing myself to betray none of what I knew about the murder of my mother by the man seated across from me.

"My own journey in this life has been filled with pain and violence, with lack and distress at times. I desire to eliminate the pain of those who suffer with no hope." Here he leaned towards me once more, brows drawn together as if in pain. "You have never, I think, known what it is to be in pain so great that you wished to die rather than continue to live."

He didn't let me answer but continued, detailing horrors of starving children, children whose bodies were riddled with parasites and disease, children with AIDs whose parents had succumbed to the disease. His eyes rested upon the floor. "I would spare you the photographs and videos I have of those who daily suffer under these conditions. All I ask is the chance to offer hope to those who pray for death."

I raised my eyes to meet his. My voice came out in a ragged whisper. "I've heard of euthanasia."

"Your mind is quick. Good, good. My father," he began, "Has for two decades been engaged in what he believes one of the greatest humanitarian efforts of all time. To those who beg for release, yes, he has offered it."

Hans rose and began pacing. "Euthanasia, as you called it. Yet I conclude that his efforts are misdirected. You see, I believe it is more merciful to offer vaccination or food to those who crave death. In this, he and I disagree. I feel that my father's efforts, well-intentioned as they are, have been short-sighted. Who would offer death when they might instead offer hope?" Hans broke off, exasperation furrowing his brow.

I had no idea how this was going to come back around to me being here.

Hans laughed, a short, forced laugh as he began pacing again, shoes clicking upon the sterile polished floor. "I am hardly the first child who wished his father would retire and pass along the family business into more capable hands."

I raised my eyebrows. Hans wanted to run Geneses?

"And yet my father will never agree to rest from his efforts. Unless." Hans looked deeply into my eyes, and I forced myself to meet his gaze, glacial and ravenous. "Unless there were something else with which he might occupy himself." He paused.

"Something which touches his heart even more profoundly than his desire to lessen human suffering."

A name popped into my thoughts. One that I *absolutely* did not come up with on my own. The name *Elisabeth,* spoken in a man's voice, and with angry emotions.

Where did that come from, I wondered? I felt an uneasy certainty that it came from Hans' mind. That he had inadvertently *spoken* in my mind like Sir Walter or Christian might do.

He spoke in a whisper. "Your great-grandmother twenty-three times removed was called Elizabeth de Rochefort. The name means nothing to you, I know, and yet I assure you that there is no other name more precious to my father. His dearest wish was to have a child with her."

I remembered, just in time, to look shocked by what Hans said. "How can your dad have a child with someone who died centuries ago?"

"How indeed?" Hans asked, carefully examining my face.

I tried to keep an innocently-puzzled expression upon it. Which, honestly, wasn't all that difficult because I still didn't see what *I* had to do with early retirement for Helmann.

And then I did.

Fortunately Hans had just turned his back to me as my face registered disgust. I grabbed for my hot cocoa, now luke-warm. The syllaberry syrup had gathered at the bottom and tasted too sweet. I struggled to swallow it down.

"My father has an unusual genetic make-up which has allowed him to live for a very long time. He was once married to Elisabeth, but none of their children survived infancy. Although she was long-lived as well, she did not survive as my father has done."

"You want me to get pregnant with your dad so he'll focus on a baby instead of trying to euthanize the world?" The words tumbled out like I'd choke on them if I kept them inside.

Hans looked at me with what appeared to be genuine shock. "I would never ask such a thing of you. Forgive me, Samantha. I have explained things most ineffectively if that is what you have concluded."

I frowned. "You don't want me to have your father's baby?"

"I hardly think an unwanted teen pregnancy would be a reasonable request to make of a young person who has suffered as you have already done in your life. Child, forgive me." Hans shook his head slowly.

"Then *what am I doing here?*" I asked.

"I wish only to ask if you would, out of the kindness of your heart, and for the benefit of millions who die and billions more who may yet—" Here he paused to draw breath. "Might you consider an egg donation?"

Chapter Eight

CROSSES OF ASH

• WILL •

Sir Walter pressed us back into the wall of the office. *Lest we should be detected.*

Right, I wrote. Our freezing cold invisible bodies would send a pretty clear "someone's rippled in here" message to Pfeffer, if it really was him.

The massive oak door creaked open and in walked my sister's dead former advisor with a dude in a suit, and a priest, and two guys dressed like monks.

Helmann, Sir Walter informed me.

I should have been freaked to be in the same room with über-bad-guy, but I was a little preoccupied seeing my friend back from the grave.

Pfeffer, most definitely not dead, scanned the desk for a moment, looking for something that was missing from the pen-holder.

Oh, crap, I thought. I'd left his pen over by the file drawers. Not finding it, he reached in his pocket and removed another pen which he turned backwards and thrust into a teensy hole on the side of his desk, like it was a key. Which it must have been, because a drawer that you couldn't even tell was a drawer a moment ago now slid open. The priest reached down inside the drawer and pulled out probably the last thing I was expecting to see. For some unfathomable reason, Pfeffer kept the elements of the Eucharist—communion—in his desk.

What??? I wrote to Sir Walter.

Peace, young Will, said my French friend. *We shall observe.*

Honestly, I wasn't sure what he meant by observe. Observe like *watch this stuff* or observe like, *I observe Christmas, you observe Hanukkah.* So I just shut my mouth. Well, I stopped with the note-writing. I was dying to ask what Pfeffer was thinking, but Sir Walter maintained radio silence as the priest chanted his way through an Ash Wednesday service in Latin. When it came time for serving the Host, Helmann seemed to *defer* to Pfeffer. Meaning he let Pfeffer eat the thin wafer first. Helmann observed Pfeffer for a few minutes while the priest paused like this was how they always celebrated Mass.

After this little pause, Helmann nodded curtly to the priest who then placed the Host on Helmann's tongue. When it came to the chalice containing the wine, Pfeffer went first again, everyone pausing for a couple of minutes. And then they finished up with it and somewhere in there while my mind must've been wandering, Helmann, Pfeffer, and the two monks got ash-crosses on their foreheads.

What's Pfeffer saying to you? I wrote as soon as the office-Mass concluded.

Wait, came the response. Classic Sir Walter.

While we waited, the priest and the monks started chanting again, but it wasn't any part of the Mass I was familiar with, just some Gregorian chant, like maybe Psalms or something.

Watch Helmann, said Sir Walter.

I watched as Helmann stood with his eyes closed. And then I remembered how Sir Walter told us Helmann couldn't change form quickly and needed chanting monks to calm him. Well, if my conscience was as smudged and dark as his, maybe I'd need monks, too. It took over a minute. Once, when my eyes flicked to Pfeffer, I thought I saw a hint of a smile on his face. Nothing with his mouth, just this look his eyes had that I recognized. Like a little pre-smile.

Why's he happy? I asked.

Please, Will, wait! This time I realized Sir Walter wasn't just telling me to wait in his usual annoying way. I could hear stress in his voice, like I'd distracted him, and he needed to focus so he could drive in bad traffic or something.

Helmann vanished.

Pfeffer closed his eyes briefly, then crossed back to the heavy oak door, allowing the Church trio to exit.

Can we talk to Pfeffer yet? I asked.

Do not change form! Sir Walter's voice was hard as stone.

I cast my gaze back on Pfeffer. He leaned against the door with his eyes closed looking suddenly like a very tired man. Opening his eyes, he noticed the pen I'd misplaced earlier. He frowned, stepped over to pick it up, and stared at the pen, like he was daring it to explain how come it wasn't in the pen-holder on the desk. He rubbed his eyes, sighed, and returned the pen-key to its place after using it to close the secret drawer.

Then he walked to the door, crossed the threshold, and closed the door behind him. I could just barely make out the sound of an electronic click, like from the card-swipe Sir Walter had used on the file drawers.

Mon Dieu, said Sir Walter. *Let us return at once to your sister. I would speak with her concerning our encounter with Pfeffer.*

Wait a sec— , I wrote. *We're just going to let him walk off, without demanding an explanation?*

58

My dear Will, the man whom you have just beheld is no longer a man with whom it would be safe for you to speak. Pfeffer is working for my cousin.

Excerpted from the personal diary of Girard L'Inferne.

Circa 1998

My little school delights me.

The children exceed my expectations. Even without the aid of hypnotic suggestion, they beg to be allowed such privileges as the donation of blood plasma, bone marrow, and even their tiny allowances to aid those in need. I saw a boy whose shoes were worn through the sole. When I asked him why he had not exchanged them for new ones, his answer silenced me.

"I sent my new shoes to a village where children have none," he said. Then he showed me how he had cleverly inserted a piece of cardboard to cover the hole in his shoe. "I need only replace this every week, and another child like me can have shoes for the first time in his life."

The angelic smile which accompanied this remark would melt the heart of the veriest reprobate in hell.

This time, I shall succeed.

Chapter Nine

FATE OF THE WORLD

• SAM •

After requesting that I make an egg donation, Hans left the room. I needed time to think, he said. Which was the first completely rational thing I'd heard since arriving. I needed time, certainly, but how I wished I had Sir Walter, or Mickie, or Will to consult with before making my decision.

My mind drifted to Christian. Could I contact him? I closed my eyes. *Christian!* I called. Suddenly, I regretted that I hadn't spent more time trying to build up my ability to converse mind-to-mind with Christian. He'd explained it was as simple as strengthening a muscle. Which I'd ignored. I didn't want to hear him any better at night, and I sure as heck didn't want him listening to my thoughts. But now, my reluctance looked foolish. *Christian?* I called out once more.

I heard only silence. I was alone. I had to figure this out by myself.

So, where was the truth in all of the things Hans had told me?

If I gave Helmann one of my eggs, disgusting though it sounded, would he stop his intended decimation of the world? If what Hans told me was true, it sounded like a simple trade-off.

But *something* bothered me about it. And until I could navigate to the core of that unease, I couldn't make a decision. Meanwhile, the clock ticked. Hans had called our meal together breakfast. If I was indeed in San Francisco, and if Hans could travel swiftly when rippled, then I'd arrived here at maybe 7:00 in the morning. Breakfast had been somewhere around 8:00. Which made sense, because no way would my dad sleep in past 8:00 even though we'd all been up 'til 2:00. I had maybe ten hours 'til my parents expected me back home again.

Ten hours in which to decide the fate of the world.

But I didn't actually *know* if I would truly be deciding the fate of billions. I didn't know if Hans was telling the truth.

Another knock on the door.

I sat up, alert.

A woman entered, bowed with hands in a position I'd seen on Sylvia's yoga DVDs.

"*Namasté*," she said. "I am Indira. I am instructed to ask if you wish for a massage? I can provide any style you like: Swedish, relaxation, deep tissue—"

"A massage?" I raised both eyebrows. "Seriously?"

Her expression remained calm as she awaited my answer.

"Um, no," I said. "I don't need a massage."

She bowed again, palms together, and exited.

Okay, that was weird.

I tried to gather my thoughts back together. What did I know about Helmann?

One: He'd experimented on his own kids. I had the journal from Pfeffer to back that up as well as Sir Walter's accounts.

Two: Helmann had purged those with the gene to ripple, both during WWII and within the last decade. Although Hans had blamed *Helga* for the more recent purges, when I'd eavesdropped on them last fall.

Three: Helmann thought it was a justifiable act to end the lives of anyone he chose. I'd seen that in the video we'd watched, and Hans' claims just now backed this up.

Four: Helmann wanted me alive even though at one point he tried to have me killed.

Another knock at my door.

"What?" I asked, irritated by the interruption.

A nurse entered the room, trailing medical paraphernalia.

"I haven't said yes," I said. A chill raced along my spine.

"I just need to take your vitals," he said. "Now," he added when I didn't respond. He held a blood pressure cuff in one hand.

"My vitals are fine," I said. But then I wondered if this was true. I still felt very strange inside if I tried to focus on it. My insides were too much like . . . Jell-o. Maybe I needed monitoring, thanks to whatever drug Hans had used to prevent me from rippling. I extended an arm, sighing.

The nurse checked my pulse, clipped something to my index finger, and took a blood-pressure reading without speaking to me.

"So, how am I?" I asked.

"All within expected parameters," replied the nurse, wrapping the cuff into a tight roll.

"That's good?" I asked, hoping for a more definitive response.

"All as expected," said the nurse, quickly exiting the room.

I sighed and closed my eyes to re-collect my scattered thoughts.

What did I know about Hans?

He'd murdered my mom and my childhood friend. Now he spoke of regrets. Did he regret his murders?

Was he telling the truth about himself? About his father?

Sir Walter agreed that Helmann had loved Elisabeth, and he said her only living descendents came from children she'd had with someone besides Helmann. So that part was probably true: that Helmann wished she'd had *his* children. The journal translations indicated strong feelings for his wife. Especially all that scribbling in the margins about "Elisabeth is dead."

But Sir Walter said Helmann had plans beyond the so-called "elimination of suffering." That he planned to reward followers with the gene I carried, one which would allow his followers to live lives of extraordinary lengths. I thought back to the video Sir Walter had sent us. Helmann had asked those assembled to imagine a future where their children lived free of war, disease and poverty *with enough time* in which to enjoy such lives.

So what did I have to do with this vision? He already had the gene for rippling and extending lives. Heck, Hans carried that gene. Helga had carried it, as had Deuxième, her child. They didn't need me for the gene.

So why did they need me? Or more precisely, one of my eggs?

Could it be as simple as Hans said? That Helmann was now old-and-wise enough to retire and pour himself into the raising of a child he'd thought he could

65

never have: one with Elisabeth's blood flowing in its veins?

The door opened again. Room Service stepped inside, his Brooks still trailing sand.

"Can I get you anything? Food? More hot chocolate?"

I stared at his shoes. "Nice Brooks," I said.

Looking flustered, he glanced at his feet.

"I guess you can't discuss running with me either?" I asked, curious how he'd respond.

"They're worth every penny," he said. A tiny grin lit his face but was quickly extinguished. "More hot chocolate?"

"No thanks."

"Is there anything else I can get you?"

I shook my head and he left. Too late, I thought of something.

"A Do Not Disturb sign would be nice," I said to the empty room. It was like Hans didn't want me to have peace and quiet in which to make an informed decision. I sighed. Of course he didn't.

I'd burned through another hour or more, yet I felt no closer to making a decision. Which was ridiculous. How could I possibly value *one tiny egg* over millions—no, billions—of lives? What if I could really stop Helmann from destroying the world with this one small gift?

I groaned and flopped onto the couch. It was a horrible couch. Who would design something at once so ugly and uncomfortable? I felt exhausted. Maybe I did need food. My mouth opened into a huge and extended yawn. I definitely needed sleep.

No, you don't! I warned myself, sitting up. "You need to make a decision and get out of here!"

What is the worst thing that could happen if you gave an egg to Helmann? I asked myself.

"How the heck am I supposed to know?" The words flew out, half-growled.

A quick knock sounded at the door and Hans appeared.

"I haven't decided, okay?" I barked out the question.

I felt a wave of anger coming towards me from within his mind. His face, however, remained impassive. Had I imagined it?

"Not to worry," he said. "I've arranged for you to view some films I made hoping to persuade my father to change his plans," he said. "I was unsuccessful with him, but I'd like for you to see *my* vision for the future."

"Okay," I said.

Hans left. Mr. Expensive Running Shoes brought in a cart with a tablet computer, set it up quickly, and left, too. I was alone with Hans' Vision For The Future.

I watched several short films of humanitarian efforts being carried out worldwide. Water purification was brought to a village that had previously suffered from yearly outbreaks of cholera. Vaccinations were offered in rural area where AIDs had ravaged the population. I watched Hans delivering milking goats to a village with no green thing in sight. The goats munched happily on dead-looking weeds. Children laughed trying goat's milk for the first time.

The videos ended and the screen went blank. It sure looked like Hans wanted to help the poor and underprivileged.

I leaned back upon the unyielding couch. The images played again and again through my head. Before I knew it, I was lying on my back, staring at the ceiling, still contemplating the differences between Hans' vision for the future and that of his father.

Just a quick nap, I told myself. *Just a couple minutes with my eyes closed, so I can think straight.* It felt so good to shut out the sterile, bright room.

I fell at once into dreams in which I watched myself within Helga's tooth-pulling room. I beheld Hans as he strolled in, casually glanced at me, pressed a cruel finger upon the bruise on my face. I remembered things I hadn't wanted to recall while awake: how Hans had instructed his sister to *kill* me.

Why hadn't he recognized me?

"*You're just one more brown-haired, brown-eyed inferior to him, dear,*" said Helga in my dream. "*You don't honestly expect him to tell one of you from another, do you?*" Her laughter rang icy and jarring in my ears.

My eyes fluttered open and I felt my heart racing. Rubbing tired eyes with the backs of my cold hands, I rose. A small sink occupied one corner of my room and I crossed to it. I let the water run over my hands, soothing and warm. I splashed some on my face.

My insides felt less wobbly than they had earlier. Was there a chance I could ripple now? I left the water running and trailed my fingers back and forth through the flow. Clear water, running freely, as it had done in Hans' videos in the African villages.

I calmed.

I felt infinite, at peace, quieted by the clearness of the water spilling over my hands.

But I couldn't ripple.

How had Hans even figured out I was a chameleon? How much did he know about me, about my friends? About Will? My heart cried out, angling toward whatever space Will occupied in the world.

I remembered his lips on mine.

But I had to focus on this room.

I remembered his laughter as I swished my hand through the willows on an early run.

I shook my head. I couldn't think about Will right now. A decision had to be made. I wrenched myself back to the present.

Maybe Hans was capable of noble action, but I knew he was capable of murder. The memory of the night my mother had been killed flashed across my mind. Other memories followed from the dream I'd just left. And there were my recollections of passages from the black book: Hans, grinning as he inflicted cruelty, looking on as a child—his sibling—tested poisoned water.

If Hans was such a great guy, why hadn't he called up my parents and arranged for a nice chat over a cup of coffee?

What had Hans done, really, to earn my trust? To make me believe what he said about stopping his father's mad scheme, or even that stopping it was what he truly desired?

Was there one solid reason I should trust this man?

I stood for several moments, hands still in water, waiting to see if my decision would change. Then I turned off the faucet. I dried my hands carefully. I stepped back to wait upon the world's worst and whitest couch.

I had my answer.

Chapter Ten

LESS LIKE A FRIEND

• WILL •

"Not possible," said Mick. She grabbed a piece of hair and started twisting it, something I hadn't seen her do in, like, *years*. "I don't believe it."

I knew what she meant. I sure as heck didn't *want* to believe Pfeffer had gone to work for Helmann. My first thought had been he was totally faking it. I mean, this was Pfeffer we were talking about. *Pfeffer*. How-can-I-convince-you-to-keep-things-secret-Pfeffer. And it wasn't like he looked any different. I mean, if he'd gone over to the dark side, wouldn't he—I don't know —*look* like it? Look more *evil* somehow? I'm not talking twirl-y-mustaches and stuff, but there should be a change.

Something to make him look less like a friend.

"I should never have believed it, *chère Mademoiselle*, had I not with my own eyes beheld it." Sir Walter sighed long and low.

He was so unnerved, he wasn't even playing with his goatee. So I had Mick to one side of me, pulling her hair like it was taffy, and Sir Walter's goatee looking all neglected on the other side.

"Tell us what you heard him thinking," I said. "I mean, you're sure he's all best-buds with Helmann?"

Sir Walter stood and looked out our window. "There can be little doubt. He has learned to conceal a part of his mind, which troubles me. I found it difficult to find his thoughts. But what little I caught was conclusive enough." The Frenchman turned back towards us. "Pfeffer tests Helmann's food."

Mick looked blankly from Sir Walter to me.

"Tests for, like, poison?" I asked.

The goatee-tugging started as he nodded in response.

"Wow. That sounds loyal," I said. Quickly, I explained to my sister about Helmann's private Ash Wednesday Mass.

"It's not Ash Wednesday," said Mickie. "Not for several days yet."

I was impressed my sister was keeping track. Of course, she was right, it was Friday, not a Wednesday at all.

"Helmann keeps to the Gregorian calendar," said Sir Walter. "The calendar of the Catholic Church of our youth."

"Well, it's still wrong," said Mickie. "How can someone like him have the nerve to take communion? I can't believe God doesn't strike him dead for it. He's got to be in a constant state of mortal sin."

"Many who deserve death receive mercy instead," said Sir Walter softly.

"I can't believe we *trusted* him," said Mick, shaking her head as she moved back to Pfeffer. "And he *lied* to us. For *years*."

"Mackenzie," said Sir Walter, "Be not too swift to judge. It is possible Pfeffer dealt by you honestly. Helmann has many methods at his disposal to alter a man's loyalties."

Hairs stood up on the back of my neck as he said this. And then a realization hit me like a punch to the gut. "Las Abs. Sam." It felt like all the air in the room was gone.

"Will, sit down," my sister said gently.

Didn't have to tell me twice. The room tilted sharply as I sank onto the couch. Mick came over, squatting down in front of me. She placed firm hands on both of my shoulders.

"I'm sure she's fine, Will. Well, I mean, she's in no additional danger because of Pfeffer." She said his name like it tasted bad.

73

"But he sent us there, Mick. Was that a trick? So we'd find her and . . . I don't know . . . turn her over to him or something?" My mind was working crazy-fast thinking how Pfeffer had set us up with a place to live *in the same town* where Sam lived. "There's got to be a reason he did that."

Sir Walter frowned. "This troubled me also, as we returned home just now. But I am inclined to be of your sister's opinion. Sam is in no *additional* danger because of what Pfeffer might or might not have planned. Indeed, if he had intended to use you in this way, those plans have surely been overthrown now that you have left Las Abuelitas."

"I don't like it," I said. The air had returned to the room, but all I wanted to do was jump on a plane *yesterday* and get back to make sure Sam was okay. Had Pfeffer figured out we'd left town? Did that mean she was safer or in worse danger? What had he meant, sending us there? Or was it all—maybe, somehow— just a bizarre coincidence and he'd never known about Sam's existence?

Well, he must know by now, being BFF's with Helmann. I noticed my hands had crept to my hair. Geez. Hair-pulling was contagious.

"We're not going back," said my sister. "Will, listen to me. Sam has Chrétien to take care of her. And she's better at rippling fast. You said so yourself. You can't go to Las Abuelitas."

I could be on a plane and over to San Francisco in ten hours.

I looked away from her, trying to find a part of me that agreed with what she was saying.

I could grab a couple thousand euros from Sir Walter, get the next flight out.

"Will." Mick placed an arm around my shoulder and squeezed hard. "Listen. This isn't about me for once."

I could be holding her in my arms by this time tomorrow.

"Will! Are you listening to me? This is about keeping Sam safe."

I grunted, just enough to let Mick know I was listening.

"I can't go sneaking around Geneses invisibly," she said. "I don't have the ability you have. If you leave us now, Sir Walter has no back-up. We need you here. Stopping Helmann is the only real way to keep Sam safe."

I hated how well my sister knew me.

"The lives of many are at stake, my young friend." Sir Walter's words cut through all my plans and left them in shreds on the floor.

The room felt too small. I needed to get out and run.

Or hit something.

Or someone.

"I'm going running," I said. My voice sounded angry. I didn't apologize.

"Please," said Sir Walter, grabbing my forearm, "Do not venture forth in solid form. You might be recognized."

I shrugged my arm free. I *wanted* to find Pfeffer and let him know what I thought of how he'd lied to us for all those years. I wanted to run 'til I collapsed from exhaustion. I wanted to stop seeing Sam's smile in my head. I wanted to kiss her brown shoulders.

My sister spoke softly. "For her sake, Will. Please."

"Fine," I grunted.

I rippled and took off into the dark and cold of a February night in Rome.

Excerpted from the personal diary of Girard L'Inferne.

Circa 2003

As they reach young adulthood, I am pleased with the progress of my Corps of Angels. They will run into a burning building with only a wet handkerchief about their faces if they believe there to be a person inside who will otherwise perish. I have also observed them plunging into icy waters, into fetid waters, and into shark-infested waters to effect a rescue of another human being.

In other words, they are willing to subject themselves to dangers I am certain none of my original children would have faced in order to save anyone but themselves.

We continue to train them as subjects of the art of hypnosis, but honestly, they exceed my best hopes quite on their own. Our casualties are remarkably low, considering the peril into which they weekly, and gladly, throw themselves.

When the New Order has been established upon Earth, I shall certainly require training in this manner for all holding positions as civil servants—firemen, EMT's, police, and so forth. It dovetails naturally with my plans that assignments for employment will be given shortly after post-birth evaluations. What shall we not accomplish, when all who serve the good of the world are trained from birth in their area of specialization?

Surely, if I were but an ordinary man, I would not sleep for joyful anticipation of what is to come!

Chapter Eleven

HARVESTED

• SAM •

The next knock, when it came, made my heart beat a little faster, but I found my resolve as strong as ever. It was the nurse.

"I want to talk to Hans," I said.

A look of mild displeasure crossed the nurse's face. "I shall make certain that *Dr. Lieberman* is informed of your request."

"You do that," I muttered as he swept out of the room, blood-pressure cuff trailing.

I paced while I waited for Hans to show up. I needed a good run. My mind felt remarkably clear, and I tried rippling a couple more times, but I couldn't.

My thoughts crept back around to Hans and what I would say to him.

How would he react to my decision? A chill of fear ran up my spine. I thought of his videotaped laughter with village children enjoying their first clean water, and I felt certain I'd be home in a few hours after a curt nod and brief handshake. Then I thought of his detachment as Helga had attempted to torture information from me, and I felt certain I'd never see home again.

A prayer, a part of the Catholic mass, echoed in my mind. I heard it spoken in the deep and earnest voice of a young man. Definitely not Hans' voice.

"Christian?" I called aloud.

No response. He wasn't near enough to hear me that way. What I needed was to call with my *mind*. I imagined throwing my thoughts far out. *Christian?*

The door opened abruptly and I jumped up, back in the here-and-now, certain I'd only imagined hearing my friend's voice.

"Well my dear," began Hans, "I understand you wished to speak with me?"

I squared my shoulders, released my hands from the tightly-balled fists they had formed. "I won't give you my eggs." My voice held steady, for which I felt grateful.

Hans' head tilted slightly to one side, his eyes remaining fixed upon mine. I thought I read a flicker of anger in those cold eyes. Without once looking away from me, Hans opened the door and uttered a quick phrase in German that I didn't understand. At the words, a stranger entered the room, pushing a wheelchair before him.

I stepped back, alarmed.

Quicker than ought to have been possible, Hans grabbed both my arms, and the second man, who looked enough like Hans to be a brother, jabbed a puff-sprayer up my nose.

I couldn't help but inhale whatever it was.

Sputtering, I cried out. "I demand that you take me home *now!*" As I spoke, I shot out my right knee with the hope of rendering Hans incapable of speech for several minutes. But my knee lifted with only a fraction of the speed and power I'd intended. I opened my mouth to shout, but had trouble making sounds come out. My tongue weighed a hundred pounds. Earth's gravity increased tenfold and I collapsed into the wheelchair behind me. With great difficulty I kept my eyelids open enough to watch while restraints were placed upon my wrists and ankles. I felt the room spin. Or was it the backward motion of the chair?

Hans walked before me down the hall. I saw Mr. Expensive Running Shoes gaping at me.

"Help! Help me! Please!" I cried out, but the words as they escaped my lips sounded like meaningless drivel. The man with the Brooks avoided eye contact as I passed. I summoned all the energy I could muster to call out for someone to help me once again. But the words never left my mouth. *Please help me!* The plea echoed within the confines of my own mind. *Christian, I'm in San Francisco. Please . . . help . . .* My head fell forward. *Please . . .* I could no longer form words, even in my thoughts.

I felt myself lifted onto a table, felt a bright point of pain as someone inserted a needle into the top of one hand.

And then I felt nothing.

***

A single bright light.

The sensation of my eyelid being lifted by someone not myself.

Lord, have mercy.

The words echoed in my head.

Was I at midnight mass with my *abuelita*? I felt so sleepy. I snuggled into her fur coat as the priest spoke the words of the Christmas Eve mass.

Christ, have mercy.

The priest sounded so young. I tried to raise my eyes to see what he looked like. Was my *abuelita's* priest young? But I was too tired. And my grandma's coat felt so warm and snuggly. I buried my face in the dark of her mink.

Lord, have mercy. I mumbled the words with the priest, with my *abuelita*.

***

Voices.

I heard someone speaking. Mass must have ended. I didn't want to get up. I wanted to remain sleeping on the pew.

"Er ist da. Und zwar jetzt!"

I knew the words. German words. They meant: *He's here! Now!*

Silence. Peace.

Then more words. In English.

"Greetings, Father." (I knew that voice . . .)

"You were successful, then, in persuading her?" (A different voice, one that sounded remote, as if it came from a TV.)

"Ah." (The voice of . . . who? I *knew* him . . .) "Here, you can just see our harvest . . . we were fortunate in our timing."

"Don't leave it there, fools!" (The TV voice was angry.) "Place it in the stasis chamber at once!"

The sound of several feet, all leaving me. Suddenly I felt alone and afraid. I wasn't in the pew beside my *abuelita*. Where was I?

Don't leave me alone! My heart cried out to the silence. *Have Mercy.* I murmured the words of the mass. I wanted my *abuelita* back again. Where was I?

Samantha! The voice spoke in the merest whisper. *I'm here. You're safe.*

I smiled. I whispered the familiar words of the mass with my grandmother. *And grant us salvation.* I relaxed again. My *abuelita* smiled, squeezed one of my praying hands with her own. Her hand felt so cold, so icy, but then I felt her arms about me and the embrace spread warmth to the core of my being.

Abruptly, a fog that had cloaked my mind lifted, and my brain functioned normally once more. My eyes darted up and down, looking for my body. It had vanished.

Sam, do you hear me?

I heard Christian's voice, strong within my mind.

I'm right here. I'm awake. How did you wake me up?

You were under an ether of some kind. Now that you are insubstantial, it no longer affects your mind.

I had strange dreams, I said.

I thank God that you're alright, Mademoiselle Sam!

I looked around, searching for the voices I'd heard or imagined. I saw a computer screen with the face of Helmann upon it. His appearance matched what I'd seen on the Brave New World video—the one where he described the elimination of billions. This didn't look like a video, though. It looked live; Helmann appeared to be waiting for someone with whom to speak.

Skype, I thought. I heard voices down the hall as well, and Helmann looked up, alert for the reappearance of Hans or someone else. The thought of Helmann, out of my reach on some other part of the planet, sent anger pulsing through me.

All will be well, now, Mademoiselle, said Christian.

Bits of overheard conversations came back to me along with the memory of what had been done to me.

No! I called out to Christian. *All will not be well. They've taken something from me. I want it back!*

I felt motion as Christian pulled us away from the center of the room and into the wall. It was a smart move—our icy forms would be a dead giveaway to a chameleon like Hans.

Sam, we must return to safety, said Christian.

Wait! I cried.

A man approached our room and crossed to the computer screen to speak with Helmann.

"I want her unharmed, Fritz," said Helmann. "Do I make myself clear? Hans has made enough mess of things today. God knows my instructions were simple enough."

Fritz's eyes darted nervously to where I'd been moments ago. Then he gasped and stood for a moment in silent shock as he spotted the operating table, now empty of me.

"What is it?" demanded Helmann.

"She is . . . she has . . . that is," Fritz hesitated.

"Yes?"

Fritz took in a deep breath. "She has vanished."

Both men were silent for several seconds. Then Fritz cleared his throat.

"Hans can easily bring her back, sir. We know where to find her, and we also know the location of all her living relations."

"That's hardly the point. Fritz, did I not warn you she would be a chameleon?" Helmann's voice sounded infinitely patient, but with anger pulsing just beneath.

"Father, I assure you, precautions were taken. She received the Neuroplex injection before Hans brought her from her home."

"Then the error must lie in *your new medication*." Helmann's tone was icy, accusatory.

"The Neuroplex has been thoroughly tested. I even used it on myself. The effects last for two days," said Fritz. "Unless, perhaps, in coordination with the anesthesia . . ."

We must leave! Christian sounded worried.

Not yet, I replied.

Hans strolled briskly into the room, joining Fritz beside the computer screen. He also looked confused by my absence.

"She managed to escape," said Fritz.

Hans bowed deeply to his father. "We beg forgiveness, Father. Fritz assured me it would not be possible—"

The angry man cut him off. "Fritz' conclusions were premature."

Hans spoke in deference. "I shall retrieve her at once."

"You'll retrieve her when I command it! You've bungled things badly enough for one day."

"Perhaps we could send an apology?" said Fritz. "Indicating Hans' mis-step?" Fritz' voice faded under the force of his father's withering glance.

"She is to be left alone for the time being," said Helmann. "Fritz, I want a thorough temperature-sweep of the building. Begin with the stasis chamber."

"Yes, sir," said Fritz, exiting.

Helmann turned to Hans, frowning. "I am most displeased."

Hans bowed as if to leave.

"You have disappointed me today, Hans. Your methods were inexcusable."

My methods were effective! I jerked in surprise as Hans' thoughts reached me, powerful within my mind.

"Forgive me, Father," Hans spoke aloud in a contrite voice.

The two men departed the room.

Now! Christian said to me. *Let us depart.*

They took an egg from me, Christian. I have to get it back.

I could feel Christian's indecision. I heard echoes of his thoughts, full of words like "deplorable" and "depraved."

86

Not today, Mademoiselle. To retrieve it, one of us must solidify. It cannot be you as you will at once experience the effects of the ether. And it cannot be me—I dare not release you.

Christian, Helmann is going to make a child—a child that's half me! It's hideous! I can't let them do this!

This is not the day, ma chère cousine, *they are sweeping the building to see if you remain. We must leave.*

I wept tearlessly as Christian carried me back to Las Abuelitas, toward home and a measure of safety.

Chapter Twelve

VIALS

• WILL •

I don't know how long I ran for, but everyone had gone to sleep by the time I got back inside the apartment. When I came solid, drowsiness pulled me under like a riptide. I passed out on my bed and slept 'til ten the next morning.

At the small table, Mickie and Sir Walter hovered over his computer tablet, watching Helmann's "Brave New World" video again.

"Yet these souls will perish, whether by our hand or another's, they have, even the youngest of them, less than a century before they will be gone and forgotten. Such a waste. And while they live their squalid existences of abject poverty and suffering, they continue to consume and destroy the very planet

that gives them life." Helmann's voice droned on and on. That was one sick bastard.

"Ah, young Will." Sir Walter pulled a chair around for me so I could watch.

I shook my head. "'S'okay," I said. "Seen it all before." I grabbed a plate and shoveled some sort of lunch meat and cheese onto it.

"Rolls in the paper bag," said Mick.

I grabbed one and tore into it with my thumbs, layered the meat and cheese inside, and took a large bite.

The roll was crusty outside, fluffy inside, fresh and slightly soured.

"Good, huh?" asked my sister.

"Incredible," I said, remembering a moment too late to swallow before talking.

Mick shook her head at my lack of manners, but she didn't get on my case. "It's like it's against the law to make bad bread in Europe," she said.

Sir Walter laughed. "Certainly, it is in *La France*."

I nodded. "I read about that in a bread book. How the government regulates baguette production."

Mick's "That's just weird," overlapped with my "It sure works."

I punched her shoulder and she mussed my hair. We were friends again.

"So what's the plan for today?" I asked. "Blow up Geneses *Romana?*"

"You wish," snorted my sister. "No, I take that back. *I* wish."

Sir Walter slid a sheet of paper along the table to me. "I returned last night and have created this map of the headquarters of Geneses in Rome."

I studied the sheet. Three floors, a handful of offices on each. Far smaller than the empty building we'd explored in Clichy-sous-Bois.

"This is great," I said. "Sorry about last night. You shouldn't have had to do this by yourself."

With long fingers fluttering like butterfly wings, he waved my apology aside.

"So we're looking for, one—" I held up a finger, "What Helmann's buying buildings for, and, two—" another finger, "What Helmann's timeline is for the end of the world.?"

Mick spoke. "Don't forget three," she said, extending a carefully-chosen finger, "How to totally make Pfeffer's life a living torment."

Sir Walter ignored my sister's rude gesture. "I believe that about sums it up."

"How about you?" I asked Mickie. "You going to tour the Eternal City today?"

She frowned.

"Your sister has graciously consented to remain within-doors," said Sir Walter. "So as to avoid unwanted detection."

"Oh," I said. "Aw, Mick, I'm so sorry."

She shrugged. "No big deal. You're the one in love with old, fallen-down buildings, not me." Then she smiled. "Just keep the Italian food coming and no one gets hurt."

"Cool," I said. It went without saying I was all for Italian food.

Sir Walter and I departed, zipping invisibly along narrow Roman streets made of an ancient cobblestone. *Hey,* I wrote out, *mind if we push pause here for a minute? It's just,* I hesitated. Sam would totally get why this mattered. I wasn't sure Sir Walter was going to. *I, uh, want to feel the road for a minute.*

I heard a low chuckle in my mind. *But of course,* was all he said.

I reached down, plunging a hand back and forth through the smoothed-over surface. It felt like a warm river that flowed every direction all at the same time. Like that bubbler thing that pushed water up from a rock at Sam's pool. I could've stayed here pushing my hand back and forth all day. But as I glanced around, I changed my mind. Rome's like, made out of stone. Roads, sidewalks, buildings, fountains, road barriers, fencing—everything's made of rock. Man, I could have some fun here. But it wasn't a real temptation. Not with the job in front of us. And in any case, not without Sam by my side.

Feeling the ache of her absence again, I tried shoving it away, down inside my shoes.

Let's go, I wrote.

A man who cannot pass his days in La France could do worse than to settle in Rome, sighed Sir Walter, rising alongside me.

When we arrived, Geneses *Romana* was humming with people. So I kind of got my wish about spending the day rock-surfing, 'cause Sir Walter said the only way to move around in a building of chameleon-aware people was to use the walls. I'd done this at Bridget Li's, walking along the length of her building *inside* the wall. Roman rock felt different, more *solid* maybe.

Shortly after our arrival, a courier on a Vespa pulled up on the sidewalk fronting the headquarters. Reception buzzed him through after he held a box up for them to read the address.

Check it out, I wrote. *Package for Signore Pepe.* That was the name outside Pfeffer's office, apparently meaning "Mister Pepper" in Italian.

"*Al Signore, immediatamente,*" said a woman behind the desk.

A young man nodded and took off down the hall with the box. It was large, like it might hold a big old-style TV. Or a body. Or who-knew what.

Our first destination presents itself, said Sir Walter. *Let us see what lies inside the package.*

"*Rapidamente,*" called receptionist to the box-carrier.

Italian sounded very French, only with an Italian accent.

Beside us, box-dude muttered something indecipherable that sounded a lot like, "Next time carry it yourself."

We slipped along the wall into Pfeffer's office, settling behind his desk as the man himself rose to take his package. On his computer, which we could see great from here, it looked like he was authorizing a payment followed by a ton of zeroes. I scanned down the page. The name of the country he was sending money to was unfamiliar to me.

Helmann is now acquiring property in the nations of central Africa, said Sir Walter.

Terrific, I wrote back.

Pfeffer returned to his desk, setting the package to one side. Hurriedly he made an adjustment to the amount on the screen by deleting two extra zeroes. Then he authorized the payment. Closing the screen on the computer, he carefully opened the package, analyzing the contents briefly. He frowned at what he saw—rows of identical vials, marked with green stripes and containing a clear liquid. Pfeffer sighed heavily. He removed the tray on top and carried it across the room, opening a hidden panel in the wall with his pen-key. He switched out the tray for an identical-looking one hidden in the wall. Locking the hidden panel, he carried the replacement tray back to the box, setting it atop a steaming packet.

Dry ice? I wondered.

From his desk, he dialed three digits into an office phone.

"Sorry to bother you, but today's package from San Francisco has arrived," he said.

We couldn't hear the response.

A sharp rap sounded on the office door, and Pfeffer rose to admit his visitor, a blond-haired dude with light blue eyes.

Franz! said Sir Walter, clearly surprised.

I was kind of surprised too, seeing as, in my mind, Franz was a mean ten-year-old kid from the black book.

"Brother," said Pfeffer, a thin smile on his face.

"Pfeffer," said Franz, returning the greeting minus the smile.

"I would be happy to take these for you," said Pfeffer.

Franz replied curtly. "Father asked *me* to place the boxes, not you."

The venom in Franz' tone made me remember how he'd liked hurting people as a boy. Apparently that hadn't changed.

"Of course," said Pfeffer. "It is only that I wish you would allow me to do more. I feel so . . . indebted. You have restored my abilities as a chameleon, given me a place among you, and yet I do so little." Here, Pfeffer placed a hand upon the box that had just arrived.

"Your service at present is invaluable," said Franz.

"Of course," murmured Pfeffer. "I only ask to serve."

Franz looked sharply at Pfeffer.

Pfeffer dropped his eyes. "That is, I should be glad to serve where ever Father sees fit."

Franz turned to leave, then stopped at the door. "I will let Father know of your wish to further our Glorious Cause in additional ways."

"I am grateful," said Pfeffer. "And, brother?"

Franz waited.

"I feel sure that I could assist you when it comes time for the Release of Angels. Would it not make sense to finish the work more quickly with additional help?"

Franz frowned. "Indeed. This is something I've told Father repeatedly."

Pfeffer looked hopeful.

Franz spoke again. "However, dear brother, he means yet to accomplish it all himself. At any rate, he has not entrusted me with the pass-phrase, even though I have demonstrated to him that the Angels must be released at thrice the speed he can manage alone."

"How did he answer your . . . suggestion?" asked Pfeffer.

Franz made a small, grunting sound.

"I see," said Pfeffer.

Neither of them said anything and I figured that was it, but then Pfeffer got this look on his face I recognized. Like he was trying to decide whether or not to reveal something really big. Knowing him like I did, I knew that look actually meant he'd committed to say something, but he just hadn't realized it yet.

Franz must've known that look, too. "Yes?" he asked.

"It may be nothing," said Pfeffer.

"Either it is something or it is not," snapped Franz, impatience thinning his mouth into a tight line.

Pfeffer's voice came out softly. "He said, to me or to himself—I know not which—that *three little words* which changed his life, will soon change the world."

Franz stepped in closer. His eyes got narrow. "You think he referred to the pass-phrase?"

"I don't know. What do you think?" Pfeffer's eyes looked all eager, like when he used to ask me questions about Rippler's Syndrome.

"Possibly," said Franz. "But it matters not if he remains determined to act alone."

"Yes, yes, of course," said Pfeffer. His eyes drifted to his desk and the box. "Forgive my wanderings, brother." Saying this, he handed the box of vials to Franz.

Franz' brow furrowed as he took it. "Only our orders are of importance. Do not forget that."

Pfeffer did this little bow, reminding me of Sir Walter, and Franz pulled the door shut behind him.

Fascinating, said Sir Walter from inside my head.

"Traitorous jerk" felt more accurate to me, but Sir Walter kept a lid on any anger he might be feeling. Myself, I was having a hard time just staying invisible 'cause I wanted to beat the crap out of Pfeffer.

The rest of the day was boring. Sir Walter wanted to stick with Pfeffer, "to get a sense of how he passes his days," and the answer was: he passed time doing mind-numbing activities like making and adjusting payments on behalf of Geneses Corporation International.

Pfeffer took off for the day an hour after sunset. The rest of the office had already cleared out, but Sir Walter stayed longer, searching through files once more. At last he seemed to finish, although he hadn't found anything useful.

Your sister awaits us, he said.

We owed her Italian, and I was down for that after the world's most uneventful afternoon.

On the way home, Sir Walter mentioned that he had arranged with the *nonna*, or elderly landlady, for some Italian home-cooking. I left him downstairs to get dinner. Once I rippled solid inside the apartment, my stomach roared with hunger. I didn't see Mick right off, which most likely meant napping or showering. Seating myself beside the window to the courtyard, I watched as Sir Walter attempted to pass our landlady a large stack of Euro bills. They were haggling over the price of dinner or something. She spoke with her hands as much as with words. After a few minutes, she walked off shaking her head and mumbling in Italian. Sir Walter stood like he was still waiting. I didn't know what for; he already had a bowl that looked like dinner.

But he stayed and, sure enough, she came back a minute later and handed him a set of keys. Which she didn't let go of right off. It seemed like she had a string of *No*-this and *No*-that to get through before she would let go. Shaking her head once more, she punctuated whatever she had to say with a jabbing forefinger that stopped just short of actually taking out one of Sir Walter's eyes.

"*Arrivaderla, Signora*," he called out, doing one of his little trademark bows.

"*Buona Notte, Signore*," she replied. She grabbed a broom that was leaning against the wall behind her and began beating the paving stones. She was muttering in Italian and still moving her head back and forth like she seriously did not approve of Sir Walter.

"Mick," I called, "Come here quick. Check out our landlady."

My sister ignored me. The head-shaking below ceased, although the mumbling continued.

"Mick, hurry up or she'll be gone."

Just then the *nonna* with the broom looked up and saw me in the window. The muttering got louder and the head-shaking started up again. I pulled back from the window, laughing, and headed down our short hallway to my sister's bedroom. I passed the bathroom, empty, on the way, and knocked on Mick's door.

"Hey! Dinner. Wake up. You should have seen our landlady and Sir Walter going at it just now." I waited to give Mick a moment to wake up, then I pushed the door open. "Wake up already."

The light beside her bed illuminated the quiet, empty room. My sister wasn't here.

I turned back down the hall, checking the bathroom more thoroughly and passing Sir Walter as he entered the apartment.

"Mick's gone," I said. Something like panic was setting up camp in my gut. "No note, no nothing. She always leaves a note on the kitchen table." It had been our system for years.

Sir Walter set a large bowl of pasta on the edge of the kitchen table, which was empty except for the laptop.

"Why would she take off?" I asked, more to myself than to Sir Walter.

"Indeed," said Sir Walter. "Although perhaps it would be better to ask ourselves who has taken her?"

Chapter Thirteen

FORGIVENESS

• SAM •

Take me to Gwyn's, I told Christian as we rose out of the valley's tule fog and into the foothills.

Are you certain we should go to the dwelling of your friend? Would not you prefer that your parents know of your safety? asked Christian.

They're going to worry for sure if they see me lying in bed looking like I've been shot full of drugs, I replied. *They think I went to Fresno for the day. I can use Gwyn's phone to call them after I . . . recover.*

Very well.

We arrived at Gwyn's, shivered through the rock wall of her mom's bakery building, and rose along the stairs. As we passed the tiny bathroom, I thought of something I was going to need.

Advil.

Apparently I'd thought it "aloud," because I could feel Christian's confusion over the strange word.

I explained. *It's a pain reliever. You had those in the seventeenth century, didn't you?*

We lacked "ad-ville," he replied. *Will I find it in an herb garden? Send me an image.*

Amused, I sent him an image of a bottle of Advil on the counter in the Li's tiny bathroom.

A decoction. I shall obtain it. Saying this, he set me gently upon Gwyn's bed.

As I solidified, a fog wove itself through my brain, as heavy as the one we'd traversed in the valley.

Christian had to wake me to deliver the Advil. *"Mademoiselle,"* he whispered. "The ether affects you still. Do you wish for the decoction of *Ad-Ville?*"

I rolled over, took the meds, and fell back into a dark sleep.

I awoke to the gloom of evening, having the sense that I'd just left a church service for the second time that day.

"You're awake," whispered Gwyn, sounding delighted. "Good. Finally someone to talk to who's not completely pissed off at me or ignoring me."

"Gwyn?" I mumbled. My mouth felt like it had been swapped repeatedly by large cotton balls.

"Drink this," she said, passing me a cup with a straw sticking out of it.

I drank something that tasted like peppermint and bitter herbs. "Sylvia-tea," I said.

"No, this is Bridget Li-tea. It's supposed to cure hangovers," said Gwyn. "I told Ma you came over so your folks wouldn't know you'd experimented with alcohol last night. She's the one pissed off at me."

"You're good," I said, nodding. I quit nodding when the room started wobbling. "And my folks, why am I here according to them?"

"They think we're just hanging after a trip to Fresno."

I frowned, remembering something Hans had said. "Did you and your mom get some text from my phone about going to a spa?"

Gwyn rolled her eyes. "Yeah, obviously Ma vetoed the idea. I won't tell you what she said about your favorite spa. Let's just say Ma doesn't appreciate Japanese culture." Gwyn's eyes grew large. "Omigosh! That text wasn't from you! Ew, it was from *him*, wasn't it?"

I nodded.

"Does he still have your phone?"

I nodded again.

"You need to get the number disconnected," Gwyn said. "In case Will or Sir Walter call you."

One more thing to do. Get a new cell number.

"So I guess Christian filled you in on . . . everything?"

"When he could be bothered to," she replied.

My brow wrinkled in confusion.

"He's the one who's been ignoring me," she explained. "He's busy praying again. Or chanting. Whatever you Catholics do. He was all telling me about your little vacay in San Francisco and then he said it was 'vespers,' and he started in on this sing-song-y Latin. I made him ripple so he wouldn't wake you up." She shrugged. "And so Ma wouldn't get all in my business about him."

I started to nod again but had to quit. The dizziness hovered nearby. "He's probably singing something called 'the hours of the day.' Nuns and priests and other good Catholics do that. Seven set times, day and night. I've actually been hearing him recently."

"Seven times *every day*?" asked Gwyn.

"And night," I said. "Although it eased up in the last century. But I'm guessing no one's updated Christian. He's probably still a seventeenth century Catholic." I tried propping myself up in Gwyn's small bed. I ached in places I didn't want to think about right now. "I think I need to pee."

"Oh, good sign!" said Gwyn, standing to help me. "I mean, it's always a good sign on the Emergency Room Channel shows. God, Sam, I'm so sorry. About what Hans did to you."

I didn't want to talk about it.

"Right," she said. "I'll just kick Christian out of the bathroom."

"You put him in the bathroom?"

"Yeah, dude, it creeped me out to have an invisible guy chanting prayers in my bedroom, okay?"

I grunted a laugh and Gwyn helped me to the bathroom.

After she got me settled back in her bed, she told me I should be feeling pretty much normal once the anesthesia left my system. "I found a recorded show on egg-harvesting from the Make Big Bucks channel." She laughed, but then cut herself off, and her eyes got soft. "I'm sorry, Sam. I'm not very good when things are horrible and serious. I feel like I have to laugh or I'll scream. I guess I just want to lighten things up. But some things aren't meant to be . . . lightened, are they?"

Reaching for her hand, I smiled. "Thanks for trying to help."

"You're welcome," whispered Gwyn. Then she sighed. "What else did I have to do with my time except surf? You were laying there looking all death-warmed-over. Catholic boy was chanting prayers. Ma's not talking to me."

"I'm glad you're here with me," I said. Tears formed in my eyes and I forced them back. "I'm not ready to go home."

"I already called Sylvia and told her you're spending the night," Gwyn said. "Ma says you can stay as long as you know she doesn't cook dinners."

My mouth formed half a smile. "Trust me, food doesn't sound good right now."

Gwyn scooted down the bed so she could wrap her arms around me. Her hair smelled like berry shampoo, which normally I'm not a fan of. But right now, it smelled like the best thing in the world to me. I let a few tears squeeze out before we pulled apart.

"I feel so . . . *mad* right now," I said. A few more tears chased their way down my face.

"Of course you do," Gwyn said, passing a box of tissue.

"And I miss Will so ba-ad." My voice cracked and I started crying hard.

Gwyn sat with me, holding me on one side, passing Kleenex. Once I'd gotten through the worst of it, she spoke. "Will's job right now is to figure out the best way to kick some bad-guy butt, which is great considering someone needs a serious kick in the pants right now."

My voice came out in a whisper. "I should have stayed with Will, Gwyn. I came here to stay safe and look what happened."

Gwyn frowned, thinking. "Coming home was the right thing to do, given what you knew at the time."

She shook her head. "Do you have any idea how much your dad loves you?"

I picked at the quilt on my lap. My dad wasn't the most demonstrative of parents.

"Sam, your dad's eyes, when he's watching you at home," Gwyn paused, casting her eyes around the room for words. "The man *treasures* you, girlfriend. That's the only way I can describe it. He gets this look in his eyes when he sees you that is different from how he looks at anyone else. Including Sylvia."

"Ew, I seriously hope so!"

"Shut up. You know what I mean." Gwyn took my hand in hers. "It would kill him to lose you, Sam. You did the right thing, coming home."

I looked down again, remembering how I'd used the exact same words to convince Sir Walter I had to come back to Las Abuelitas. "Yeah. I know."

The sound of Christian softly clearing his throat made us both look up.

"If I am interrupting, I can vanish once more," he said.

"Well, that's just dumb, since you'd still be here anyway," said Gwyn, patting the bed beside her. "Come on over. Join the convo."

Christian took a chair at Gwyn's desk instead, after bowing slightly.

"God, I love how you do that, but you have absolutely got to quit bowing at school," said Gwyn, shaking her head sadly.

Christian flushed. "As you command."

"Oh-boy-there-we-go-again," said Gwyn, blurring her words together to obscure them from Christian. "Which brings up something else," she continued, "Now that the girls of Las Abs High have noticed your existence." Sighing, she placed one hand on Christian's shoulder to steady herself as she leaned and grabbed a notepad off her desk. "Sorry," she said, indicating the personal contact. Of course she didn't mean it.

"I've made some notes for you. If a girl says any of what's written here to you, you want to run the other way because she's after your virginity." Gwyn paused and cleared her throat. "You know what that is, right?"

I rolled my eyes.

"You will pardon me," interrupted Christian. "I am no virgin."

"Really?" Gwyn's voice came out in a low purr.

"He was married, dweeb," I said, throwing a one-eyed stuffed tiger at her.

It was very ugly, but she hugged it close, glaring at me.

"But I am puzzled," said Christian. "You say the soliciting of sexual congress is permitted within the halls of learning?"

"Say what?" asked Gwyn.

I remembered things Will had told me about life in the court of Louis the Fourteenth. "Gwyn's not talking about . . . prostitution. In our century, well in our country, anyway, some kids choose to have, er, sexual contact outside of marriage."

"The *unmarried* females are promiscuous?" asked Christian.

"Very," said Gwyn. "So stay away from girls who give you their number or say they want to hook-up or fool around or . . . just keep clear of the girls around here. They're not all like me, 'kay?"

My fingers gripped the fur of another stuffed animal, but I stopped myself from actually throwing it. I was in Gwyn's care, after all.

"I am here to guard the safety of *Mademoiselle* Ruiz. I shall not permit myself to become distracted," replied Christian. Then his face turned a deep scarlet. "That is, it shall not happen again. I shall never forgive myself for allowing a distraction to prevent me from protecting you."

"He means his chanting thing," murmured Gwyn. "It's what distracted him last night."

"I beg forgiveness, *Mademoiselle*," said Christian rising to bow deeply.

"Yeah, um, sure. I forgive you," I said, knowing it would matter to him.

"So, you pray seven times every day?" asked Gwyn.

Christian bowed. "I celebrate the hours daily."

"That's cool," said Gwyn.

I turned my laughter into a cough. *Cool* from the girl who said, minutes ago, that it creeped her out?

"But I shall no longer do so facing the east, nor shall I lower the lids of my eyes. I believe neither is required of me by God."

"Um, yeah, I think you're good there," I said. "So my window faces east, I guess?"

"Yes. I was turned from you last night, or Hans could not have assailed your person." Remorse creased his face.

Why did my freaking window have to face east? I felt anger rise at Christian for his mistake, even though I'd forgiven him. It looked like forgiveness was going to be more of an ongoing activity.

"Still, you saved her in the end, didn't you?" asked Gwyn, brightly. "Tell her how you did it. How you could hear her."

"Your thoughts called to me loudly," Christian said to me. "Sir Walter said this might happen. He believed you to be gifted in this ability which is not shared by all chameleons." He straightened proudly. "It is a de Rocheforte trait."

"So I've heard," I said. "But I can't speak my thoughts to Will or hear his thoughts. We write stuff out, using images."

Christian nodded. "He possesses not the trait. Your communication with him will be difficult always."

Gwyn laughed. "While she's invisible, you mean. They do just fine when they're solid."

Or on the same continent, I added to myself, thinking again of the slow drift of tectonic plates as South America said farewell to Africa.

The Will-shaped space in my heart contracted, dwarfing my body's other pains. It gripped me, this longing, so vast that it could swallow continents. I missed Will. I needed him. How could I be expected to face what I'd just faced, without Will at my side? I was calling Sir Walter tomorrow. Forget about safety and phone etiquette. I *needed* Will like I needed air and sunshine. Like I needed to run. I refused to live without him.

And then I thought about Helmann's Brave New World video. About a holocaust that would leave humanity in shattered pieces. I couldn't ask Will to leave Sir Walter's side. He had work to do. And so did I. I would lock away this hurt, this ache that matched the shape of Will's body no longer curved against mine.

I had to recover my egg. I had to thwart Hans and Helmann in every way possible.

Now all I had to do was convince Christian to help.

Excerpted from the personal diary of Girard L'Inferne.

Circa 2005

Our first purge has begun. After decades of collecting data on those who carry the chameleon gene, we have begun to eliminate them in numbers small enough to raise no suspicion. Hans, especially, understands the need for secrecy, in the more sensitive areas of the world, such as the United States. He pleases me, in his diligence to be certain the deaths might have happened to anyone.

Any hesitations I felt six decades ago, when I made available the medication which counteracts Helmann's disease— these hesitations are laid to rest now. The medical records of the recipients lead us infallibly to eliminate potential carriers.

The way is being cleared for the future. For the day when I shall offer to the deserving the gift of life eternal. For their children at any rate. Although, who knows but that we may, in time, find ourselves able to fuse the gene for invisibility into the DNA of an adult. I am certain we shall not lack for volunteers should the day arrive!

I estimate we can eliminate ninety-five percent of all living carriers in the next several years. Those who escape us? Well, once I have the run of the planet, it will be a simple enough step to convince the jealous to turn in their neighbors or their family members.

It has been done before.

I hesitated briefly over removing the last of Elisabeth's descendants. But I must show strength and not weakness in this *matter. Who are they to me? Merely the offspring of her bastard bratlings.*

Chapter Fourteen

ONLY MADMEN DRIVE IN ROME

• WILL •

"You think she was kidnapped?" I asked. "Did Pfeffer 'hear' us somehow?"

Sir Walter frowned and glared, the nearest I'd seen him to angry. "Formerly, Pfeffer *never* gave any indication that he could hear the thoughts from my mind unless we were *both invisible*. I tried for years to train him, but it was in vain."

"Like me," I said grimly. "But let's say he *did* notice us: where would he take her?"

Sir Walter brought a fist down on the kitchen table in the first display of anger I'd ever observed. The bowl of pasta rattled and settled beside the computer. A flicker of light caught my attention: the monitor, coming to life, out of screen-saver mode.

"There's a note!" I said, leaning over Sir Walter to read a brief message that had been typed onto the computer screen.

I went to Saint Peter's. Got stir-crazy. Back for dinner. Make it good! ;)

"WHAT?" I roared. At Sir Walter. 'Cause he was the only person in the room. But it wasn't *him* I was pissed at and next thing I knew, I'd kicked a dining chair that bumped the table as it fell. The bowl of pasta teetered and slipped, dumping dinner all over the fallen chair.

"Church? Really? *Now* she gets religion?" I paced back and forth, uttering foul things about my sister and her sense of timing. I really wanted to kick another chair over, but I knew Sir Walter would be the one paying for damages. I settled for pounding my fist into my left hand. Repeatedly.

Sir Walter's soft laugh filled the dead space. "Perhaps an invisible run would be in order?"

Somehow, him asking that just took all the fight out of me, and I sagged onto the couch. "I should've known to check the computer," I mumbled. "We always leave notes on the kitchen table. It was so obvious."

Sir Walter's mouth curved up but just on one side. "*Calquecop le pa que be quand las denses s'en soun anandos.*"

"Am I supposed to understand that?"

"It is a saying in the tongue of my youth: *Sometimes the bread shows up after the teeth are already gone*," he replied.

"Hmmph," I grunted.

"It is a way of saying that bad timing happens, my young friend."

He was trying to help. I made an effort to be less grizzly bear. "That sounded like Spanish. You spoke Spanish when you were a kid?"

"*Occitan*," he corrected. "It is similar to Spanish. Or rather, to Catalan."

I sighed, stretching my hands high above my head. "So you figure she's okay, then?" I asked.

"I think it unlikely Pfeffer will venture to St. Peter's cathedral this evening." He tugged at his goatee as he answered my question. Meaning he was just a little worried.

Right then I heard Mick's special knock at the door.

"You better get it," I said, folding my arms over my chest, anger returning.

""I'm so glad you're back," said my sister, entering. "Locked myself out. It smells like heaven in . . . here." Her eyes found the upside-down bowl of dinner as she removed sunglasses and some kind of head-covering. "Oh. Bummer."

"Yeah," I said. "A little casualty of your need for fresh air."

She looked at me, puzzled, a questioning smile on her face.

"We thought you'd been kidnapped," I said.

"I left a note." She pointed to the computer.

"Yeah, well, first we thought you'd been kidnapped. Then we saw the note and realized you'd just been selfish."

My sister closed her eyes and did her little count-under-the-breath thing. "I needed to get out, okay, Will? This apartment gets a little claustrophobic with that old grandma sweeping all day and shaking her head at me if I get too close to the window."

My anger evaporated as I thought of the *nonna* muttering at my sister all day. I laughed. "Dude, she's hysterical, huh?"

Turning, I asked Sir Walter about the exchange I'd seen between him and the old grandma.

"Ah, yes," said Sir Walter. "It now appears most fortunate that I secured the use of her deceased husband's Fiat." He looked sadly at the pasta. "I believe we shall dine out this evening." Taking one of my sister's hands in both of his, he smiled. "A little celebration for things feared lost but happily recovered."

"You think it's safe for us to go out?" Mick asked.

"*Now* you think of that?" I asked, rising to clean up the mess of pasta.

I had the satisfaction of seeing my sister flush red and stop herself from responding in kind.

"I'm really sorry, Will," she said. "Forgive me?"

I nodded.

"I left a note," she said.

"Screen-saver kicked on," I replied.

"Oh," she said. "I didn't think of that."

She seemed so genuinely repentant, I didn't have the heart to mutter "obviously."

"We don't have to go out for dinner," she said. "I know I took a risk earlier today—"

Sir Walter interrupted. "No, no. I believe the population of Rome should be sufficient to keep apart Pfeffer and ourselves."

"Don't forget Franz. He knows what you look like, too, doesn't he?" I asked.

Sir Walter shrugged in a way that I translated as, "*Yes, but it matters not.*" Or maybe just, "*I've made up my mind, dweeb.*"

He turned to my sister. "You were wise to conceal your appearance."

"Yeah," she said softly. "Something Pfeffer taught me."

"For when we used to visit his lab," I explained. I didn't mention how they used to force me to dress like a girl. Seriously, the sooner some things are forgotten, the better.

We grabbed hats and scarves, me and Sir Walter swapping, which was pretty hilarious, seeing him wearing my Nintendo stretch-cap.

"You really want to look different, you could shave," I said, tapping my chin.

He looked at me like I'd just suggested he cut off his right hand.

My sister defended him. "He looks plenty strange wearing the hat."

Apparently our landlady agreed, shaking her head and clucking under her breath as we piled into her car. Sir Walter made me and Mick sit in back.

"You will be more hidden," he said.

I shook my head. If he wanted hidden, we could grab my sister and ripple. But Sir Walter was in "be nice to Mickie" mode right now, and he knew she hated that form of transportation.

We pulled into the alley fronting our apartment building. Cars lined both sides of the narrow street. Most were parked half on the sidewalk, half on the street. I didn't see how we were exiting this road without taking a few side-mirrors out, but Sir Walter managed it okay. The alley dumped into a little roundabout circling a fountain, and that was where things got interesting.

A group of guys my age were out on Vespas, two or three to a bike, zipping around the circle like it was a race. They called insults to one another, laughing as they passed us by, some of them reaching out to thump the hood of our car. There was no way Sir Walter could enter the roundabout without taking out a couple of the mopeds, so we just sat there until one biker took off down another alley, followed by the rest of them.

We reached a wider street where two-way traffic was a possibility, barely, and joined a handful of other cars, all in a hurry, like their *nonnas* were gonna give them what-for if they didn't get back for dinner.

Sir Walter drove a little too slowly for some of them. A car would be coming our way, and we'd see, to our left, that someone had decided to pass us. It would look like collision was inevitable, but then Sir Walter and the oncoming car would each part just a tiny bit toward the outside, and maybe up on the sidewalk, and the passing car would zip through. Crazy.

We made another turn, onto a still-bigger street. I tried counting lanes, but it was tricky as the Roman drivers didn't seem to stay in a lane for very long. I could see white stripes on the pavement, but clearly these lines meant nothing to the drivers. Apparently traffic signals didn't mean much either. Even red lights. Eventually, though, enough cars at the front of traffic would stop for a red light and that would force everyone behind to stop as well. Except for the motorized bikers. They would zip between cars, or down the sidewalk, and line up in front of all the cars waiting for the light to change. When the signal turned green, the cars would pass the motor-bikes and race towards the next traffic light where the cycle repeated. All without staying in lanes.

Although it was February, and cold, many motorists drove with a window down so that they could communicate via hand-gesture, apparently a method preferred over turn-signal blinkers. Sir Walter did okay with all of it. I thought it was sort of funny, since I didn't have to drive. Beside me, Mick clutched a beaded rosary necklace I was sure she hadn't owned before her trip to Vatican City. Her lips hadn't stopped moving since we'd left that first roundabout.

We hit a downhill stretch where you could get a look ahead to see how bad the traffic really was. White lights coming towards us for miles, red lights stretching into the distance until reaching a really large roundabout. I saw at least eight cars-widths of fluid, lane-changing traffic. We inched towards the roundabout. As we got closer, I saw a uniformed official directing traffic from atop a small cement column. Not a job I envied. I leaned my head against the window, wondering how much farther to dinner.

None of us were prepared for what happened next. A motorcyclist took advantage of a slender aisle between several cars and rushed forward to catch the policeman's "Go" signal before it switched to a "Don't even think about it" signal. The biker wasn't going to make it. The Mercedes in front of us was attempting to sneak through while the policeman shook a threatening hand at the motorcycle. The car behind us apparently assumed Sir Walter would do the same. At the last minute the car in front of us changed his mind without notifying the guy behind us, who then rammed into us so hard that our hood crumpled into the Mercedes. Mick's head jerked up from praying.

And then there was this massive chain effect, like, once a few cars saw us get sandwiched, they thought, hey, looks like fun, let's all try it! Must have been a hundred cars smashing into each other's bumpers. And probably three-hundred angry, gesticulating Italians shouting at one another and the one policeman. No one seemed to feel it was important to stay inside their car.

Sir Walter was trying to get our car started again, but the engine wouldn't turn over. I rolled my window down, sticking my head out to see how bad it was up ahead.

Sir Walter cursed, looked behind us to confirm what Mick and I could both see. "Grab your sister and let us disappear."

"What?" I asked. "Why?"

"I do not wish to have our identities brought to anyone's attention while we stay in Rome. I will instruct the *nonna* to report the vehicle as stolen."

He extended one hand for me to grab, looking in all directions to see if it was safe to disappear.

Everyone's attention was directed away from us. "Go!" he said.

My hunger disappeared the moment my body did. That was a relief anyway. The three of us eased through the screechy metal doors, and then Sir Walter must've decided passing through all that metal and all those angry Italians was too much, 'cause he angled us towards a strip of dirt planted with trees every ten or so feet. That felt a lot better. For Sam's sake, I tried to pay attention to what the trees tasted or smelled like, but honestly, I wasn't picking up on anything much.

Eventually, we made our way back to the alley where our apartment sat. As soon as we solidified, Sir Walter excused himself.

"I believe there is a vendor selling pizza around the corner," he said.

Pizza sounded good. Bed sounded good. Never, ever driving in Rome again sounded good.

We ate and crawled off to bed.

Any hopes I had for sleeping in late were dashed way too early the next morning. Mickie and Sir Walter were talking in very excited voices that I couldn't sleep through. I stumbled into the kitchen.

"The sun's not up," I complained, grabbing a roll off the table.

Mickie looked at me, her face wrinkled with worry as bad as I'd ever seen it.

"What?" I asked.

She looked ready to burst into tears.

Sir Walter indicated the computer. I looked and saw an news article about last night's car pile-up. With a photo showing about a mile of cars, although only those in front were really visible.

And then I saw what had my sister so upset.

Me. Sticking my head out the window, which I'd done for, like, all of two seconds. In front of me, looking ridiculous in a Nintendo stretch-cap, sat Sir Walter.

Thanks to some stupid cell phone camera, we were officially headline news.

Chapter Fifteen

AROUND ALL THE TIME

• SAM •

"Hey, Christian," said Gwyn. She sidled herself next to him in the one-person passenger seat of my Blazer.

"Really, Gwyn?" I muttered, pulling the car into reverse.

She'd called, insisting it looked like rain and would I please swing by the bakery to pick her up. The bakery was directly across from the school parking lot.

"Over there," she said, pointing to the far side of the lot. "I saw a good parking space."

What she saw was an opportunity to hang out thigh to thigh with Christian. She flung an arm around his neck as I revved over a speed-bump.

"Hey, careful, Sam! Not all of us are seat-belted in here!" She smiled at Christian and murmured, "Sorry," indicating the drape of her arm along his shoulders.

She was patently *not* sorry.

"Oh, darn," she said as another car took the spot. "Guess we'll have to circle around again. I didn't see David Lopez aiming for that parking spot."

I'd bet crazy kinds of money she *did* see him. I was familiar with the species *Gwynicus Prowlicus* and its devious ways.

Later, over lunch, Gwyn timed her seat-grabbing perfectly. That is, she waited until she could tell which seat Christian meant to take and then angled herself in so that he spent a brief moment upon her lap.

As he stood and apologized, she blinked at him innocently, something she'd perfected through years of hiding bad behavior from her mom.

Christian flushed while speaking to Gwyn. "Allow me to point out that this might be avoided, had you allowed me to remain standing until you had chosen your seat."

Gwyn had told Christian he should quit doing things like remaining standing until the girls were seated. Or rising from the table if a girl got up to buy another soda. As far as I could tell, Gwyn's ideas of Christian's habits came from watching Jane Austen movies with her mom rather than from actual knowledge of seventeenth century court life in France.

But Christian was too polite to say anything to embarrass her. Or maybe he found it all amusing. Or maybe he wasn't listening. His vigilance on my behalf had definitely scaled way up since my kidnapping.

I found myself keeping my eyes open as well. I scanned faces in the halls instead of tracing the flow of cracks in the concrete as I moved from class to class. But no one was looking at me. They all stared at the guy walking beside me. He'd altered his gait since coming to California. I wondered how he'd been able to do it so well until he told me that walking lessons had been part of his daily routine as a young courtier.

"We studied the rules of motion and how to present ourselves most attractively to the world," he'd said. "I understand an entire art-form has grown from our efforts and survives to this day—the 'ballet,' Sir Walter informs me."

All I knew was that Christian had figured out how to blend in and yet still attract a heck of a lot of stares. As the three of us walked together to biology, every girl we passed turned her head back over her shoulder to keep her eyes on Christian.

"Dr. Yang's going to wonder why the sudden outbreak of neck strains in high school girls," I murmured to Gwyn as we sat for class. "It's ridiculous."

In her seat beside me, Gwyn scribbled for a few seconds and passed a note to me.

Sad-looking eyes—check.

Amazing hair—check.

Ass-to-die-for—check.

What part of this confuses you?

This time when I rolled my eyes, they ached from repetitive motion strain. I had to admit she was right about Christian's eyes, though. They did have this sort of sad-puppy-dog look to them. *Haunted,* Sylvia had called them.

Gwyn reached back to pull a stray leaf from Christian's long hair. "Flowing locks of gold," she'd said when he wasn't in hearing range, "Hair that belongs to a bass player in a really cool band."

I could hear a girl seated behind Christian quizzing him on what biology was like in French schools.

"Do you study reproduction?" she asked. "Or anatomy?"

I glanced back to see her adjusting a tight tee-shirt to display her own body parts to advantage.

Christian's face was red when he turned forward. Gwyn stared at the girl looking like she could shoot lasers from her eyes.

She passed me another note.

OMG Can you believe the girls at this school?

I snorted back a laugh while she waited for me to respond. On the board, Mr. Polwen had written: HUMAN CLONING—ETHICAL OR UNETHICAL?

Gwyn sent me another note.

Do you think Christian gets lonely here?

Ignoring her, I scribbled notes on a controversial cloning facility that had come to light last fall. I'd heard about their claimed success with humans. The location of the facility had been kept secret, but in the photos you could see the Cyrillic alphabet, so it was somewhere in the former Soviet Union, people surmised.`

Gwyn kicked my foot and looked at me with an eyebrows-raised expression that asked, *Well, don't you have an opinion?*

Probably, I wrote at the bottom of a scrap of paper. I left it on my desk where she'd see it. My stomach was doing sick flops as I tried to copy Polwen's notes on zygotes and blastocysts, the names for the earliest stages of human embryo development. I *had* to get my egg back. And soon.

Class dismissed and Gwyn linked one of her arms through mine, the other through Christian's.

"Looks like rain again," said Gwyn. "Do you mind driving me?"

I made a choked laughing noise.

Gwyn guffawed. "Okay, it's not going to rain. I just like your company." She winked at Christian.

The two carried on a discussion of the merits of American versus French pastries, about which Christian knew little and all of it centuries out of date.

They'd be pretty cute as a couple, I had to admit. Gwyn climbed in the front of my Blazer cab again, snuggling against Christian for the three-hundred-foot drive across the parking lot and Main Street.

Our school's three cheerleaders waved and called out, "*Bonjour*, Christian," as I idled in front of the Las Abuelitas Bakery Café.

"*Au revoir*," said Gwyn, planting a quick peck on his cheek as she stared down the trio.

The door closed and I pulled out into the Las Abs rush-hour of school-letting-out.

"You suffered distress today," said Christian. "During the lesson which the biology master taught. Are you recovered?"

I swerved the car around Main Street's large pothole. "How did you know . . . what I was feeling?" It was true, the discussion of creating life in test tubes had me pretty upset.

"I felt it," said Christian. "Like an assault almost physical in its nature."

"You felt . . . my feelings?"

"Indeed."

"Can you do this with other people or just me?"

Christian shrugged. "The thoughts of others I catch easily. Feelings, I am less accustomed to . . . overhearing. But I think that your feelings were of a strong nature. And we are both of the family de Rochefort."

Okay, I thought. *Super-freaky that Christian has a window into my soul.*

"I'll try to keep my thoughts to myself in the future," I said.

"Just as you wish," said Christian. After a brief pause he added, "Perhaps you felt it inappropriate that I 'listened' to you?"

I pulled the car down our long drive. I didn't want to appear impolite. "It was nice of you to ask how I was doing."

Inside the house, Sylvia had left a note on the fridge white-board. "Shopping," the note said.

"Samanthe?"

I closed the fridge. Whatever I needed right now, it wasn't in there.

"I have been considering our wisest course of attack whereby to remove the egg from the possession of our enemies," he said.

Half my mouth curved up into a sad smile listening to his funny turns of phrase. "What did you come up with?"

He frowned. "I am unsatisfied on all counts. To go alone would be the wiser course, but I cannot allow myself to be parted from you again."

"I thought I might go on my own," I said.

His eyebrows raised; the lines furrowing his forehead made him look older than a high school boy.

Which he was.

"That would be unthinkable," he said. "I beg of you, Mademoiselle, place me not in the position of being unable to account for your wellbeing."

"Yeah, I didn't figure you'd go for that," I said.

The hard part of having Christian around all the time was just that: he was around all the time.

Chapter Sixteen

BESETTING SINS

• WILL •

Mick and I were good at packing up quick, and we left Rome before the sun had risen. Sir Walter led us invisibly towards the outskirts of the great city where we stopped briefly at a car dealership, with really sweet rides like DeLoreans and Mercedes and Alfa Romeos. Sir Walter bought a midnight blue Alfa Romeo *Giulietta* and the world's smallest Mercedes, paying cash.

"If we're splitting up," said Mick, "I think it needs to be you two who stick together." Her eyes held back tears.

"No, no," said Sir Walter. "The Mercedes is to compensate our landlady for the loss of her vehicle." He arranged to have the car delivered to her.

"The Alfa Romeo's for us?" I shook my head. "Flashy, much?"

Sir Walter shrugged. "It is considered the safest compact car on the market."

We piled in the car and Mickie started crying. "It's all my fault."

I wrapped an arm around her. "Don't."

"No, it's the truth. And I'm not just talking about yesterday. I never should have taken the work Pfeffer offered all those years ago."

"That work kept us in shoe leather and groceries," I said, trying to turn around the Mickie-guilt-fest.

"But I took the job because I wanted . . . what's the word?" She paused, sniffled. "I wanted *glory*, Will. I wanted to do great research and become known and respected."

"There's nothing wrong with that, Mick."

Her sobbing got a whole lot worse. "I was willing to endanger *you* to get what I wanted. I brought you into the lab so Pfeffer would be sure to keep me on."

I made a small snorting sound. "Well, you can quit beating yourself up on that one. You think I would have stayed home, knowing you'd met someone who was researching Rippler's Syndrome? Mick, I would have snuck in to see him if you hadn't taken me."

"You're—just—saying—that." She made these little hiccups-sounds between each word.

I shook my head. "Sorry, Mick, you're stuck with a deceitful, sneaky little brother. I totally would've gone to see him on my own."

She looked at me. "Really?"

"I swear."

"It doesn't excuse that I was willing to use you," she said, wiping her eyes on her shirt-sleeves.

"Hmmm, so I'm a lying deceiver and you're guilty of, um, I think it's called 'vainglory.' Both pretty bad. What a team we make, huh?" I bumped her from the side, trying to make her laugh, which she wouldn't do.

"We each carry within us the seed of a great evil," said Sir Walter.

"Yeah, dude, what's your sin of choice?" I asked.

"Will!" murmured my sister.

"My besetting sin, that is, the evil by which I am most sorely tempted is *sloth*," he said.

"You're fond of sleep?" I asked.

Sir Walter laughed. "No, no. I am fond of sitting by whilst others are allowed to work great harm."

"You're not sitting by this time," said Mickie.

"Indeed," replied Sir Walter. "There is, I believe, hope for me yet."

Eventually, last night's interrupted sleep caught up to me and Mick. We crashed out, and the next thing I was awake for was crossing the border into France. With fake passports—proof that deceitfulness had its uses.

"I propose that we make a stop in Nice," said Sir Walter. "My cousin has leased a building there rather closer to the *Musée National Marc Chagall* than makes me content."

He then explained we might actually be able to learn what use the buildings were being put to, seeing as this one had been acquired a couple years back.

Sir Walter had a new plan for keeping Mickie safe, as well. "I like it not that we must abandon you for so many hours at a time, my dear. I propose placing you invisibly within the walls of our hotel during the hours we must be gone."

I shook my head, 'cause no way was my sister going for that.

To my shock, she nodded and said, "Okay. Good idea."

I turned to her. "Who are you and what did you do with my sister?"

She looked down, her long lashes hiding her eyes from me. "It's the least I can do," she murmured. "One less thing for you to worry about."

"Thanks, Mick," I said. "And, by the way? It's really relaxing, hanging inside a wall."

"Yeah," she said. "Chrétien told me about it."

"Huh?" I asked.

"I placed Chrétien within the walls of my family's castle following the death of his wife and daughter," said Sir Walter. "For nearly four-hundred years he rested there."

"Dude!" I exclaimed. "Four-*hundred* years?"

"He wished to end his own life," said Sir Walter. "I convinced him instead to rest, to heal."

"Still," I said. "Four-hundred years . . . What about eating and sleeping?"

"Those are only required when one moves about as a chameleon," replied Sir Walter. "However, if one is still, it is possible to remain indefinitely invisible."

That made sense. "So what convinced him to, um, come out of hiding?" I asked.

"I asked him to protect the life of *Mademoiselle* Sam, explaining that she is like a long-lost grand-daughter," said Sir Walter.

I felt a sick gnawing in my stomach, wondering if Sir Walter secretly hoped Chrétien would "heal" by falling in love with Sam. I seriously couldn't let myself start thinking like that. Only how do you get rid of that sort of idea once it moves in?

Sir Walter put us up in a really swank hotel with crystal chandeliers and marble everywhere. One great thing about Nice was we got to try a local special, *Salade Niçoise*.

The salty black *niçoise* olives tasted so good you kind of wanted to keep gnawing on the pits. Unfortunately, you couldn't take more bites and gnaw at the same time. I popped out a pit in my hand, setting it on the white tablecloth beside two others.

"Could you be any more cave-man?" murmured my sister.

I was glad to see Mick's sarcasm back, 'cause it freaked me hanging around the version of my sister that cried and apologized for everything.

Following dinner, Sir Walter placed Mick into a really nice patch of very ancient stone wall. Then we rippled and took off toward Helmann's building. Like the structures surrounding it, this building had red roof tiles and was painted off-white. There was absolutely nothing special about it, except for the location.

Helmann, like his former associate Herr Hitler, said Sir Walter, *would like nothing better than to obliterate the art of the Jewish people. Along with their race, that is. He is disturbed by how the beauty of Chagall's work calls to the hearts of so many nations.*

Sick bastard, I wrote.

Quite.

The inside of the building appeared every bit as empty as the one we'd viewed near Paris. We started with our zig-zags on the ground floor. We'd nearly finished the third level when Sir Walter spoke, sounding excited.

Pass before me, he commanded. *As if in a circle.*

We were holding hands, facing the same direction. I didn't really see the point, but there's times it's better to just do what Walter de Rocheforte tells you. I swung out in a little half-circle 'til I must've been facing him.

Okay, I wrote, *now what?*

You noticed nothing unusual? He asked.

Nada, I wrote.

Reverse the motion, this time lending your full attention to what you can sense.

I raised up one hand in this "whatever you say, dude," gesture even though obviously it wasn't like he'd see me do it. But when I brought my hands back down it made me think of something.

I had five senses, right? So I already knew Sam and Sir Walter killed me on smell and taste. But I'd always been able to *see* stuff just fine when I rippled. I could *hear* just fine, too. That left one last sense: touch. And me and Sam were both good at noticing what something *felt* like.

This time, when I wheeled out around Sir Walter, I extended my free hand and held all the fingers out wide.

I kind of noticed something. Like the air was gooey or super-thick.

What the heck? I scribbled on my note-pad. Then I moved ahead and back several more times. That was some freaky air right there.

What's wrong with the air? I wrote. *Why's it all thick and moist?*

139

I believe we have discovered something of importance. Pass through me, Will, and tell me what you notice.

I had a sick feeling I knew what was here in the building with us. Which was confirmed when I walked "through" Sir Walter's invisible body.

It's the same, I wrote.

Indeed, he said.

So Helmann's stuffing these buildings with corpses, you think? Like some creepy Nazi cemetery?

That is no corpse, replied Sir Walter. *It is a living being before us. It may even be the body of a Geneses employee. I do not think Helmann would go to such lengths to dispose of his enemies.*

Dude, I wrote, as quickly as I could. *Stop talking! It'll hear you!*

Indeed, I have been attempting communication, but with no success, said Sir Walter.

You want to talk to it?

I would welcome the chance to discover anything that might reveal to us my cousin's intentions. Unfortunately, the person you have encountered seems to slumber. It is impossible to be certain, without bring him into solid form, but I can hear no active thoughts, no trace of conversation within the mind.

I thought of something worse than being overheard. Pulling hard on Sir Walter's hand, I yanked us back several feet. *What if it—uh, he or she—knows how to do that thing you did with getting the bullet out?*

Pardon? Sir Walter sounded confused.

140

It's just, I don't want someone from Geneses that close, you know. Like, what if that person reached inside me and yanked out my heart, you know?

Sir Walter chuckled. *Be at peace in that regard, my young friend. Firstly, because you are thinking of two entirely distinct actions: the removal of an object which does not belong in your body is quite different from the removal of an object which is knit to you by a thousand strands, even invisible. Secondly, it is extremely unlikely that this individual has received training in this area of expertise.*

Again with the chuckling. I didn't see anything funny about it.

My cousin Helmann never mastered the art as did I. As children, during an exceptionally snowy winter, we played at a game of my invention, Helisaba—that is, Elisabeth—Girard, and myself. I would hide a small object within the walls of the castle and the other two would seek it out. Never could Girard find the object, save with the help of Elisabeth. After a few tries, he refused to play, saying the game was impossible.

Years later, he sought me out to teach him this ability, which came easily to me. I attempted to teach my cousin how to trace the air in search of subtle differences in its texture, or its weight, or its moisture-content. None of these could he perceive. He scorned my lessons and accused me of lying about things that were not possible to detect.

Loser, I wrote. *It's not like it's even that hard.*

Ah, said Sir Walter, *for you, it is possible, but for my cousin, it was supremely difficult. Think of your own abilities:*

you can see and hear clearly, but you say that odor is difficult for you to sense.

Oh, I wrote. *Yeah, I guess. I can't taste, either, like Sam can.*

In any case, my dear young man, I am quite certain Helmann's enormous ego would never permit others to learn what he himself has no mastery over. In addition, it took me many centuries to develop the skills I possess. I do not exaggerate, Will, when I say that I have never met nor heard of anyone who is my equal in this area.

I didn't need any convincing in this department. I couldn't imagine training my fingers to detect what was invisible-bullet and what was invisible-flesh.

Okay, I wrote. *So this person's not going to come screaming at us and pull our brains out. Got it. But what's Helmann sticking live people in empty buildings for, anyway?*

This, I do not understand, said Sir Walter. *But I intend to discover. And Will? There are five bodies stored here.*

Chapter Seventeen

PINACLE OF RESPECT

• SAM •

I crunched mournfully through a bowl of Sylvia's homemade granola. Missing Will had become an ache that pressed upon me without mercy and without respite. It was another six days before our every-other-Friday phone call. I'd passed the half-way mark yesterday.

Sir Walter was taking no chances that anyone would be able to figure out that any of us were connected, or important to one another. "Your danger would increase significantly if my cousin suspected you to be in league with me," he'd said. Sir Walter had checked where my parents' long-distance phone calls came from. He'd acquired phones registered to owners in those locations. Not fail-safe, but at least calls from

Nayarit, Mexico or Ontario, Canada wouldn't stand out as unusual to anyone who might be monitoring calls to my family.

I shuddered. *Monitored* described me all too well.

Sylvia was keeping a close eye on me, too.

"What is it? Did I overcook the granola again?" She pulled the lid off the half-gallon jar, sniffing the cereal.

"No," I said. "I'm just not in a granola mood, I guess." I carried the bowl to the sink.

Sylvia caught something in the way I shuffled.

"Aunt Flo here for a visit?" she asked.

I guffawed. Syl had a million ways to describe menstruating, and none of them involved the word "period." She opened the freezer and pulled something out.

"You need chocolate," she said. "Lucky for you I froze some chocolate croissants from Bridget's last fundraiser."

Chocolate croissants sounded good. Really good. I sat back down at the kitchen island as my stepmother clattered through a narrow cupboard of baking sheets, lined up on end. She found the one she wanted for re-heating croissants. Then she plunked two more on the marble in front of me. Warped from use, the pans rocked back and forth, chattering to one another in the quiet kitchen.

"After croissants, we're making double-chocolate chocolate-chip cookies," she said, smiling.

"Bet you don't miss having your period," I said, figuring I'd just go with her assessment of the cause of my doldrums. I remembered the day I'd asked her why she and my dad didn't have a baby. I was eleven and longing for a sibling. Sylvia had told me of her first husband's vicious abuse, how he'd landed her in the hospital with heavy internal bleeding. "*They took out all my baby-making-parts to stop the hemorrhaging, sweetie,*" she'd told me. "*They saved my life, and got me help to leave the relationship, but only after he'd destroyed something infinitely precious.*"

Across from me, my step-mother frowned, clutching a sponge. "Do I miss the aches and mood shifts? Not so much. But, the power to reproduce . . ." She applied the sponge to a stubborn spot on the counter. "Something irreplaceable was stolen from me, Sam."

I swallowed. Eerie coincidence, Sylvia's choice of words about her abusive first husband.

"Promise me you'll never grant anyone that amount of power over you," said Sylvia, crossing over to rub my back. Then she sighed. "Sorry for the heavy. Turning forty-one must really be getting to my biological clock. It seems more final than forty, somehow."

I turned to hug my step-mom. "You still managed to become a great mom, you know."

She smiled, blinking back tears, and kissed the top of my head. "And you're a great daughter, Sammy."

Down the hall, Christian opened his door, keeping up the illusion that he spent his nights downstairs.

"*Ooooh-la-la*, that's more like it!" Sylvia said, all signs of sorrow brushed aside. "Now you're a handsome California *hombre*."

Christian flushed. Sir Walter had provided his son with contemporary clothing, but it had been contemporary for *Paris*, not central California. Sylvia had recently suggested a trip to La Perla, Las Abs' one and only retailer of clothing. I had to admit the fit of his new jeans was an improvement over the hyper-fashionable Parisian jeans. He looked friendlier, somehow. Less of a stand-out in our homogenous town. Not standing out was good.

"Gwyn dispatched unto me an electronic messenger," announced Christian as Sylvia passed him a croissant.

"She *texted* you," I corrected. So much for not standing out.

Christian bowed his acquiescence. "She states that she is *bored* and wishes for an escape from her mother's *patisserie*. Sorry—bakery." From a back pocket, he removed his personal knife and fork from a container called a *cadena*.

Sylvia sighed and shook her head.

"The personal knife and fork? Really not necessary," I murmured to him, repeating what Sylvia must have told him already a dozen times.

Christian ignored me, and I remembered his response last time. *Your belle-mère lacks servants. It troubles me greatly that she takes it upon herself to launder my clothing and clean the dishes upon which I dine. Allow me this small courtesy, the using of my own fork and knife. These, at least, shall not be added to her labors.*

"Honey, ask Gwyn if she'll bring some of those dark chocolate chips with her," said Sylvia.

I sent a quick text.

My step-mother turned to Christian. "Today, I am instructing you in the fine American art of making chocolate chip cookies!"

"Most excellent," said Christian, reaching for a second croissant.

Sylvia bustled from pantry to counter to fridge, setting the ingredients upon the island.

"*Mise-en-place*," said Christian. "I saw this style of preparation demonstrated upon the small electronic theater."

"The TV," Sylvia automatically corrected him. "So what's *mise-en-place* mean anyway? I've never known."

Christian shrugged, looking just like Sir Walter. "It means simply that prior to cooking, everything is brought to its proper place."

Its proper place. The opposite of me and Will. His proper place was here, at my side, like the cubes of butter beside the bag of sugar. Not far away on another continent.

Christian licked his fork and knife clean and replaced them in the *cadena*.

"So," began Sylvia, "Does everyone in France carry their own, er, personal silverware?"

Christian turned to me, alarmed as to how he should answer.

"It's an old-fashioned thing," I said. "The knife doubled as a weapon in a pinch."

"Mm-hmmm," intoned Sylvia.

"During the reign of Louis Quatorze, knifings were so common in the streets of Paris that the king ordered all knife-ends to be blunted," added Christian.

"Wow," said Syl, her back to us.

"I bet not everyone complied, though," I said, bumping Christian's shoulder.

His knife had a wicked looking point and resembled a dagger more than a butter knife.

Gwyn's arrival a few minutes later put a stop to the discussion of seventeenth-century cutlery.

"You have no idea how bad I need chocolate chip cookies," said Gwyn, flopping onto a bar stool beside Christian. Leaning well into his personal space, she held a jar out for Sylvia. "As requested. Dark chocolate chips."

"Does not your mother prepare these cookies daily?" asked Christian.

Gwyn shook her head at him, hair flying, grazing Christian's face. "That's so cute that you think she lets me eat them." She chucked him under the chin. Then she put her hands on her hips and frowned, clearly in preparation to impersonate someone.

"*On-ry foh custumah! Foh custumah!*"

"Your mom doesn't talk like that," I said, a little shocked at Gwyn's irreverence.

"My aunties do," retorted Gwyn. "I was doing them."

"And I'm *sure* they deserve your respect," said Sylvia, trying to look severe.

"Oh, yeah," said Gwyn. "My culture's all *over* respect for elders." She winked at Christian, her four-hundred-year-old crush.

Sylvia passed the flour to Gwyn. "Measure eight cups into the bowl. We're doing a quadruple batch."

Christian sat with his brows pulled together, clearly trying to puzzle something out. "Forgive me, *Mademoiselle*," he said to Gwyn, "But is the culture of the Chinese indeed given to respect for elders? Because you display less of this toward your mother than I have ever encountered, in all my years."

Gwyn turned to him with eyebrows pulled high. "Is this sarcasm?"

"Indeed, it is not," declared Christian. "I have often observed your irreverence towards the woman who gave you life."

A smile played at one edge of his mouth. He *was* trying his hand at sarcasm.

Gwyn stared at him. She let out a little huff of indignation. Then she grabbed a pinch of flour and flicked it at him. "I—am—plenty—respectful," she said, punctuating each word with another flick of flour.

"That type of behavior belongs outside," warned Sylvia.

Christian, epitomizing respectful behavior, obeyed my step-mother at once, stepping out through the sliding glass door. And Gwyn couldn't resist chasing him, flour-sack in hand.

Sylvia chuckled. "They make a very cute couple. I would have thought he was more your type, but I guess not?"

"No," I agreed. "Not even close." I hadn't spoken much about Will recently with my step-mom. It hurt too much.

Gwyn and Christian burst back inside, laughing. A gust of wind brought in the scent of pine through the door.

"War's over," said Gwyn. "Christian has agreed that I'm the pinnacle of daughterly devotion."

Sylvia passed Christian a towel. He was *covered* in flour. He walked to the sink and dusted himself off.

My stomach growled, loud in the silence.

"Guess I'm still hungry," I said.

"Me, too," murmured Gwyn, eyes devouring Christian.

"It's all these good smells," said Sylvia, scooping the first dough-balls onto the cookie sheets.

As Christian reached for a cookie-scoop to help my step-mother, I caught the soft nutty scent of flour on his clothes. It mixed with the scent of pine from outside.

The smell of Will.

I left the kitchen so I could have a good cry by myself, and Christian, may God bless him for it, let me go alone.

Excerpted from the personal diary of Girard L'Inferne.

Circa 2006

It is with great pain that I admit that not all of my new children are progressing as I had planned. So bright, their promise even three years ago. But as they pass through puberty we see signs of discontent, of rebellion even. Those who were first to volunteer for tasks requiring self-sacrifice three years ago now hang back, eyes to the floor. Matron keeps me informed as to names, refusals to participate. They will be terminated, of course, before they realize it might be possible to escape.

In addition, I see all too clearly that a high number suffer from mental psychoses. I had thought that it was possible such persons could serve me as Helga has served me. But even her usefulness is now tainted. While she thinks my eye wanders, she acts in ways contrary to my wishes. I can no longer trust her.

The fault, unfortunately, stems from my own DNA. Fritz is optimistic that the markers for such psychoses can be eliminated, eventually, so that a cleaner strain of my own make-up might be passed to the leaders of the new humanity for which I labor. But I have no wish to wait as long as he says this will take.

Not if there are other possibilities.

Chapter Eighteen

SAM-COUNTRY

• WILL •

Sir Walter didn't figure it was safe for us to stay in a playground-for-the-rich like Nice for too long. "Pfeffer knows my habits," he said. "And I am ashamed to admit that in addition to sloth, I have been guilty of *luxuria*, the sin of indulging too heavily in the good life, as a result of a few rather judicious investments this past century."

Mick laughed. "Not really a temptation Will and I had to face before meeting you!"

"I believe we should return to my more humble dwelling outside of Carcassonne," said Sir Walter. "Neither Helmann nor Pfeffer know of its existence."

We arrived at the small house early in the day. Into the living room where Sam and I had kissed, where she'd slept at my side. I felt this awful hole open up inside my guts. Once again, I tried stuffing all my Sam-feelings down to my toes. The insides of my sneakers were getting crowded.

I turned my attention to the conversation between Sir Walter and my sister.

"And the proximity to Montpellier, where Helmann has another building, means we can study for an extended time a building owned by Geneses."

"I wonder if this one will be stuffed full of bodies," said Mick, her brow crinkled. "You said they seemed to be sleeping?"

"So it appeared to me, *Mademoiselle*," replied Sir Walter.

"Maybe this is stupid, but do you think Helmann is imprisoning people?" she asked. "Like what you did for me back in Nice, except with malicious intent?"

"Sir Walter and I talked about that," I said. "Like, maybe Helmann is piling up his enemies in empty buildings across Europe."

Sir Walter spoke. "However, Helmann's policy has always been to kill his enemies."

"So maybe these are people he wants to wake up and question or torture or something," I suggested. "Like he couldn't get to it right away, but he wants to be able to find them later."

Stroking his goatee, Sir Walter grunted. "It is as good a suggestion as any. But why acquire the use of buildings for this purpose?"

"It wouldn't have to be *for* that purpose," I said. "It might just be like, hey, I caught these dudes in the *banlieues* and I want to be able to find them again and oh, look, I own a building right over there."

"Perhaps," said Sir Walter, giving his beard the deep-massage treatment. "*Monsieur, Mademoiselle*, if the building in Montpellier does, in fact contain invisible bodies, I propose that we bring one of them into solid form."

The color drained from Mick's face, but she didn't voice an objection.

"It'll be okay," I said. "You know how fast me and Sir Walter can ripple away if we need to."

She nodded. "It's what we're here for. To figure how to stop Helmann."

"I propose making the attempt by myself," said Sir Walter.

Mick looked relieved.

I felt bummed, but if he went by himself, at least my sister could spend the day normally, inside her own skin instead of inside a wall. I could do that much for her.

"Sure," I said.

It could have been a really nice time for me and Mick, except every hour in this house felt like torture to

155

me. Everything here was Sam. My loneliness for her got so thick I could've used it for a pillow.

Wandering down the hall, I saw the little room that had been hers. I kind of hovered at the doorway 'cause there was this voice in my head going, *this is a dumb idea, Will. You know it's gonna make it worse, right?*

I crossed over the threshold and into Sam-country. The little white bed was all made in the corner. And suddenly I couldn't make myself go another step, 'cause what if it smelled like Sam in here? Man, that would probably kill me. I leaned against a wall beside the door and sank down to the ground, my knees bent up in front of me. My eyes closed on a tiny prayer. *Please, let her be safe. Please let her be okay. Please.* I knew it probably irked God how people only talked to him when they needed something, and I was no exception, but it felt good, reminding God to maybe think of her.

When I opened my eyes, they felt all wet, so I didn't get up right away, because really, the last thing I needed was my sister worrying about me. I pulled my sleeve across my face a couple times and just sat there, hanging in Sam's once-upon-a-room, wishing I could see her face again.

Outside, a little bit of sun was trying to shine through the clouds. It would almost make it, a patch on the wooden floor growing brighter, but then new clouds would roll past and the floor would get dark again. I stared at it: light, dark, light, for long enough that the little spot on the floor moved, creeping over towards that white Sam-bed I didn't want to think about. Finally the sun won the fight and this shaft of light shot through the window and under the frame of the bed, lighting up something white-colored on the floor.

My pity party had gone on long enough at this point, and I stood up to grab the whatever-it-was. It looked a little like a pillow case or maybe a kitchen towel, and I figured I'd save Sir Walter crawling under the bed when he noticed it twenty years from now.

I could feel the sun warm on my skin as I reached for the white fabric. The south of France definitely had the advantage in winter weather over Paris. Down the hall, Mick was muttering again, the computer on the receiving end of her complaints. I glanced at the item in my hands, about to ask Mick if she'd seen a laundry pile.

Then the words stuck in my throat. It wasn't a dishrag or pillowcase. It was a girl's tee shirt. One of those little skimpy shirts without sleeves and skinny little straps for the shoulders and I thought my heart was going to fall on the floor in front of me, I swear, because this shirt was Sam's. I thought about just taking it straight to the trash, which was what anyone with a brain would've done, but of course I didn't have a brain when it came to Sam, so I just buried my face in it in case it had any Sam-smell left.

Which it did.

Man, I'm such an idiot at times.

Before long Mick noticed me standing there in the hall huffing like a glue-sniffer, and she saw my face, wrinkled up like an old apple, and she went all big sister and tried to come give me a hug.

I dropped the shirt on the ground.

"I'm going for a run," was all I managed to say before tears started leaking out my eyes.

My big sister stepped aside and let me go.

Chapter Nineteen

FOCUS ON THE PRIZE

• SAM •

I couldn't get Christian to agree to return to the small Geneses lab in San Francisco. And I understood it was crazy to try. So, once I realized he wasn't going to change his mind, I only had one small problem left to overcome: how to ditch Christian so I could go alone.

Encouraging him to take Gwyn up on her repeated date offers was futile. He wouldn't hang out with Gwyn *sans moi*—without me. He wouldn't do anything *sans moi*. I had only one option, so far as I could tell.

Sir Walter had explained to us that by staying in invisible form, it was possible to put off actual sleeping. But eventually, every active rippler would need true sleep. In Christian's case, he could go six days before he had to get a full night's rest. Just one stretch of six to eight hours would do, and he'd be good for another week of life spent mostly visible with invisible guard duty each night.

Christian's need for sleep once a week had almost been a deal-breaker for Will, who became frantic at the thought that I'd be unguarded for eight hours once every seven days.

I'd come up with a solution I thought was obvious. "How about if I sleep rippled during the time Christian sleeps solid? That way I'm safe."

Will had called me a genius and planted a kiss on my shoulder. Sir Walter had nodded and said it was a good solution. Christian had proposed my spending every night invisible, but Mickie had vetoed that idea.

"It will stunt her growth," she said. "Sam doesn't need that on top of everything else. Plus she's got parents. With only one night a week there's a much smaller risk they'll come barging in and flip out thinking she's gone."

We'd picked Sunday night as Christian's night of rest. My dad rarely visited my room, but Sylvia popped in sometimes, and this was *least* likely to happen on a Sunday when she hounded me with *get-to-bed-because-it's-a-school-night*.

All of which meant I had eight hours in which to retrieve my egg. I figured I had to allow two hours each way for travel and an hour buffer in case Christian got up early. He always came to wake me up, and he'd figure out pretty quick I was gone if the air over my bed wasn't ice-cold. So, that would give me three hours to figure out how to steal something from a (probably) secure facility which might or might not have invisible guards and which would certainly have cameras.

I spent Sunday surfing the internet trying to learn more about human egg cells. Having picked a time during which Christian was engaged in chanting, I had the screen to myself. What I discovered unsettled me. I hadn't thought through the implications of what I wanted to do today. I'd had a vague idea that I was going to San Francisco to "get my egg back." But it wasn't like I could just pop it back inside me. Eggs were living cells, with expiration dates. Hans and his sibling doctor, Fritz, were presumably keeping my egg alive artificially. Retrieving my egg wasn't what I needed to do: *destroying* it would be my job.

I tried to reason with myself that it was just a cell like the dead skin cells that flaked off my arms in the shower. And in a way, it was just a cell. But it was a special cell. One that represented half of a potential little Sam who could run around and play.

I shook off the willies by reasoning that the *last* thing I wanted was for one of my eggs to become a little Sam who could run and play. That was what Helmann wanted and what I needed to prevent.

A long, quiet Sunday drew to a close at last. Christian said goodnight to Syl and my dad, which was my cue to turn in. He wouldn't truly let himself sleep until he'd seen me ripple each Sunday. Tonight his thoroughness irritated me.

"I'm going, I'm going," I said as he rippled solid up in my bedroom.

"It was not my intention to hasten you, *Mademoiselle*."

"Sam," I said. "My name is Sam, not *Mademoiselle*." My fear of the next several hours came out as anger directed at Christian.

"Forgive me," we both said at the same moment.

I guffawed and Christian smiled.

I took a calming breath. "I really appreciate all you're doing for me. I'm sorry if I seem ungrateful."

Christian shrugged just like Sir Walter. "You are giving up a great deal of personal freedom in order to remain with your *famille*—your family."

I flushed. He understood me a lot better than I gave him credit for. "Yeah, well, in any case, I want you to know I am grateful for everything you're giving up to be here."

"*De rien*," he said. *It's nothing.*

I took in another couple of deep breaths and calmed myself. Within moments, my skin faded and I disappeared from sight. *Dormez bien, Christian*, I called out. *Sleep well.*

Vous aussi, he responded. *You, too.* Then he rippled to return invisibly to his room downstairs.

He could hear my thoughts. I hadn't considered how that might hijack my plan.

Think sleepy thoughts, I commanded myself. I decided to listen closely to Christian's thoughts, which would keep my mind occupied *and* serve to notify me when he drifted off to sleep.

So I listened while he chanted a Psalm or two. I heard his prayers to God (for my safety, for the well-being and success of Sir Walter, Will and Mickie.) And I heard as his heart called out a night-time prayer for the souls of a dead wife and child: his own? I wondered. Finally, I heard only silence.

I rose and rippled solid, hurriedly throwing on black sweats and a black jacket. Cliché, but there's a reason people wear black on missions requiring stealth and anonymity. I caught my reflection in the mirror. I looked tough and determined, which made me smile, but the smile basically ruined the effect.

Next came a little exercise I'd devised for myself but had been unwilling to practice while Christian could see me. I walked into my bathroom and opened the junk drawer where I kept a splinter removal kit. Opening the small box, I removed a bright sharp sewing needle.

Taking the needle in my right hand, I held out my left. My goal was to train myself to ripple fast enough that I wouldn't poke myself with the needle. Hans and Ivanovich had been scary-fast with needles. I needed to be faster.

It took ten tries, but finally I vanished before the needle made contact. What I discovered was this: I had to disconnect from my fear of the needle. If I focused on my goal (rippling) instead of my fear (the pain), then I could succeed. These were things Coach had drilled us with again and again. I smiled. Who knew? Maybe I'd be a better runner now, too.

"Focus on the prize," I murmured, shaking my head at the parallel with running.

I made two more attempts and beat the needle both times.

The clock beside my bed informed me I'd used one precious hour, but I'd made it a lot more likely that I could vanish quickly under threat. I took a few steps towards my window, rippled and exited my house from the second floor. The liquid embrace of the glass was certainly reason enough to try this, but I also wanted the chance to make my way down through "thin air," something I hadn't tried since the showdown with Helga in France. Once again, the air felt heavy and liquid-like. I "swam" my way down to the ground and took off running for San Francisco.

Snow drifted down as I left Las Abuelitas. When I dropped in elevation below a thousand feet, the snow turned to a soft rain. Will had told me about running invisibly in the rain: it was as magical as he'd described. The rain fell through me as I raced along the road, outpacing most cars, which slowed for the wet roads. The rain should have tickled, and it almost did. This would be what it felt like to be tickled if you weren't ticklish. Pleasant. Funny. Soothing. It put a smile on my invisible face.

I felt invincible. I would march into Helmann's medical facility and destroy that egg. No one would see me. No one would know it had been me. I was a ninja, dark as night and twice as invisible. I threw my head back in laughter, drinking in the rain that couldn't reach me, could only tickle its way through me to the ground.

By the time I reached San Francisco, the rain had stopped. In its place, a thick fog swathed the city. Moving through fog felt like passing through a dusting of flour. Along streets still busy at midnight, I glided in silence. I arrived at my destination—a narrow side street—and looked up at the building that housed my egg. Top floor—the tenth. I pushed upwards and swam my way past the second floor, third floor. Curious, I tried something different from a swimmer's stroke. I imagined myself pushing off like a hawk. The fourth through eighth floors flew past me. I imagined stopping and I halted. I could see the windowless tenth floor just above me. I took a slow breath—I imagined doing so, anyway—and passed through the stone exterior of the building.

A thousand grains of sand flowed through me, more substantial-feeling than the fog or drops of rain. I yearned to linger here, to sense the motion within the solid wall. But I had a job to do. I pushed through the exterior until I found myself inside the building, hovering two feet above the floor. Which just didn't seem right. I lowered myself so that I could at least pretend the floor supported my feet. I'd entered a room I didn't recognize, but the building was narrow. A single hallway ran it's length. From the hallway, I felt sure I could find the room I needed.

Gliding across the room, empty but for a few humming computers, I approached the door and slid through it. *Solid wood. Nice.* The building was old. I felt a second twinge of regret that I didn't have time to simply *play* in the facility, moving back and forth through its fascinating surfaces. Something to tell Will about the next time we talked. My heart squeezed tight and I set the thought aside.

Lights glowed clinically bright in the hall. I felt exposed. Then I remembered Christian's use of the wall as a place to hide. The type of person who worked in *this* building would be all too aware of what a sudden cold spot in the room meant. I flowed into the wall. Only wood and hollow spaces, a few wires, prickling and zing-y with what? Electricity? I moved forward down the wall, passing the room where my egg had been surgically removed.

I shuddered and moved on to find the room Helmann had referred to as the "stasis chamber." Or maybe the stasis chamber was something inside the room. I would soon find out.

I took a deep breath and looked into the next room, the one that held my egg.

Unfortunately, my egg wasn't the only living thing in there.

Hans, bowed over a microscope, sat in the quiet room.

Excerpted from the personal diary of Girard L'Inferne.

Circa 2007

I am led to a conclusion most unexpected and unpleasant: populating the world with leaders who bear my DNA will not serve me.

Not only do I fear the appearance of mental illness, which has been statistically significant, but now I observe an even graver problem. Perhaps forty-five percent of my newest children exhibit an intolerable lack of obedience. I will have obedience. This rate of failure is not acceptable for the future. I will not waste further effort creating progeny who cannot, because of stubbornness or mental illness, serve the greater good.

Of course, my Corps will still serve me in other ways.

Chapter Twenty

SLEEPER

• WILL •

When I returned an hour and a half later, I could hear my sister speaking excitedly in this loud voice she reserved for actual people, as opposed to when she muttered to the computer or to herself. Sir Walter must have returned while I was running.

I shoved the door open and walked inside. Mick's forehead was wrinkled as she paced before the fireplace. When I entered, she looked over at me all worried.

"*Bonjour,* young Will," Sir Walter said to me. "Your run, was it pleasurable?"

"Sure," I said, mopping my sweaty forehead with a shirt-sleeve. "It was great. What's up?"

Sir Walter glanced at my sister.

"It's okay," she said. "Ask him."

"I have visited Montpellier and found the building occupied, once again, by invisible bodies. However, they were of too great a size for me to bring into solid form and then return, should that prove necessary," said the old man. "I am wondering, considering your own size, which is superior to mine—"

My sister interrupted. "He needs you for back-up."

I frowned. "Yeah, sure. Can I grab a shower first?"

"But of course," said Sir Walter.

Walking down the hall to the shower, I noticed Sam's white shirt was gone. Probably Mick picked it up. I thought about asking her for the shirt back, but this time I listened to the voices telling me, *Dude, seriously not a good idea.*

I cleaned up, feeling better both from the run and the prospect of doing something. As Sir Walter and I sped towards the southern coast of France, a tiny question ate at me.

You sure we're doing the right thing, chasing down bodies in empty buildings? I wrote. *Pfeffer seemed to think there was some project coming up that Helmann wanted to tackle himself. Shouldn't we maybe focus on figuring out what that is?*

The "release of angels," said Sir Walter.

Yeah, I wrote, remembering the odd phrase. *I'm thinking whatever an "angel release" is, it's not good news. Shouldn't we try to find out more about that?*

Helmann is not in the habit of posting his plans for all to see, my friend. It is not simply a matter of walking into one of the headquarters of Geneses and looking at a calendar, said Sir Walter.

You found important stuff, I wrote. *Like that video.*

I was fortunate. As were we in overhearing Pfeffer and Franz. Sir Walter paused. *I am, as you Americans say, simply "going with my gut" in this investigation of Helmann's Montpellier building. It strikes me as most ominous, my cousin's acquisition of property in the midst of those he desires to eliminate from the human race.*

Uh, yeah. I'd call that ominous for sure, I wrote.

We traveled in silence for several minutes.

And yet, said Sir Walter, *I feel certain my cousin waits for something. Almost, I can feel him as he holds himself in check . . . waiting . . .*

Hey Sir Walter? Can you hear the, uh, "signature of his thoughts" or whatever you call it?

Hmmm, sighed my friend. *He learned, whilst we were children, to cloak his thoughts within the confines of his own mind. It was in response to my ability to "hear" him that he developed this shield. But I catch his emotions, at times, when we are near one another.*

Can he hear your thoughts if he's close by? I wrote.

He is, in this area, deaf as the proverbial pot.

I didn't recognize the proverb, but I felt relieved.

The ability to transfer thoughts is a de Rochefort trait, said Sir Walter. *And Helmann has not a drop of de Rochefort blood within his veins.*

Guess that's why I'm stuck writing you, huh? No de Rochefort in me either?

Sir Walter laughed. *You have the heart, if not the blood, of a true de Rochefort. You remind me greatly of Chrétien.*

I figured this was a compliment. Until I thought about how Sam might think the same thing, in reverse. That depressed me.

We'd reached the outskirts of Montpellier. Sir Walter guided us towards a newer part of town. *This isn't at all like that part of Paris where Helmann's other building was,* I wrote.

Sir Walter replied, *In recent times, there were great projects of redevelopment within this town. After Algeria gained independence from France in the last century, the population of Montpellier grew dramatically. I fear it is no mistake that Helmann has acquired property within a population of immigrants to France.*

Wasn't the south of France one of the last hold-outs for safety if you were Jewish during the Second World War? I wrote.

Yes, replied Sir Walter. *Even today, France harbors the largest population of Jews in Europe—more kosher restaurants exist in Paris than in New York.*

Helmann must hate that, I wrote.

Indeed, said Sir Walter.

Sick bastard, I thought for probably the hundredth time. I needed to upgrade my insults.

We arrived and since Sir Walter had already visited the building, we didn't have to do the boring-as-heck zig-zag through all the floors. Instead, we shot straight up to the top floor where he'd located bodies. I'm pretty used to the whole idea of not having any substance, but there was something creepy about standing in a room of invisible dudes. And what would we learn when we brought a body out of hiding?

Sir Walter dropped my hand to go "grab" the body. There wasn't anything for me to watch until he came solid with the body. So who were we waking up: friend or foe? I stared into empty space, waiting.

Then, I saw Sir Walter come solid, arms around a man who looked asleep. For a minute, Sir Walter gazed at the sleeper, waiting to see if he'd awaken on his own. When this didn't happen, Sir Walter wafted a vial of smelling salts below the man's nose.

We waited.

And waited.

Maybe three minutes passed. The dude on the floor didn't look North African. He was pale as sunrise. And blond, his hair cropped in a buzz-cut.

Coming solid beside my friend, I asked, "You think he needs another whiff?"

"Perhaps," said Sir Walter. He waved the vial under the guy's nose again. I could see why Sir Walter needed me along. Thin and wiry, the young man sleeping on the floor was close to my height. Sir Walter remained solid at the guy's side, looking puzzled and frustrated.

"*Levez-vous!*" he said aloud. *Wake up.*

The guy didn't even twitch.

Gently, Sir Walter jiggled the guy's shoulders.

Nothing.

Sir Walter did his sigh that meant, "*I am feeling very frustrated right now, but I'm too French and polite to say anything.*"

He jostled the young man's shoulders one more time, a bit harder. Still nothing.

After another minute, Sir Walter stood. "If you would be so good as to replace this body, I should like to bring the others into view."

One at a time, Sir Walter brought out four additional blond-haired guys, all of whom looked more or less the same age. And all of whom looked like they were sleeping. None woke up for Sir Walter.

After a couple more "*I'm really frustrated*" sighs when the fifth guy wouldn't wake up, Sir Walter spoke to me. "We return to your sister," he said, "If you would be so kind." He indicated the sleeping form.

I crossed to the man's side. They all had this look up close that I didn't like at all—like guy-versions of Helga. I wrapped an arm around him on either side, and rippled us both invisible.

Then Sir Walter and I slipped through the building walls and shot back to Carcassonne with nothing to show for our afternoon's work.

What do we do now? I asked as we journeyed. *Do we go back to sneaking around Geneses offices?* I was really hoping to suggest San Francisco.

Before you joined me in France, I paid visits to several offices. In Tokyo, I discovered the video which I sent to you. In the Paris and Berlin offices, I found nothing of interest. Helmann's Moscow office revealed a rather disturbing interest in cloning technology.

Clones? I interrupted. *Like, clones?*

Human reproductive cloning, yes. He seems both fascinated and repulsed by the idea. I do not know which impulse will win out. The Catholic Church frowns upon the idea.

Huh. All I could think of was *Star Wars* and the clone army Emperor Palpatine created, which seriously creeped me out as a kid.

In San Francisco I discovered his recent obsession with acquiring real estate. And I remain persuaded that understanding his intention in this area is deeply important.

Okay, I wrote. *So we try somewhere else. Flip for it, huh? Flip?*

Flip a coin, dude. Heads, Barcelona—tails, London.

What a . . . unique means whereby to make decisions of great import.

We didn't talk the rest of the way. When we got back, the house smelled like pesto, the one dish my sister knows how to cook.

"I found basil taking over the pots in your little greenhouse," said Mick. "It's so warm in there, you could have a garden year-round."

I felt a moment's guilt, thinking how my sister had been pulled away from her little garden in Las Abs. Over dinner, we discussed the visit to Montpellier.

"It was just weird," I said.

"Weird in what sense?" asked my sister.

"It was like those guys weren't alive or dead." I frowned. "Like they were in some different state of existence."

"*Mon Dieu*," whispered Sir Walter, holding his fork half-way between the bowl and his mouth. "My cousin was fascinated in the eighteenth century by Doctor Mesmer."

Mick shook her head. "Mesmer?"

"Mesmer, like *mesmerize?*" I asked.

"*Exactement!*" said Sir Walter, fork still hovering in mid-air.

"I think you're on to something," I said.

"WHAT?" asked my sister, so loudly that Sir Walter's fork dropped from his grasp. "Sorry," she murmured.

I turned to my sister. "Hypnosis! What if the sleepers had been *hypnotized?*"

"That would explain the sound sleeping," said my sister. "So, how do you wake up someone who's been hypnotized?"

Excerpted from the private diary of Girard L'Inferne.

Circa 2007

I am informed that a descendant of Elisabeth yet lives. I have investigated ten generations of Elisabeth's offspring and I find diligent, entrepreneurial souls who leave a legacy of self-sacrifice. They are uniformly intelligent; of tendencies to mental illness, they show none.

From her genes, then, will I offer the reward of longevity to my servants in the Glorious New Order. Well, my dear Helisaba, you could not bear me a child while you lived, but your descendants shall live as princes in the New World Order. Princes who will serve and obey.

Chapter Twenty-One

CORPOREAL FORM

• SAM •

As I crossed the threshold, two things happened: the overhead lighting dimmed slightly, and Hans looked up, clearly startled by the change in lighting. And then something even stranger happened. It was as if someone had flipped a switch allowing me to hear inside Hans' head. Radio-Hans was broadcasting severe distress at the moment: *Father has discovered me!*

Hans jumped up from the microscope and towards a computer.

Quickly, he closed pages on the screen.

I caught another transmission from inside Hans' mind as he scanned his computer screen: *It is neither*

Father nor Fritz . . . As I "heard" these bits, I could feel relief rushing through him.

"Greetings," he said.

He was greeting me?

"This is a surprise," he said aloud. "Judging by the precise amount of warm air you have displaced, I believe I must be in the presence of Miss Samantha Ruiz. Or perhaps you would prefer *Señorita* Ruiz?"

As he spoke, I caught an odd subtext—an unpleasant sensation as he uttered the word "*Señorita.*"

"To what, I wonder, do I owe the extreme pleasure of your appearance?" Hans laughed softly. "Or rather, your lack of appearance?"

Well, this wasn't turning out at all as I'd planned. So they had a method for detecting the presence of ripplers? I recalled Helmann asking for a "temperature sweep" of the building. The change of lighting must have been the cue that alerted Hans. I slid inside the wall to see if the lights would change again. Sure enough, the lights returned to full power in the room I'd left.

Hans clicked through screens monitoring the building's other rooms. He was searching for me. *Radio Hans* told me he was angered by my disappearance.

I stepped back into the room and the lights dimmed. I felt Hans' elation at my return. My ability to "hear" him was certainly improved. Must have been all the nights I'd spent listening to Christian.

"Come, now, you've traveled so far. How are we to converse if I alone have vocal chords?" He chuckled, but the way he presented himself on the outside didn't match what he felt on the inside. "Perhaps we could share a cup of hot chocolate together? There were so many things I wished to say to you but was unable to as a result of the abruptness of your departure." His voice was smooth and soothing; his emotions were sharp, dangerous.

It was similar to the first time I'd overheard his thoughts. Aloud, he'd calmly asked Helmann's forgiveness. In his mind, he'd raged in self-defense. It seemed I couldn't hear all of his thoughts like I could Christian's. Perhaps I only overheard Hans' thoughts if they were charged with high levels of emotion.

"Miss Ruiz?" He paused. "Samantha? Let me first offer to you my deep regret for the, ah, methods I employed upon your last visit."

Radio Hans made clear he didn't feel any regret.

He continued. "However, I am most happy to report that all of my hopes and plans are now well underway." His emotions agreed with his spoken words this time. "Perhaps it is the cameras that make you hesitate? Allow me one moment. They don't record sound, you know."

During the time it took him to say these things, he'd risen, turned out the hall and room lights, and dashed around the four corners of the room. I couldn't see him in the dark, but I could hear him moving.

The lights came back on. "There we are," said Hans. He pointed to cameras in the corner. He'd placed sticky-notes over the lenses.

Why had he turned off the lights to do this? In a flash, I realized he didn't want his associates to know he'd stopped the video feed. Before I could think through the implications any further, he addressed me once more.

"Will you now honor me with your corporeal form? There are so many things I could tell you, my dear, if you would but ask it of me."

That convinced me. If Hans really was changing the course of Helmann's plans, didn't I owe it to Will, Mick, and Sir Walter to find out everything I could?

I came solid. "What can you tell me?"

Hans rose and strode towards me.

"Stop right there!" I ordered.

He halted and held his arms wide, smiling. "I mean you no harm," he said aloud.

But *Radio Hans* said otherwise. He *absolutely* meant me harm.

"Tell me about your father's plans to erase half of humanity," I demanded.

He didn't reply right away. Not aloud. But from his mind I caught more than just an emotion this time. I heard a full sentence: *More than half—we rid the planet of five billion!* I felt his glee as he thought this. So much for Hans the humanitarian.

Hans spoke, head tilted to one side. "Do you recollect what use my father is making of your egg?"

"You said he wanted a kid. You said it would distract him so that you could run things."

From Hans' mind, I caught a flash of anger, quickly extinguished, as he turned from me. He indicated the microscope I'd seen him peering into when I arrived. It was set up to look at something inside what resembled a four foot tall thermos. "In here lie wonders, Samantha! Come, come—have a look!"

"Is my egg in there?"

His mouth stretched wide. I'm sure it was meant to be a grin, but it reminded me of Helga's feral smile. "So much more than that!"

Without realizing it, I'd crept forwards, almost within reach of Hans.

"It is a perfect copy of *you*," he said. His arm stretched towards me, a casual gesture.

I recoiled.

"Oh, come now, my dear," said Hans, "Have I not already obtained all I desired from you?" He turned back to the device. "Herein lies your double. Will you not have a look?"

In that instant, he reached for my arm and his grip was like iron. Immediately, I rippled away.

Radio Hans got louder now that I was invisible. And none of it was pretty. *Filthy half-breed . . . Spaniard-tainted . . . Blood of Moors and Mayans . . .*

He despised me.

His voice, however, spoke in tones of infinite calm. "Do you still fear me?" He shook his head sadly, as if in regret. "You have just proven how safe you are, even when within my reach. Do you see in my hands anything with which I could harm you?" He held his hands wide for my viewing. As he did so, I saw a flash of an image, courtesy of *Hans-vision*: his jacket pocket was *stuffed* with needles, weapon of choice for Geneses employees, apparently. I thought I'd seen a revolver and a knife as well.

I couldn't let myself get near him.

"She will be raised as a queen, you know," said Hans, "This tiny replica of yourself. She will never know loss, or grief, or lack. Imagine that, Samantha. A version of yourself who never suffers the ache of her mother's death." He lowered his voice. "Yes, my dear, I know of that tragedy."

Because you caused it! I thought.

Suddenly it occurred to me to wonder whether the "radio" worked both ways.

I know what you did, you bastard! I sent the thought as clearly as I could towards Hans.

"I confess, I have considered creating a second-self of my own," said Hans.

He didn't seem to notice my silent messages; I tried one last time: *You're evil! I hate you! Do you hear that?*

He couldn't—I would have caught some flare of emotion if he'd heard me insulting him like that.

He spoke again. "They say that twins have no need for anyone else—that they inhabit together a private and complete world. Would not that level of companionship be marvelous?"

Two of Hans was *not* something the world needed.

He gazed again into the microscope, ignoring me for the moment.

And then, seeping slowly inside me, I felt the mystery and wonder of being in the presence of my own *self*, in a Petri dish. All that I was. All that I could be. It was terrifying and tantalizing: who would I have been without seeing my mother killed before my eyes? Without believing, as I had for years, that it was my fault? I saw myself with Gwyn's easy laughter, Sylvia's confidence. I could have been so different.

My heart went out to this tiny duplicate Sam. And the thought of what I'd come here to do filled me with dread. But *that* Sam, the one in the thermos, would be brought up by Helmann, author of the dark experiments in the black book. I could not allow that. Not in a million years. Not for anything.

"All of your cells, busily replicating themselves," said Hans. "While you yourself stand invisibly here. You feel the immensity of what we carry out, do you not? Perhaps there might be a place for you in the future I imagine." He sighed. "But we will never know if you refuse to come solid and converse *like an adult.*"

His anger pushed through with that last barb, but I felt his yearning as well: he really wanted me back.

And now I wanted the same thing. I realized that I could get him to *think* the truth even if he spoke nothing but lies aloud. I came solid.

"Here I am," I said. "Tell me, Hans, one more time: what is your dream for the future?"

I stood well back from him as he began repeating what he'd told me the day he'd kidnapped me. But this time I didn't pay attention to his words. I focused on what was playing on *Hans-vision* instead.

Destruction. Deaths of millions. Of billions.

His true feelings didn't "play" for long; they came as flashes of emotion—brief, intense, and then gone, like sparks quickly stamped out.

I interrupted him, trying to coax forth another burst of truth. "What do you want most in all this?"

He paused, clearly irritated by the interruption. But I got what I wanted. I saw images from his mind, sharp and clear: Hans, standing over his father's grave; Hans, behind a podium as head of Geneses. And one more image.

My clone, dead at his feet.

I caught it all in that instant. He feared his father meant to supplant him by creating a child with

Elisabeth's blood who would rule at his side. Hans was jealous of me.

My mind was spinning. He'd seemed so eager to protect me last fall, telling his sister to stay away from me. But that was the thing—he'd *only just* realized why his dad wanted me. He'd only just realized that a Sam-clone spelled the end of all *his* dreams.

While I was working through these thoughts, Hans had crept up on me. He'd reached inside his coat. Lightning-fast, he sprang at me, a knife glittering in his outstretched hand.

Chapter Twenty-Two

MESMERIZED

• WILL •

I jolted awake early the next morning, just as the stars began to wink out before dawn. I'd realized something important. Throwing off my covers, I ran down the hall to get Sir Walter up. His room lay empty. I ran to Mick's room, about to pound the door. But then I realized there was a fire blazing in the living room. I wasn't the only one up early. I flew into the living room where Mickie and Sir Walter sat talking.

"Couldn't sleep either?" asked my sister.

"The pass-phrase is for *them*!" I said. "The dudes who were hypnotized!"

Mick looked at me, eyebrows raised, waiting for more.

"Yes," murmured Sir Walter. "But, of course."

I explained to Mick that Pfeffer and Franz wanted to get a *pass-phrase* from Helmann so they could start "releasing angels," whatever that meant.

"Did the sleeping guys *look* like angels?" asked my sister.

"They look like *Helga*," I said. "I mean, like boy versions."

"Like members of the so-called Aryan race?" said my sister.

Sir Walter nodded.

"Maybe it's a good thing you couldn't wake any of them," said Mick, looking worried.

"Our next step must be to discover the pass-phrase," said Sir Walter. "This is indeed a matter of grave urgency."

"Yeah, that'll be easy enough," I said, shaking my head. "What was that you were saying about Helmann keeping important info to himself?"

Sir Walter ignored my comment. "Pfeffer seemed to think he might know the pass-phrase, or a hint as to its nature."

Mick turned pale. "If you feel you need to go back to Rome . . ."

I shook my head. "It's crazy thinking we can guess it. Franz wasn't exactly encouraging to Pfeffer that either of *them* could guess it."

"His hesitation was not as to the *ease* with which the phrase might be found," said Sir Walter. "Franz warned against trying to use it without their father's permission. I think Pfeffer had a pretty shrewd guess what the pass-phrase might be."

"That 'three little words' thing?" I asked.

Sir Walter quoted Pfeffer. "'*Three little words that changed my life will soon change the world.*'"

"Oh, no," murmured Mick, looking like she was going to be sick. "Oh, man . . ."

"*Mademoiselle*, are you ill?"

"Mick?" I crossed to my sister and knelt before her.

She sat still, staring into the blazing fire.

"You figured it out, didn't you?" I asked quietly. Then I turned to Sir Walter. "She knows the password, but she's afraid we'll use it if she tells us."

"Of course I'm afraid," she snapped. "But I'm not going to let my fear stand in the way." She deflated, sagging into the couch. "I know what's at stake here, Will. Give me a little credit."

Sir Walter looked expectantly, giving my sister a minute to pull it together.

"Get the black book Pfeffer stole," she said.

Chapter Twenty-Three

SHE HAD SPIRIT

• SAM •

A month ago, I wouldn't have escaped. Heck, this *morning*, I wouldn't have made it. But all my practice at evading a sharp jab with a needle paid off. I rippled away before Hans reached me. The lights dimmed instantly.

He stumbled through the air that had been me. I slipped back inside the wall, instinctively seeking cover even though I was invisible.

He looked up as the lights came back full power. And then, finally, he allowed his inside feelings and the outside expression of them to exist in harmony.

It was not pretty.

He grabbed a chair and hurled it across the room. The computer suffered the same fate. He cleared a long counter, smashing each item against an opposite wall. Finally, after shoving everything off his desk in one large swipe, he paused. Hands on hips, he gazed about the room.

The only thing remaining upright in the room was the large thermos-like object holding a developing copy of me. After grabbing a pair of gloves from a drawer, Hans approached the clone-container. I found myself drifting along the wall to watch. With practiced and precise motions completely unlike what he'd used to trash the office, Hans disassembled the container. He removed a tiny disk—an actual Petri-dish—and set it carefully on the desk. Then, fumbling for a moment within his inner jacket pocket, he brought forth a syringe holding a clear liquid.

I knew what he meant to do. Hans would accomplish the task I'd come here to perform. But the task felt completely different now that I'd seen that possible-Sam: the one who could grow to maturity free from my pain. I'd seen her, and there was no way to pretend I hadn't.

As I watched him destroy the tiny organism, felt his horrible delight, I was glad I hadn't had to do it myself. It was the difference between observing a kill and pulling the trigger. I didn't know what the law said about week old blastocysts, but I knew Hans' intent was murderous.

It put my step-mother's annual heartache about a miscarriage in a completely different light. I hadn't understood why she felt sad about someone she'd never met. But I got it now. She grieved for someone she *had* seen, if only in her imagination.

At that moment, *Radio Hans* settled into a round of self-congratulatory cheer.

I left the building.

Quickly, I made my way out of San Francisco. I drifted across the San Joaquin Valley, eerily still in its blanket of winter fog. Up into the foothills I ghosted, silent and swift, until I neared Las Abuelitas.

The highway before me curved sharply: Deadman's Curve. Home lay just ahead. I rippled solid a few miles short of my house, craving a good run. The air felt icy after my hours of insubstantiality, but the ground beneath my feet comforted me. I focused on the sound of my shoes slamming down upon bits of gravel. The air passing through my lungs burned, a fierce and fiery cold.

As dawn drew near, a lone bird called, and the sky passed from sterling to pale gray in the east. The back of our house, facing west, lay in darkness. As I drew nearer, I rippled invisible again so no one would notice me returning. I passed our pool, flat and still in the breezeless dawn, a heavy mist rising because Syl kept the pool heated through winter. Dad had forgotten to cover it last night, which would make my step-mom crazy when she noticed. A warm swim sounded wonderful after my shaky run. But my parents would rush me to the doctor to check for signs of insanity, swimming before sunrise on a winter's morning.

Then I smiled. I could swim. I just couldn't come solid. I glided towards the water, curious what I'd feel. Crossing to the deep end, I crouched and dove head first. I could sense the instant that every part of my invisible body crossed from air into water. A thousand tiny fingers whispered past me as I shot through. Passing through air never really felt like anything, but water? It made me think of slithering my fingers back and forth through a bowl of seed-beads Sylvia kept upstairs.

"They're therapeutic," Sylvia had said, shrugging, when I asked her what the seed-beads were for.

It was a great comparison. Seed beads had smoother, slipperier edges than grains of sand. Pushing around through my swimming pool felt slithery as well. I'd expected the water might feel thick and stretchy like glass. Water seemed more . . . tickle-y. A thousand times more playful. I kicked off the sides, back and forth. Pushing through my pool required less effort than "swimming" upwards through air. No, that wasn't exactly right, I decided. It came back to something Sir Walter had said about *expectations*. I expected water to require effort, and I adjusted my motion accordingly. When I'd "jumped" down from Sir Walter's castle tower in France, I'd expected to "fall" and had been surprised when I found it took effort to make my way to the ground. *Expectations*: they all fell apart when I lacked substance.

The kitchen lights flicked on and I heard Dad's truck revving up as he backed out our long driveway. I felt reluctant to leave the pool, just like a little kid when the lifeguard says it's time. But Syl would come knocking on my door if I didn't start making noise in my room.

I took one final glide through the pool, from end to end, and stepped back into air. I didn't have to dry off. Cool! When I slipped through the sliding glass door, a delicious hug, I heard Sylvia humming. She was making French Toast, and her version was definitely worth getting back inside my skin for. I ghosted upstairs and lay on my bed, waiting for Christian to come "wake" me.

Several minutes ticked past on my clock. I'd cut it pretty close if I wanted to hide what I'd done last night from Christian. As I thought this, something inside me twitched in annoyance. Because, no, I *didn't* want to hide this. Hiding things always backfired. So I was telling Christian everything, and he could just *deal* with it.

The drive to school passed in silence after I launched the first grenade at Christian. I could feel the emotions rolling off him. His seemed clearer or crisper than those I'd felt from Hans. Christian felt angry, but there were other quieter emotions as well. *Helplessness*, I thought. And . . . *panic?* Yes, he felt very panicked by what I'd revealed.

"Christian, I'm sorry for all the things you're feeling right now. I didn't act right by you. I see that."

"No, *Mademoiselle,* I believe that you do not see at all clearly in this matter."

We drove another quarter mile in silence.

"Do you understand the reason for which I agreed to accompany you to your village of . . . of origin?"

"Yeah." I sighed as I turned onto Main Street. "You're here to keep me safe."

"*Non, Mademoiselle.* Safe-keeping: that is but my job. It was never the *raison* . . . the *reason* for which I agreed." Christian stumbled in his English, probably because he was so angry with me.

"It wasn't?" I looked over at him, puzzled.

"My reason for accompanying you is this: my father, having discovered a last living descendant of the woman he loved, could not bear to lose her. He loved you for yourself, already, *without doubt*, but upon discovering your identity? My father felt paralyzed. He knew not how to, at once, pursue the downfall of a man most wicked and keep safe a child most *précieuse*."

I drove right past the school parking lot. If Christian noticed, he didn't say anything about it.

"*Mademoiselle*, you are young. You know nothing of loss, of what the loss of a child can do—"

"*What?*" I slammed on the brakes and shoved the car into reverse. Turning to the right, I drove two streets down and into a quiet parking lot. We were completely alone, cut off from anyone's view by the large yews bordering the cemetery grounds. "How *dare* you?"

I grabbed Christian's arms and slipped into invisibility. From my formless state, I hurled image after image at him. Hans, striking down Maggie and my mother. Me, staring at the cold ground where they'd lain my mother's ashes. Birthdays without her. Kids jeering at me for my odd silence. Hours spent weeping at her grave.

I felt Christian join me, becoming insubstantial beside me.

Forgive me, he said.

I couldn't form words. Tearlessly, I mourned. For mom, for the tiny Sam-in-a Petri-dish, for the happy childhood I'd missed out on.

With the compassion of one who'd known suffering, Christian enfolded me, whispering soothing words to me in French. Eventually, even when you're invisible, the tears run out, the grief quiets.

Forgive me, he asked of me once more.

Yeah, I replied. *I do. I guess Sir Walter left out some of my . . . history.*

Who can guess at the sorrows borne by another? asked Christian.

As he spoke, I saw an image flash through his mind and roll into mine. Christian, kneeling beside a grave—the grave of his wife and daughter. I felt his emotions wash over me: Loss. Grief. Despair.

No one should be asked to bury their child. Christian's words reached me as a whisper. *The child of my flesh, she was not. The child of my heart, she will always remain.*

You had a daughter? I asked. *Sir Walter said you were married, but you're so young . . .* I let my words trail off. I couldn't tell if Christian wanted to continue talking or wished for silence.

In a display of his confidence in me, despite my youth, my King, Le Roi-Soleil, commanded that I be married to Marie-Anne, one of the Queen's ladies-in-waiting. Marie-Anne was pregnant already with Louis' child when we were wed. I knew little of love, less of being a father.

But I loved them, murmured Christian. *By God's holy wounds, I loved both as my own.* He fell silent.

I felt like a horrible person for having yelled at Christian. How lonely, to have lost someone hundreds of years ago. My own separation from Will seemed like nothing compared to the depth of that loss.

Something inside me shifted and I vowed to be kinder to Christian.

That's why you agreed to watch over me, I said. *For your dad's sake. So he wouldn't have to go through . . . what you went through.*

Indeed, replied Christian. *He has seen what you have seen of my past. But I do not desire that he be forced to live through it himself. Mademoiselle, I must beg forgiveness for my thoughtless speech earlier.*

No worries, Christian. I felt him puzzling his way through my words. *It means 'I forgive you.'* An idea came to me and I solidified in the empty cab of my car. "Come with me," I said aloud.

Beside me, Christian's form shimmered back to solidity. The sun caught the gold of his hair and it gleamed.

Opening my door, I stepped out, gesturing for him to follow. I led him to my mother's grave and sat. The grass over the plots looked barely alive; Las Abs wasn't at its best in February.

"I showed you the bad stuff. When things were worst for me," I said, staring at Mom's headstone. "But it wasn't all bad."

To one side of her grave, a trio of violets had pushed through the cold earth.

"Show me," said Christian.

I hesitated, looking around.

He spoke again. "It is not necessary for us to assume chameleon form in order to share thoughts. Although, touch is helpful, certainly." He smiled at me, tilting his head to one side. "Have you never tried this with your . . . *petit-ami?*"

"With my boyfriend?" I shook my head. "It's not as easy for me and Will. I'm pretty sure we have to be invisible to, um, shuffle things back and forth."

Christian extended an elbow gallantly my direction. I snorted a tiny laugh, but threaded my own arm through the crook of his. Closing my eyes, I brought back small happy memories. Mom and me, making snickerdoodle cookies together, then giving up and just eating the dough. Dad waltzing with my mom late one night when they thought I slept. All of us eating s'mores around a merry campfire with a million stars wheeling overhead. I sent Christian image after image: things I had sealed off, even from myself, for years.

The ground grew cold and then freezing beneath our jeans. I opened my eyes and we stood, Christian pulling me up beside him like I weighed less than a feather.

"I fear we are badly *en retard*—late—for classes," he said.

I groaned. "Sylvia's already gotten a phone call from school, that's for sure. We should head over to school. I'll make something up." I sounded braver than I felt. I'd never skipped classes.

"Wait," said Christian. "Before we leave, if I might presume . . ."

In the still and cold of the cemetery, Christian sent me an image of his beautiful wife, Marie-Anne. In his memory, she stared at him with an impish grin as they sipped wine together. Dipping her finger in the goblet, she flicked some of it at him, laughing.

"Looks like she had spirit," I said.

"She was, in temperament, very like your friend, Mademoiselle Li," said Christian.

Then he sent me one last memory. A single lovely thought. A small girl, clutching one of his fingers with her chubby hand. More than a baby, but not yet old enough to walk on her own. She had long curls of gold, eyes black as night and skin like porcelain. She laughed as she took an uncertain step forward. She was more than pretty; she took my breath away.

"My Madeleine, while she lived," Christian murmured.

The image faded and I found my eyes clouded with tears. Blinking them back, I gave Christian's arm a squeeze. "She's so lovely."

He pulled a handkerchief from his jeans and dried his own eyes. "She was, indeed."

I wondered where he'd found a handkerchief in Las Abs. It must have survived Sylvia's Paris-purge.

"*Mademoiselle* Sam, I beg of you, let us have no more secrets. No more clandestine voyages of questionable safety." Here he smiled at me and it was like sunshine after a foggy morning. "If you believe you must risk your life for something important, please allow me to come alongside and provide assistance. For the sake of those who love you."

"Deal," I said. "And there's something else. I've been thinking about my secrets. Your dad said how the time for keeping what I can do hidden from everyone is maybe coming to a close."

"*Mademoiselle?*" Christian looked alarmed.

"I don't mean I'm telling *everyone*. Just, I think it's time I tell my folks the truth. And I thought maybe Bridget Li, too. Gwyn's mom."

"I confess I should find great relief in this," said Christian.

"Tonight, then, when my dad gets back from the berry farms, okay?"

"As you suggest," he said, with a tiny bow.

I was in plenty of trouble when I drove home after a half-day at school. The vice-principal hadn't been half so incensed as Sylvia. She was in kitchen-scouring-mode, never a good sign.

"When your father gets home tomorrow," she said, attacking a pile of crumbs by the toaster, "We are working out the details of a prolonged grounding."

"Dad's staying the night in the valley?" I asked.

She shook her tea-towel fiercely over the sink. "You know your dad and his berries."

I nodded. "I'm sorry, Syl. It won't happen again."

"She took me to see the resting place of her mother," said Christian. "The fault is mine, and I will share in any punishment you think fair."

"Oh, no." Sylvia set the tea towel onto the counter gently, like it was made of glass. "Oh, Sammy, come here." She didn't wait for me, instead closing the space between us, her arms wide. Sylvia gave great hugs even though she was shorter than me. "I didn't even think about what time of year it was."

I hadn't either. We were only days away from the anniversary of my mom's death.

"I'll explain about school to your father," she whispered, holding me tightly. Pulling back, she looked me in the eyes, compassion written across her face. "You need some alone-time?"

I did. I felt exhausted. Maybe Christian could get by without a good night's rest, but I suddenly felt like I was about to fall over where I stood. "I'll be in my room," I said.

"I shall *ground* myself as well," said Christian, bowing to both of us as he crossed to the hall behind the kitchen, as if retreating to his room. Of course, I knew he wouldn't stay there for long.

Hearing Christian's door close, I dragged myself to the stairs. Tread by tread, I ascended, growing more exhausted with each step. I felt Christian's icy form passing me. There was some comfort in knowing I could sleep in safety, with him invisibly watching my room. Kicking the door shut behind me, I flopped on my bed.

Right before I drifted off, I thought of one last thing. "Christian? We'll talk to my folks tomorrow when Dad's back."

Very well, Christian replied.

In the back of my mind, remote but persistent, I heard Christian singing again, the French song of love and loss. I caught a fleeting image: Christian, smiling over the form of a young woman with a tiny baby in her arms. And then I drifted to where I heard and saw nothing at all.

A few hours later, Sylvia stuck her head in to see if I wanted dinner. I wanted sleep a whole lot more, and whatever incoherent thing I mumbled must have gotten the point across. She closed the door and left. This time in my mind, I heard Christian chanting Psalms. *Vespers*, I said to myself, remembering the old-fashioned word as I drifted back under clouds of warmth.

Christian woke me one more time that night. My clock read 1:39AM. This time he wasn't chanting Psalms or prayers.

"Fire!" he called. "Your house is afire!"

Chapter Twenty-Four

HELISABA ES MORTA

• WILL •

My sister held out her hand for the aged journal Pfeffer had stolen two years earlier. Sir Walter gave the black book to her.

Seeing it again made me stop and think how Pfeffer must've been on our side back when he sent the book to us. As my sister flipped through pages, I spoke. "I've been so pissed off at Pfeffer, I didn't even think how he gave us that book. That's not something he'd have done if he was on Helmann's side at the time, huh?"

Sir Walter nodded. "Those are my thoughts as well. I fear Pfeffer was . . . *persuaded* to join Helmann."

The thought of Helmann *persuading* anyone made the hairs on my arms rise.

"Here," said Mick, her voice all soft and scared-sounding. "Is this what you're looking for? Three words that changed your cousin's life forever?"

Her finger pointed to some scribbles in the margin. The same thing written several times in a row.

Helisaba es morta.

It meant: Elisabeth is dead.

"*Mon Dieu!*" whispered Sir Walter, the rest of his breath escaping heavily. "*Mademoiselle*, I believe you have discovered it."

Chapter Twenty-Five

BURNING THINGS

• SAM •

I sat upright, feeling my heart pound from the sudden awakening. "Are you sure?" I couldn't see or hear anything fire-like in my darkened room. I maybe smelled smoke, though.

"You must change form at once—I shall carry your *belle-mère* to safety."

My eyes flew wide as I saw a flare of light outside my window. "The house is burning!" I said, stupidly.

"Quickly, *Mademoiselle*, please, assume your chameleon form!"

I tried to calm my mind, knowing full well Christian wouldn't leave to help Sylvia until I vanished. I thought of Illilouette Creek and felt my skin begin to melt away. Then I stopped cold, rippling back solid.

207

"Mom's painting of Yosemite!" I cried. "I have to save it!"

"Which painting?"

"The one over the couch, by the kitchen."

Christian nodded. "It is too large for you. Run to Sylvia. You can ripple with her, *non*? I shall rescue the picture."

"Okay," I said. Grabbing my cell, I rippled to safety. I would call 9-1-1 from outside the house once I had Syl.

Passing invisibly through the door of my room, I caught the scent of smoke and the odor of things that shouldn't burn. I shot down the hall to my parents' room. Downstairs, I could now hear the crackling of a fire gaining momentum. Had I jeopardized Christian's safety, sending him after the painting? Surely he'd have enough sense to judge whether it was too dangerous.

I came solid beside my step-mom's side of the bed. She turned in her sleep. Inhaling as I leaned over to take her in my arms, I felt my lungs burn from the spreading smoke. Sylvia coughed as I embraced her. *Thank goodness she's short*, I thought.

She mumbled in her sleep.

Her voice cut off as I rippled us to the safety of nothing.

The odor of incineration grew stronger once I'd vanished. I took several swift steps to a large window overlooking our deck and pool. I barely noticed the grip of the glass as we passed through. Falling earthward, I saw a dreadful beauty reflected in our swimming pool. Flames engulfed the entire lower level of my home and glimmered in reds and golds on the surface of the water.

Christian! My mind cried out, seeking his thoughts. His presence felt near, but he wasn't responding at the moment. I dashed across the pool with it's grimly beautiful reflection of the inferno. Down the stairs to Sylvia's garden I carried my step-mom invisibly. The slope of the hill sheltered us from the view of the flames. Setting Sylvia carefully upon the stone bench beside the fig tree, I brought us both solid.

"The house is burning," murmured Sylvia as she came awake in the cold night air.

I fumbled with my cell, new and unfamiliar. "Unlock, you stupid thing," I muttered, punching buttons. I had a text. I flipped past that to free up my number-pad. 9-1-1. I pressed the buttons too quickly and only *one-one* appeared on my screen. Hitting the cancel button, I dialed once more, successful this time.

One ring. Two.

"Please state the nature of your emergency," said the voice on the other end.

"Fire!" I shouted. "My house is burning down! Send a fire truck!"

Sylvia grabbed my cell and rattled off our address, which I have to admit, it hadn't occurred to me to report to the operator. A minute passed while Sylvia remained on the line, nodding and grunting, "Mmm-hmm" every few seconds.

The flames engulfing the house rose steadily to the second floor and I heard a loud explosion from the far side where our garage lay.

"Oh dear God!" said Sylvia, passing my cell back to me as she sprang up the garden stairs. "Christian!"

I dashed behind her, holding her from moving any closer to the inferno. "It's okay! He got out!" I could hear him praying on the other side of the house.

"What? How do you know? Are you sure?"

I answered only the last question. "Yes, I'm sure." The window over our kitchen sink exploded, sending glass arcing across the night sky—a terrifying rain of reflective mirrors each capturing the glow of flame.

"He's out front," I said.

Sylvia grabbed my arm. "We're going to find him."

We passed in a wide half-circle around to the south side of the house. The heat coming off of it amazed and horrified me. *Christian!* I called out once again. Rounding past the now-empty burn pile, we heard sirens wailing as the volunteers of the Las Abs fire department roared towards our home.

Christian stood outlined against the black sky, arms raised high overhead.

Sylvia laughed in relief as we spotted him together. "I don't think the firemen will have any trouble figuring out where to turn in."

"He's not trying to attract attention," I said, hearing an echoed prayer from his mind. "At least, not from the fire department." I could hear him chanting one of the psalms that asked for aid.

We ran up the slope, skirting the driveway where it hugged the burning mass. Christian, seeing us, dropped his arms and ceased chanting. He closed the distance between us in two giant strides, scooping me into his arms.

"*Merci, Seigneur!*"

I heard his whispered thanksgiving in one ear. Then I felt his embarrassment, rolling over and past me. He set me down and, seeing Sylvia, murmured, "Thanks be to God!"

Looking past Christian, I saw Mom's painting of Yosemite lying on the entrance to the driveway. The fire truck roared around the last curve toward our house.

"The painting," I cried.

Christian looked behind and saw the canvas, saw the approaching truck, and vanished. Half a second later he reappeared at the top of the drive, hauling the precious artwork off the road not a moment before the firemen drove across where it had lain.

Sylvia, standing beside me, blinked and rubbed her eyes, but said nothing.

The fire truck came to a noisy halt along our driveway.

"Anyone still in the structure?" called a tall man as he jumped off the truck.

"No," Sylvia called. "We're all out."

I turned my back on the firemen and their activities. Suddenly, I couldn't watch the flaming house anymore.

Las Abuelitas' single police vehicle screamed down the highway and pulled beside our drive, the county sheriff arriving just behind.

A dark-haired officer approached us, carrying blankets. I recognized Officer Thao; Coach had repeatedly tried to get his younger brother Phong to run cross country.

"How thoughtful," said Sylvia to Officer Thao, wrapping a blanket around my shoulders before taking her own.

"Thanks, Thao," I said. I clutched the soft fleece close. It gave instant relief from the biting night air. I hadn't had a chance to realize I was freezing in the brief time since I'd carried Sylvia from her room.

"I've got the heater running in the patrol car," said an officer I didn't know.

"Come on," said Sylvia. "Let's get inside."

Christian placed a gentle hand between my shoulder blades, aiming me to the top of the driveway and the warmth of the patrol car. From within his mind, I heard as he continued to chant. *Deus in adjutorium meum intende. Domine ad adjuvandum me festina.* Although my years of catechism had long since faded, I could understand the words: *God come to my assistance, Lord make haste to help me.*

"What he said," I mumbled, my first real prayer in many years.

The officer and his officer buddies passed out stretchy hats and gloves and one pair of socks which Christian and Sylvia both insisted I wear.

"I'm fine," I said, shoving the socks away. I leaned my head against the glass of the vehicle window. I was anything but fine. I was making a mental inventory of everything I cared about on the first floor of our home: *the family pictures on Dad's desk; the ugly pillow I'd made in second grade for Mom's birthday; my flip-flops, sitting by the sliding glass door; the Ghirardelli caramel squares in the pantry; my princess Ariel cereal bowl* . . . the list wasn't long. I didn't want to think about my bedroom right now.

Sylvia sighed, long and heavy. "I should call Dave."

I hadn't thought about Dad, other than being thankful he'd been gone.

"Can I borrow your cell, Sam?" she asked. "Mine's upstairs . . ."

Uncurling the fingers that gripped my cell, I passed the phone to her.

"It's trying to make me read a text, honey," said Sylvia. "What do I press?"

"Here," I said. My step-mom was hopeless with electronics. I stared at the unfamiliar number and accidentally punched the "view" button instead of the "ignore" button. Everything on my new phone seemed backwards. My thumb hovered over the "back" button as I glanced down at the new text.

I know where you live.

I gasped involuntarily.

"Honey?" asked Sylvia, still reaching her hand out for the phone.

I turned the gasp into a cough. "I'm fine. Just inhaled a little smoke or something." I hit the "delete" button, changed my mind and hit "no" once and "back" twice and passed her the cell.

Beside me, cramped in the patrol car's back seat, Christian looked at me with his brows raised. *Wherefore are you thus alarmed?*

Wherefore? *Do you mean "why" am I freaked?*

Yes, wherefore? Why?

Ignoring his bizarre English, I flashed him an image of the message upon the cell phone screen, explaining that it was from a San Francisco prefix. Hans.

He is vengeful, Christian said, *Like his father.*

214

My heart sunk within me. *You think he set the fire?* I already knew the answer.

Indeed.

I sat, lost in thoughts dark and despairing. Was it possible that my visit to the Geneses lab had brought our house down in flames? Or would he have tried it anyway? I stared out the car's front window, craning to see past the fire truck. The flames were gone now. My house resembled a skeleton: a smoking, reeking collection of bones laid bare. As I watched, the roof over the garage groaned and collapsed inward.

So much for my Blazer.

Christian reached over for my hand and held it, squeezing softly. *I am so grieved, Mademoiselle, for all that you have lost.*

You saved Mom's picture, I said. *That's the only thing I really cared about.*

Your cell phone, said Christian, *It made the sound of an angry hive of bees while you slept this last night. Would that have been the messenger?*

Text message, I corrected automatically. *Yes, probably. If I'd seen it, maybe none of this would have happened.*

Surely, you could not have foreseen this destruction.

No, I agreed, *but I might have sensed Hans, heard his thoughts.*

I felt Christian's surprise. *You can hear Hans as you hear me?*

Sort of. Except I only get stuff from him when he's really emotional. Angry. Frustrated. Happy. Then I hear him.

I see.

Maybe I could have heard him muttering, "Your house is toast," or something, I said.

Mademoiselle, can you hear him, now?

I paused, listening. Beside me, Sylvia spoke softly to my dad. He sounded really upset. I blocked that sound out and searched for the sound of Hans, gloating or celebrating.

There was nothing.

He's not around, I said. As I sent the thought to Christian, I felt sure I was right. *We're safe.*

Mademoiselle, you will forgive me for speaking in contradiction, but we are anything but safe. I believe the events of this night have proven that Las Abuelitas is no longer safe for you or your family.

Well, what are we supposed to do about it? Call the police?

I felt Christian hold himself back from retorting in kind with my sarcasm.

We must leave, Mademoiselle. We must depart Las Abuelitas.

Chapter Twenty-Six

THE ANGEL

• WILL •

Mick gave me an extra big hug as Sir Walter and I got ready to go. I wanted to bring her with us, to watch invisibly, but Sir Walter pointed out that if anything happened to us, there would be no one to bring Mickie solid.

"And no one left to warn Sam," she whispered, eyes brimming.

"It'll be fine, Mick," I said, sounding braver than I felt.

We arrived back at the building in Montpellier and approached one of the sleepers. It was a lot easier for me to "feel" where the invisible body was, now that I was trying to notice. It was like I was using a muscle and noticing it get stronger with use. Sir Walter tried the French version of the phrase first.

"*Elisabeth est morte*," he said, the words echoing off the walls of the empty room.

We'd brought the guy solid and leaned him against me so that my arms were wrapped around him. If he seemed immediately hostile, I'd be ready to ripple him back to insubstantiality. What with Sir Walter muttering beside me, the whole thing felt like a weird séance.

The French phrase didn't work.

Sir Walter switched to *Occitan*, the language in which the black book had been written. "*Helisaba es morta.*"

I felt life returning to the sleeper's body. I couldn't get a good look at his eyes from behind like I was, but Sir Walter's expression told me the pass-phrase had worked this time.

"Greetings, *Bonjour*," said Sir Walter.

Finding his arms loosely held by my own arms, the blond-guy turned to look at me.

"Hey, there," I said, "Easy now."

"You speak English?" asked the former sleeper. "I was to have been assigned to France. Where is the doctor?"

"The doctor . . . could not be here." Sir Walter was improvising; I could tell. "We came instead. And you are called?"

"I am Eric," he said, trying to shrug free of my grasp.

Sir Walter gave a fraction of a nod, indicating I should let him go.

"How far has the medical emergency progressed?" asked Eric. "I stand ready to assist."

Leaning out of Eric's sight, I raised my eyebrows at Sir Walter, all *what the heck?*

"And your companions?" asked Sir Walter. "Are they prepared to assist in a medical emergency? Or do you expect them to act . . . differently?"

I was really wishing Sir Walter would do his "talking inside my head" thing with me now, 'cause I didn't really know where he was going with this line of questioning.

"Of course they will assist. We are no cowards," said Eric. He looked deeply offended. "We are members of the Angel Corps. Have they been deployed ahead of me?"

"As you see," said Sir Walter, "You alone stand before us."

Eric looked worried. "Have I been left behind? Disqualified in some way?"

"I'm here to test you," said Sir Walter. "To hear, in your own words, what you are prepared to do and to uncover where your loyalty lies."

"I am prepared to lay down my own life, if necessary, to bring assistance to others. I know that I may become infected, and I accept this. Like Dr. Girard, I fear neither plague nor death." He paused for a moment. "I am a loyal servant of the good doctor."

Sir Walter raised his hand to his goatee, the signal that I should transport Eric back to invisibility.

In an instant, we were gone.

Sir Walter sighed heavily. *Will*, he called inside my head, *I do not like leaving him here awake, but I fear our only other option is to strike him a blow to the head.*

I paused, considering how to "write" the laughter I was feeling at my friend's funny way of putting things.

And then I wasn't laughing anymore, because invisible Eric wriggled free of me and rippled solid in front of Sir Walter.

Sir Walter registered shock and threw a single thought to me: *A chameleon?*

Chapter Twenty-Seven

THE TIME FOR SECRETS IS PASSING

• SAM •

A loud rap sounded on the window of the patrol car next to Sylvia. We'd steamed up the windows too bad for me to be sure who knocked. My step-mom opened the door on Bridget Li.

"Come with us," Gwyn's mom said, her voice low and urgent.

"*Now!*" said Gwyn, standing behind her mom. "We're getting you to safety. Come *on!*"

"What are you talking about?" asked Sylvia.

Gwyn reached out a hand. "Sam, now!"

My step-mom looked at me and then at my friend. Gwyn's eyes were over-large and focused on me.

"Let's go," I said. "I'll explain in Bridget's car."

As we stepped into the icy pre-dawn air, my eyes flew wide. There had to be fifty or more cars lining the side of the highway, gawking at the smoldering ruin of my home.

"Christian up front," barked Gwyn, reserving the back for herself, Sylvia, and me.

Her mom's Mini Cooper held us, barely. In the front seat, Christian hunched over his long legs, easily as squashed as us. Although he didn't have two cats crawling over his feet, trying to find a place to settle.

I looked at Gwyn and mouthed, "*Cats? Really?*"

"What's going on?" Sylvia demanded.

While I hesitated, Gwyn answered. "That was no accident, your house burning down. Ask Sam. Someone tried to kill her. And they didn't mind taking you out as collateral damage. We're taking you some place safe, for the short term." Looking at me, Gwyn added, "I hope its okay I told Ma about . . . everything."

"Sure," I said, nodding. Sir Walter's words in France echoed in my head once again. *The time for secrets is passing.*

Sylvia took my hand and held my gaze. "Sammy?"

"Gwyn's telling the truth," I murmured. Then I cleared my throat and spoke more clearly. "I have an unusual genetic make-up, Syl. There are people who would like to harvest my genes for their use. And," I hesitated, "There are people who would like me dead."

"You're kidding."

"Most regrettably, *Ma Dame*, she is not deceiving you," said Christian.

Between the two of us, Christian and me, we told Sylvia everything. She demanded a demonstration, which Christian obligingly provided, and to her credit, she didn't freak out. My step-mom *rocked* self-control.

After only a minute or two of silent reflection, she spoke again. "Where are we going?"

Bridget answered. "A rental I have in Midpines. It's a complete dump. Mice-infested—"

Here Gwyn, smiling, pointed to the cats.

Her mother continued. "But the oil heater is powerful, and there's something else waiting there that you're going to need."

I looked out the window. It was still dark, but I recognized a motel sign with a tiny burro. I remembered this place. Bridget flicked her turn-signal and we pulled down a drive just past the motel.

Sylvia sighed. "Dave's going to need directions." She passed my cell to Bridget, who'd just parked the Mini beside a dark shack. "You better tell him. I don't think I could."

"*Non!*" cried Christian. He grabbed the phone before Bridget could take it. Holding it in the air and waving it he explained. "My father has spoken to me about these small electronic *espions* . . . ah, spies. To speak into them is to broadcast to all. To *all*," he said with added emphasis.

"Electronic 'spies'?" murmured Gwyn.

"It's okay," I said. "I know how to tell Dad where we are without telling anyone else." I punched in the numbers for my dad's cell. "Dad? It's me. Sam."

"I'm on my way, honey." My dad's voice, strained and anxious, brought tears to my eyes.

"We're fine, Dad. Try not to worry. Bridget Li has given us a place to stay for now."

"I should come to the bakery?"

"No, Dad. Um, do you remember where I puked in the mini-van you were test driving? Don't say where! Just tell me if you remember where it happened."

"Sure, honey." I heard a short laugh. "That would be hard to forget."

"Okay, so listen close. Don't tell anyone where you're going. We'll explain why later. Just drive to that place where I puked in the car, and then go one more drive down and turn into it. You'll find us there. Same side of the highway, okay?"

"Sammy, are you sure you're okay?"

"Yeah, Daddy." My voice cracked as I said goodbye.

We piled out into the cold night air.

"I forgot to have the electric disconnected," said Bridget as a sensor light illuminated our path. "Fortune smiles on you."

We shuffled inside the small cabin. Inside felt as cold as outside. Or nearly. The cats set to work, scurrying across the cold linoleum floor, and Bridget fussed with a panel of dials beside an ancient wall heater.

"Doesn't take long to warm such a small place, at least," she said.

I sank into a scratchy brown plaid couch. The cold made its way through, slowly freezing the backs of my thighs, but I felt too tired to stand.

"Gwyn, give me a hand with the bags," said Bridget.

"Ask Christian," replied Gwyn, yawning hugely.

"*Gwyneth Li!*"

Gwyn rose, rolled her eyes dramatically as she passed me, and followed her mom outside.

"We're going to need cash," said Sylvia. "You didn't happen to grab your wallet, did you?" she asked me.

I shook my head.

"Our ATM cards have probably all melted," murmured my step-mom.

"Forgive me, *Ma Dame*," said Christian, "But my father left me a strict list of things to be avoided should we find ourselves within circumstances such as these." Christian straightened himself and closed his eyes, reciting. "*Do not make use of:* passports, ATM cards, cards of credit, vehicles owned by yourselves or close friends or family, cellular telephones owned by the same . . ." He continued through a litany of *don't use* items concluding with, "Your true names."

Bridget and Gwyn re-entered, dropping duffle bags on the floor before us.

"Mmmm, it's warming up nicely," said Bridget, smiling.

"It's freezing, Ma," said Gwyn, unzipping one of the duffels and withdrawing a poofy down jacket.

"Those are for your friends," said her mom.

"Put on your own oxygen mask first," retorted Gwyn. She threw me a jacket. "Just sayin'." She tossed another jacket to Sylvia.

"We packed what we could for you," said Bridget. "I'm afraid we have nothing for Christian."

"Who apparently sleeps fully dressed," said Gwyn, eyeing his apparel. "Dude, that's got to be bad for the health of the foot, there, sleeping with your shoes on."

I guffawed. "Christian pretty much doesn't sleep. So he doesn't need, uh, sleepwear."

Sylvia looked at him, opened her mouth, closed her mouth, and shook her head. "I don't need to know everything," she mumbled.

Gwyn handed a stack of clothing and a pair of Uggs to Sylvia. "These should all fit you." Stepping closer to me, she whispered, "Seeing as how you totally outrank me in the boob-department, I didn't bother packing you a normal bra. I brought you a sports-bra. More one-size-fits-all, I figured."

I felt my cheeks warm as I took the clothes. "I'm sure this will be fine," I murmured. "How did you even know . . ."

"About the fire?"

I nodded.

"It's like Sir Walter said. Nothing goes on in Las Abs without Bridget Li knowing. I had a bad feeling you might need to disappear for awhile, so we grabbed some clothes." She giggled. "Disappear. That's totally funny when you think about it."

I changed clothes with Sylvia in a cold, dark bedroom. Pulling on the sports bra, I felt an ache to be out on the roads, running. My running shoes were probably melted into a puddle of goo. Gwyn had brought flip-flops for me. She knew I'd never fit in her size 6 shoes. My heel hung sadly off the back of the flip-flops.

When we stepped back into the main room, I noticed the temperature had improved significantly. Unfortunately, the warmth had brought with it an unpleasant odor. My nose wrinkled.

"Mouse-poop," said Gwyn. "Ma says it's in the heater, so the smell should burn off pretty quickly."

On the floor, sitting cross-legged, Christian pulled his eating knife through what had been a blanket minutes ago.

"Um, Christian? What's with the wanton destruction?" asked Gwyn.

Setting one piece aside, he pulled his knife through the blanket again. "I am constructing a . . . how do you call it? *Un manteau.*"

"A jacket?" I asked. "A cloak?"

"A cloak, yes," he replied. "We have no money. I have no jacket. I would prefer to make one rather than thieve for one." He slipped his eating knife inside its case and withdrew a flat piece of leather, folded over upon itself. Inside lay several coils of thread and a bright golden needle.

"So, what," said Gwyn, "You're like a bodyguard-seamstress?"

Christian laughed. "I was, before my father discovered my existence, apprenticed for three years unto a tailor."

"Dude, how could your own dad not know you existed?" asked Gwyn. Then her face flushed. "Oh. Same as my dad, I'm guessing."

Christian looked up as he drew a length of thread through the needle. "Sir Walter married not my mother. Nor did he know that my mother had borne me. He learned of me during my fifteenth year and at once brought me to live with him at the court of *Louis Quatorze, à* Versailles."

Sylvia drew in a rapid breath. "My French is a little rusty, but did you just say something about Louis the Fourteenth?"

While Christian drew long stitches through the fleece, I explained to Sylvia the possibilities of extending life as a chameleon. Gwyn's mom listened with eyes wide, murmuring to herself in Chinese.

"*Wo De Tian Ah*," she breathed out as I finished. "Everlasting life. No wonder someone's trying to kill you. Although kidnapping you would make a lot more sense, wouldn't it? So they could use you like a . . . a donor bank?"

"*Ma!*" said Gwyn. "Not helpful." She wrapped an arm around my shoulder, protective.

"Why didn't I hear the smoke alarms?" asked Sylvia suddenly. "Did you hear them?"

I shook my head. "Hans must have removed the batteries. Or rippled away with the detectors entirely. I think Hans wanted me dead, for sure. But I don't think he was acting on orders."

"That is my conclusion as well," said Christian. He frowned as he pulled out his knife to clip a knotted thread. He drew a new length through the tiny needle. "Yes, *Mademoiselle*, I feel certain Hans acted outside his father's wishes. After obsessing for so long upon his deceased wife, Helmann is not someone to disregard the death of her last remaining heir."

We had to do some more explaining for Sylvia here. By the time we'd finished, we heard a truck pulling down the drive. Christian looked alarmed, but Syl and I reassured him that we knew the deep rumble of my dad's pickup.

Bridget pressed her face to the window, using her hands to block the inside light. "It's him," she confirmed. "Gwyn, you'll need to drive the Mini back. I'm not having you wreck that truck."

"We're going to need my dad's truck," I said. "I mean, this is nice as a landing pad, but we can't stay here."

Christian added, "Those at Geneses are surely aware of your friendship with *la famille* Li—with Gwyn and Bridget. Eventually, our enemies will search all of the dwellings owned by these friends."

"If only they thought we died in the house fire," I said.

"This is going to hit the news, honey," said Sylvia. "Your dad is a big name in valley farming. The police and the fire department know we survived."

"Not to mention the several dozen onlookers who came to watch," said Gwyn. "We got there late compared to some, but everyone was passing the word you'd made it out okay."

Bridget opened the door for my dad, who rushed to gather me and Sylvia in his arms.

During our explanation to my dad, he lapsed several times into whispered Spanish, reminding me of Gwyn's mom. The sun had risen by the time we finished.

Standing by a side window, hands on her hips, Bridget spoke. "So, you need a car that won't be recognized as belonging to you, and I just happen to have one." She pointed out the side window. "I have the pink slip for that vehicle. My last renter couldn't pay me or even afford a new battery, and I told him I'd take the truck."

"First order of business is to get that battery taken care of," said Sylvia. She'd been jotting down notes for several minutes.

"I've got jumper-cables," said my dad. "But I'll need the keys to the other truck."

"Keys?" Bridget blanched. "I forgot them."

"Really, Ma?" Gwyn shook her head and marched outside. We watched as she felt under each wheel-well.

When she strode back into the cabin, she held up a key. We all stared at her, dumbfounded.

"What?" she asked. "As-seen-on-TV, dudes. Don't tell me I'm the only one here who watches the Infomercial Channel." She shook her head in disbelief.

Taking the key, Dad stepped outside. He returned several minutes later shaking his head. "Your renter wasn't kidding when he said he needed a new battery. That one's deader than last season's berries."

231

Sylvia removed a pen from her mouth. Bite marks disfigured one end. "Buy new battery," she murmured as she wrote. Finishing, she resumed chewing the writing instrument, her wide eyes fixed on a spot beside the wall-heater.

I shook my head, slowly. "I can't ask you to do this," I said. "It's me Geneses wants, not all of you."

"*Mademoiselle*," said Christian. "You have already the proof that Hans will not hesitate to harm the ones you love in order to reach you. And when Helmann discovers the loss of your egg and your *jumelle*—how do you say it in English?"

"My clone," I whispered, nodding. "He'll force my family to reveal where I am."

"He would harm them to learn this, *certainement*, *Mademoiselle*."

A shiver ran through me.

My father cleared his throat. "Did you just say *Geneses* wants you?"

"Geneses is Helmann's company," I replied.

"It's just . . ." my dad broke off, scratching his head. "Anyone else caught the news today? About Geneses?"

We shook our heads.

"It's all over the radio stations." Dad frowned. "There was a massive outbreak of a plague in central Africa. Thousands dead, apparently within hours of contracting the virus. And the only relief organization who'll set foot in there right now is some group backed by Geneses. Angel Corps, the media's calling them."

My dad paused and looked at us long and hard. "Are you sure a company with that sort of integrity would hire murderous thugs?"

I sighed. "Yeah, Dad. We're sure. You're going to have to trust me on this one."

"Hush!" said Christian, straining to listen for something.

"Another car," whispered Bridget.

"Quick," cried Gwyn. "Do that hug-thing where you ripple away with someone."

I looked to Christian. *I'll get your father; you must secure your belle mere—your step-mother.* His silent words resounded in my head as I looked in alarm at Gwyn.

"Get your family to safety!" demanded Gwyn. "Ma and I will be fine. It's probably nothing, anyway. Some lost tourist looking for Yosemite."

I nodded and threw my arms around Sylvia, rippling to safety with her. Beside me my dad was cut off mid-gasp as Christian vanished with him.

Outside, a car door slammed and someone approached the cabin.

"Can I help you?" asked Bridget, opening the door.

"Oh, good morning. I was about to knock," said a friendly-sounding voice. "I'm here hoping to interview

233

the Ruiz family? I was told this was the place to find them."

As he craned his head around Bridget and smiled at Gwyn, my suspicions were confirmed. I'd heard that voice before. It came from a man with a thing for expensive running shoes.

Chapter Twenty-Eight

SELF SACRIFICE

• WILL •

It took me a split-second to come solid behind Eric, ready to defend Sir Walter with one of those blows-to-the-head.

But Eric didn't look like he wanted a fight. He looked like a kid who just dropped his ice cream cone.

"Please," he said, "I must know if my name has been struck from the Corps."

Sir Walter frowned. Obviously neither of us could tell Eric what he wanted to know. And now we had the issue of his status as a chameleon to deal with.

Eric spoke again. "If this is about my hesitation during the fire, when I was eleven, please allow me to prove myself. I am a different man today than that young child. I am a member of the Angel Corps. I passed the tests."

"Yes, my dear young man," said Sir Walter, stroking his goatee again.

I got ready to vanish with Eric again, but Sir Walter shook his head, a sharp negative, just as I was going to ripple.

"The thing I must determine is whether you are, in fact, an angel of mercy or an angel of death," said Sir Walter.

As soon as the words had left Sir Walter's lips, Eric collapsed, out cold.

Onto me.

I grunted, smacking hard on the floor.

"Fascinating," said Sir Walter.

"Heavy," I said, rolling now-sleeping-Eric off of me.

"I think we discovered the trigger that induces a hypnotic sleep," said Sir Walter.

"You think?" I asked. "A little heads up would be nice though, next time. How the heck did you know the password?"

Sir Walter laughed. "I did not intend to send him to sleep. I merely asked the question that came to mind. It was a happy accident, my friend, if such things are ever accidental."

We stared for a few moments at blond-haired, blue-eyed Eric, sleeping on the floor again.

"Let us return him to his hidden state," said Sir Walter. "I also should like to, er, *ree-pill*. I am spending so much time solid that my stomach begins to demand meals at regular intervals."

My stomach growled loudly. "Sure."

Sir Walter placed an arm upon my shoulder as I vanished with Eric.

I replaced the body and began writing questions to Sir Walter about the "angel." *So, obviously he's talking about Helmann, right? All that 'Dr. Girard' stuff?*

I believe we can assume that, said Sir Walter. *My cousin is only too likely to have called them, out of unadulterated pride, his 'Angels.' But I am disturbed that I knew not of this new generation of children.*

You think Eric's his kid? Like, part of a new batch? I asked.

Do you not think so? asked Sir Walter. *Based upon his appearance, he could be a sibling to any of them: Hans, Fritz, Franz, Helga . . .*

Yeah, I agreed. *Never seen Fritz or Hans, but this dude looked like Helga, all right. And the other sleepers looked like Eric. You think they're clones?*

No, said Sir Walter. *They are at a minimum of eighteen years of age. I think not that Helmann was engaged in cloning that long ago.*

Guess they didn't look like twins, quite, I wrote. *So what have we got here? Kids trained as medical experts or something?*

Indeed, agreed Sir Walter. *Loyal, even as his earlier children were. And yet . . . there was something less threatening in Eric's demeanor. Certainly he believes himself ready to act in self-sacrifice, for the good of others.*

He said something about a plague, I said. *That can't be good.*

Agreed, said Sir Walter. *Does my cousin mean to infect the nations with disease and then offer selective healing?*

We'd drifted to the windows on one side of the room as we spoke. Outside, the sun settled, brooding and red, spreading in a thin ooze as it slipped behind the horizon.

Let us return and consult with your sister, said Sir Walter. *She has proven her worth several times over in these mysteries.*

That and she's probably bored senseless by now, I wrote back.

We glided silently across the room, toward the front of the building. I was just thinking how I hoped Sir Walter would let us take the stairs when I felt something brush through my knees.

What the heck? I wrote to Sir Walter.

Something troubles you?

Walk over here, I wrote. *There's something invisible.*

An object hollowed and containing many small objects, said Sir Walter.

Can we grab it into solid form, you think? I wrote.

I shall attempt it, he said.

Sir Walter dropped his hand from me, which I *noticed* this time, and a moment later, he appeared in solid form, arms around a large Styrofoam box that looked very similar to the box delivered to Pfeffer's office in Rome.

Coming solid, I knelt to lift the lid, confident I'd find the same packets of dry ice cooling tiny vials.

"What do you make of this?" I asked, peering into the fogged interior.

As Sir Walter knelt beside me, a phone rang from inside one of his pockets.

A phone that only two people had the number for.

A phone that was only to be called in case of absolute emergency.

"It is your sister," said Sir Walter, examining the caller ID.

Chapter Twenty-Nine

NOTHING WORTH HEARING

• SAM •

The young man stood smiling on the porch, looking as though he'd very much like to come inside.

Which I'm sure he would have.

"I'm a reporter from the *Bee*," he lied, flipping through a notepad. "Like I said, I'd really love the chance to interview the family about the fire. Anything to do with David Ruiz is big news down in the valley . . ."

Bridget scowled at the young man. "I don't know who said they'd be here."

The man from Geneses flipped through his notes. "Ah, one of the officers on the scene . . ."

"Officer Phong?" asked Bridget, substituting the name of Officer Thao's little brother.

She thinks fast, I said to Christian.

"That's the one," lied the man. "I remember it 'cause it rhymed with 'ping-pong.'"

"Yeah, well, Officer Phong must've misunderstood. I'm down here cleaning the place out with my daughter so the family can come here, but they aren't here yet. The cabin is a mess right now. They went down to a hotel in Fresno. Or maybe it was Merced."

"It was Hanford, Ma," said Gwyn. "Wasn't it?" She picked up a broom leaning in one corner and began sweeping the floor.

Bridget shrugged. "One of those three. Take your pick."

The man leaned in. "Are you sure they're not here? I don't want to bother them. I just want a few minutes to ask some questions." He paused. "I'm not an idiot. You've got three cars parked out front."

Bridget laughed. "Yeah, well, I dare you to start that red truck. My last renter left it for dead."

"The blue truck's mine," said Gwyn. "Ma's driving makes me get car sick."

"There's nothing wrong with my driving," snapped Bridget.

"Unless you like to keep your breakfast *inside* your stomach," retorted Gwyn, turning back to sweep the floor.

"Okay," said the man with the Brooks, "I'm sorry to have taken up so much of your valuable time." He held his hand out to shake Bridget's. "Sorry to disturb." I saw a flash of something in his other hand. As he shook hands with Gwyn's mom, he reached up with the other hand and, covering her mouth, he puffed an inhaler in one of her nostrils as she inhaled to cry out.

But before Bridget could get any sound out, she sagged and then collapsed.

"Miss," said the man in an alarmed voice. "Miss, your mom seems to have fainted."

I had to save her! Could I take this guy on, I wondered? I had to try.

Do nothing! Christian's voice commanded. *I beseech you!*

"Can you help me get her to the couch? Maybe some water?" suggested Hans' employee.

Christian! They're in danger! I called out, itching to ripple solid and attack Brooks-man.

Wait—please, Mademoiselle! If he means to do more than search the dwelling, we will attack together!

As Gwyn rushed to get a cloth wet, the man reached around and squirted the same thing in Gwyn's nose, catching her as she collapsed. He set her on the couch and then dashed to the back bedroom, shoving the bed across the room, opening and slamming the closet door. He darted to the bathroom, threw the shower curtain to one side, checked a linen cupboard.

Exiting the back of the house, he cursed and sprinted back through the front door, punching buttons on a cell as he ran.

Wait and listen, called Christian, sensing the part of me that strained to come solid.

"They're not in Midpines," said the man. "The truck is the same make as the *spic's* truck, but it belongs to the *chinks*, apparently. They said the family got a hotel room for the night, but they acted like complete retards arguing over where, exactly. I've got Hanford, Merced or Fresno."

The man from Geneses nodded one more time. "I'm on it." He drove off.

I rippled solid with Sylvia in my arms. "Christian, you follow him—I'll stay and help here."

"Following that *imbecile* would accomplish nothing," said Christian as he came solid with my father beside the couch. "We already know his purpose: he wishes to locate you."

"*That* was an example of a Geneses employee?" asked my dad. His quiet voice told me just how angry he felt at the moment.

"Yeah," I said, rubbing Gwyn's hands. "That's Geneses for you. We're all racial inferiors here except for maybe Christian."

Bridget shook her head once and opened her eyes, looking confused.

"Did I miss something?" asked Gwyn, eyes fluttering.

"Nothing worth hearing," I said, reaching my arms around to hug her.

"We need to get out of here," said my dad. "I want Sam safe from that . . . that poor excuse for a human being."

"We need cash," said Sylvia.

"And a battery," said my dad.

"For which we need cash," said Sylvia. "Not credit cards. They're too easy to trace."

"I've got five-thousand in cash back in the bakery," said Bridget. "That's more than Mrs. Gutierrez at the bank could probably come up with on such short notice. And I don't think you want to stick around Las Abuelitas even one more day."

"Definitely not," I agreed. "But we can't take your money."

"You have five-thousand *in cash* sitting in our home?" asked Gwyn, crossing her arms over her chest.

Her mom nodded.

"God, you are *so* Chinese, Ma. Have you not heard of banks?"

"It's for emergencies," said Bridget.

"Yeah, well I had an emergency need for jeans last week, and you said we were broke."

"That wasn't an emergency," snapped her mom.

"You're crazy, Ma, you know that? Seriously, when exactly do you think you're going to need that much money?" Gwyn shook her head.

"Today," said Bridget, smiling smugly.

Gwyn opened her mouth to say something but changed her mind. And then changed it again. "That was pretty smart of you, Ma."

"We can't take your money, Bridget," I repeated.

Sylvia raised her eyebrows. "We can and we will. Dave's truck is yours 'til we can pay you back."

Bridget nodded her approval.

"Excellent," said Gwyn. "That's worth what, thirty-thou'?"

No one responded.

Gwyn shook her head. "Am I the only one who's seen Crazy Chuck's Chevy Circus commercials?"

Sylvia turned, covering her mouth to hide her laughter.

"It will take me an hour and a half to get there and back," said Bridget. "Longer, if you want me to pick up a battery."

"I don't like staying here that long," said Sylvia. "All the roads out of here take us close to Merced or Fresno and the sooner we clear those areas, the better."

"Not all roads," said my dad.

"Tioga Pass is closed, Dave. It's January. We have to go west to leave the area."

"I know some back roads to the valley," said my dad.

"I'm so sorry," said Bridget. "I wasn't thinking of how I'd boxed you in by saying what I did about hotels."

"You were brilliant," said Sylvia, smiling. "I could never have thought on my feet like that."

"You may well have saved their lives," said Christian. "Do not perspire upon things of small importance."

Gwyn stared at him. "Did you mean to say, 'don't sweat the small stuff'? 'Cause, dude, that was some creative use of English."

Suddenly, I remembered something. "Christian, how long did it take you when you brought me back from Geneses two weeks ago?"

He drew his brows together. "Perhaps the half of one hour?"

"That's what I thought!" I said smiling. "It took me over two hours. Pretty much what it would take speeding by car."

"I am unusually swift when incorporeal," said Christian.

"I'll say!" I agreed. I turned to everyone else. "Christian can take Bridget to get the money and the battery. He can get there in less than a quarter of the time it would take by car."

However, Christian point-blank refused to leave my side. ("I swore an oath to my father, and I will uphold my oath.") So the three of us, Christian, Bridget and myself, rippled and traveled together. Christian explained that we'd all be able to move at his speed so long as we touched.

Following a crazy-fast zip through the foothills, we approached Las Abs. As we arrived, I caught an echo of an emotionally-charged thought that came from Bridget's mind.

New car.

Well, if anyone would recognize an unusual car in Las Abs, that person would be Bridget.

I looked both directions, curious what she'd seen. I found the new car, and my blood froze. Driving slowly along Main Street I spotted a small sports car that I knew very well. I'd ridden inside it last year.

It's Hans! I cried out to Christian.

Chapter Thirty

WEIGHT OF THE ATLANTIC

• WILL •

"I think you should come back right away," said my sister. Her voice, crackling over the connection, was plenty loud for both of us to hear.

"Are you unwell, *Mademoiselle?*" asked Sir Walter. "Are you in danger?"

"It's not me," said Mick. "It's . . . those people we don't like. They're doing . . . things we don't like. And you need to come look at it *now.*"

My heart hammered as I rippled back solid and grabbed the phone. "Mick? What is it? Is it—" My voice cracked. I couldn't make myself ask about Sam by name.

"It's not about *her,*" said my sister. "It's something else. Can you come back, like, *now?*"

248

"Sure," I said.

Before I'd hit "end," Sir Walter had rippled away to hide the Styrofoam box once more. Then he came solid and reached for my arm. Together we vanished and raced like a silent wind back to the tiny house.

My sister sat hunched over Sir Walter's computer. When we solidified in the room, she waved us over. "Geneses is up to something. I mean, it all looks nice on the surface. They come out looking like saints, really, but I've got a bad feeling about it."

Sir Walter and I read the news headlines about an outbreak of deadly plague within a small central African country. Volunteers connected to Geneses International had taken the point on trying to contain and cure the disease.

"Please tell me this group of volunteers doesn't have a name related to heavenly beings," I murmured.

"The media are calling them *Angel Corps*, you know, like Mercy Corps or Peace Corps," replied my sister.

"Oh, no," I said.

Sir Walter brought a hand across his face.

Between us, we caught Mickie up on what we'd discovered in Montpellier.

"If Helmann is using the *Angel Corps* to 'help' victims of disease," said Mickie, "I think we can expect massive casualties."

"Like the video," I said.

249

"*Mademoiselle*, would you please search for other instances of this disease? In other locations?" Sir Walter's right hand clenched and unclenched. I'd never seen him nervous, but maybe this was what it looked like.

My sister bounced around on several news sites, repeatedly closing pop-up notifications. The disease seemed to be contained within the one country for now. But I started thinking about California's diverse population, just full of people-groups Helmann would like to eliminate. *Not Sam, not Sam, please, not Sam . . .*

"What does Geneses' official site report?" asked Sir Walter.

Mickie opened a new window and we waited for the Geneses page to load. When it came up, there was just some crap about how proud the company was of its brave volunteers, and how the *Angel Corps* would have every advantage of immunological technology Geneses could provide.

A new pop-up covered part of the article, and my sister quickly closed it.

"Wait," I said, "What was that? Something on central California?"

"Just an interest group on berry farming. It's very active today. I'm part of a couple of groups that I thought might help me keep tabs on Sam and her family," explained my sister.

"Oh," I said, returning my attention to the article on Geneses' home page.

Sir Walter tapped the screen. "Bring it back," he said. "The notification."

Mickie tapped her fingers across the keyboard. "I'm sure it's nothing. Usually it's just complaints about LA taking farm water or something."

But when the chat group site opened, it was full of entries featuring the name "Dave Ruiz." Sam's dad.

"Oh, no," murmured my sister. "How did you guess?"

"Our enemy rarely strikes upon only one front," said Sir Walter.

As we read through the posts, I felt every one of those six-thousand miles between Sam and me.

"Everyone's talking about Sam's house!" cried my sister, reading faster than me. "It burned to the ground."

The weight of that distance gathered and settled in my chest.

"Sam's dad is big news in farming circles," continued my sister. "His name comes up all the time on some of these chat sites."

"Click upon the linking article," said Sir Walter.

There it was, in the Fresno Bee. An article on berry-grower David Ruiz and the tragic blaze that left him homeless.

How much did all the water in the Atlantic weigh, I wondered? It rushed in behind the six-thousand miles, filling my lungs with a crushing load.

"Sit down," murmured my sister.

I sank into the chair beside her.

My sister took my hand as she scanned the screen. "The former occupants are unavailable for comment, blah, blah, blah, several eyewitnesses *saw the family safely outside the house* while the fire department was there." My sister gave my hand a quick squeeze.

I heard a pounding surf roaring in my ears.

Sam would be okay. She had to be okay.

"This news article is insufficient," said Sir Walter. "Return to the chat forum, please, *Mademoiselle*." His voice sounded thin.

My sister wiped her eyes with the back of one sleeve. "Here's something," she said. "Everyone wants to interview Dave Ruiz about the fire, but no one can find him or Sylvia. Or Sam. Here's something else. Bridget Li's name is popping up." My sister ran a finger down the screen, reading silently.

I wanted to read, but my eyes kept going out of focus with tears: the wide Atlantic was leaking out of me.

"Bridget's saying she doesn't know anything." My sister let out a short laugh. "Reporters are swarming Las ABC, and Gwyn's telling them to buy a coffee or get the hell out of the café."

"We have to go," I said. With the ocean roaring in my ears, the words sounded small and far away, like someone else had spoken them.

"Indeed," said Sir Walter. "I would be willing to gamble that *Madame* Li knows the truth of their location. And when we are closer to Chrétien, I shall be able to communicate with him from within our minds," he said.

Mick looked up. "Really?"

Sir Walter nodded. "Let us prepare to leave."

"Thanks, man," I choked out.

As Sir Walter turned, I saw a face so pinched with grief that I forgot about the weight of the ocean upon my chest. I'm not much of a hugger, but I threw my arms around the old man.

"I'm sure she's fine," I said. Only I wasn't sure of anything.

We rippled to travel back to Nice, at my sister's suggestion. I felt grateful to her, knowing how rippling made her feel sick. From Nice, Sir Walter chartered a private jet to get us to California.

The worst part of it all was how we couldn't communicate with Sam. Her home phone number wasn't working, for obvious reasons, and Sir Walter wouldn't try her cell.

"If she has been . . . detained by our enemies, I do not wish to alert them as to her connection with us," he said.

Mickie reached over to take my hand.

"I'm fine," I lied, closing my eyes, wishing I could sleep to pass the time faster. But I had too much adrenaline pumping through me. I tried to get comfortable. The leather seat felt slippery and cold and too big, like no matter how I sat, I couldn't anchor myself to it properly.

I looked out the window; the vast ocean looked immeasurable. Staring at it made me feel like we weren't really moving at all, like we'd never reach the next continent.

Mile after slow mile, the engines droned, until the noise started making me a little crazy. At some point, Sir Walter offered me special headphones. But then it was too quiet. I threw the headphones down and let the engine-noise fill my head.

Chapter Thirty-One

APOCALYPSE

• SAM •

You are certain it is Hans? Christian asked from inside my head.

I'm sure, I replied. *I rode in that car with him last fall.*

As we watched, Hans pulled his car into a sharp reverse, in the middle of Main Street, and peeled out, leaving dark stripes upon grayed asphalt as he drove out of town.

I caught another thought from Bridget Li. *Tourist.* Meant as the worst variety of insult.

He appears to have departed, said Christian.

I guess, I said. *Let's just go forward with our plan. I'll keep my, uh, ears open for any sign of him returning.*

We passed through Bridget's rock wall, which startled her, and then the three of us materialized within her kitchen.

"I'm not dreaming this, am I?" murmured Bridget to herself. She gave her head one good shake and then crossed to a stack of cleaning rags. Moving these out of the way, she uncovered a small fire-safe. It looked like one in my dad's office. I wondered briefly what he'd kept in ours, what had survived the fire.

Bridget fumbled with the lock and opened the safe. Quickly, she passed us the money. "I'm going to stay here," she said. "So I can keep an eye on things around town."

I told her the identity of the rude tourist.

She nodded. "If he comes back, I'll hear about it."

"Be careful around him," I warned.

She grinned. "I survived the Cultural Revolution in China. Well, I was a baby, but I survived, didn't I? The Li family has always been fortunate."

Bridget made a call to have a car battery delivered directly to the bakery. "Joe's Auto owes me," she said.

Once we had the battery, Christian and I said goodbye to Bridget and returned to Midpines.

Gwyn and Sylvia were talking quietly when we arrived and came solid again. I took the battery, which was just crazy-heavy for such a small object. Crunching noisily through a thick layer of digger and sugar pine needles, I carried it out to my dad. He was fiddling under the hood of the truck. He pulled an old transistor radio from his pocket and turned it off, removing his earbuds.

"You can have my old iPod, you know," I said as he wrapped the earwires carefully around the piece of ancient technology.

He shrugged. "I like the radio."

"You hear anything interesting?" I asked.

He took the battery from me. "Boy, you're getting strong, kiddo, just like your mom was."

I smiled.

"I always told her she was strong enough to be a farmer," he said, heaving the battery into place.

"And she laughed at you," I said, remembering their banter, "And said you were stubborn enough to be an artist."

He fiddled with things under the hood of the truck. "I did hear some interesting stuff on the radio, actually. More on Geneses International and that group of volunteers. Angel Corps, they're calling them."

"What's the news saying now?"

"Same plague showed up in a neighboring country. Red Cross basically told 'em, 'Hey, be our guest,' and let the Geneses volunteers go in first, like the Marines, you know."

"Weird," I said.

"You know, Sammy, I grew up with bullies like that racist who came knocking here earlier. We didn't have all the stuff you kids get in schools now about tolerance and diversity."

Dad had finished with the battery and dropped the hood. The metallic reverberation echoed through the pines.

"That guy got me thinking, remembering what high school used to be like if you were a Hispanic kid in an Anglo school. And then I got this really bad idea I couldn't shake," he said, walking to the driver's seat. "Probably just your old man getting paranoid." He shook his head. "I haven't heard anyone use language like that in a long time."

He turned the key and the truck started up. We each made a thumbs up at the same time and then laughed together. I felt my heart swell.

"I love you, Dad," I shouted, over the roar of the truck.

He grinned, his sun-browned face creasing along a thousand lines. He turned the engine off. "I love you, too, Sammy. Let's go tell your step-mom we're ready to roll."

We crunched back through the dense carpet of pine-needles to the little cabin.

"Hey, Dad? You didn't tell me your idea. The bad one you said you couldn't shake."

He frowned, wiping his hands several times on his jeans before reaching for the door handle. "Yeah, it's probably crazy." He rested his hand on the handle.

"But here's the thing. There's a deadly sickness in a tiny country in central Africa, and Geneses just happens to have a group of volunteers there? So, I wondered, if everyone running Geneses thinks like that racist who came here, what if the people at Geneses are the ones making everyone sick?"

"Oh, no," I whispered. "Oh, no!

We entered the cabin, and I quickly shared what my dad said with Christian.

"Wait a minute," said Sylvia. "You think this *Helmann*-person is killing thousands of innocent people?"

"We heard about it on a video he made," I explained. "He plans to get rid of billions: the weak, the sick, and those he called the 'inferior races.'"

"A second Holocaust," murmured my step-mother.

I nodded.

"We should go to the media with this," said my dad, fumbling for his cell. "I've got the number for someone on Channel 2 News in here."

"I beg of you, *Mon Seigneur* Ruiz," said Christian. "You will not live to see another day if you present yourself to the public in this manner."

"Christian's right," murmured Sylvia. "They *want* to find us."

"In any case, we need to talk to Sir Walter first," I said. I looked to Christian. "What do you think? Does this constitute a cell-phone emergency?"

Christian fixed his eyes upon the linoleum floor for several seconds. "I believe my father should be told of your father's idea."

"Use my cell," said Gwyn. "Someone's probably monitoring all of yours." She indicated me, Sylvia, and my dad.

"What time is it in France?" I asked, preparing to call a number I'd memorized. For emergencies only.

"Nine of the clock," said Christian. "In the afternoon."

"Night," corrected Gwyn.

I dialed. The phone went straight to voicemail.

"They're not picking up," I said.

"Probably a dead battery," Gwyn said.

"Do not leave a messenger," said Christian.

"Message," Gwyn corrected automatically.

I hit "end."

"It is apparent to me what we must do," said Christian. "Sir Walter instructed us to return to him should Helmann begin his *apocalypse*—what is the word in English?"

"Apocalypse," we all said together.

"Then we're going to France," said Sylvia.

Gwyn shook her head. "You'd have to use your passports to travel to France. Hans, plus maybe

260

Helmann, will be tracking credit cards and passports for sure, watching for the Ruiz family to pop up somewhere," she said.

Christian frowned. "In which case, your arrival in France would mean certain death."

"What about fake passports?" I asked.

"This isn't the movies," replied my dad. "You can't just go to Fresno and get a fake passport."

Gwyn guffawed. "Well," she said, "Not in the time frame you're looking at, certainly. And not four of them for five-thousand dollars."

We all turned to look at her.

"What? I saw it on the Crime Channel," she said.

"We have to go alone," I said. "Me and Christian. It's the only way." The thought of returning to Will, of re-crossing that great divide—it made me almost giddy.

"Young lady," said my dad, "You are not getting on a plane. Someone wants to kill you, and Gwyn is right about your passport being a sure way to track your movement."

"We need not show our passports to travel," said Christian.

"We'll catch a plane," I said, "But we'll do it invisibly."

Chapter Thirty-Two

KIDNAPPED

• WILL •

As soon as we touched down at Fresno Yosemite International, Sir Walter rented the fastest car Hertz had available. Mick was sleeping by the time we got close to Las Abuelitas. I spoke softly to Sir Walter. "I'm worried about someone seeing me and Mick when we're supposed to be in France."

"I am in hopes your sister will agree to spend the afternoon hidden," replied Sir Walter.

Mickie woke up, rubbing her eyes as we drove slowly past Sam's house. Only a skeleton remained— blackened and dead-looking. I wondered how it made Sam feel, her home gone like that. But mostly I wondered where she was now.

"You got any sign of Chrétien on your, uh, radar?" asked my sister.

Sir Walter shook his head.

"How close do you have to be for it to work?" I asked.

He shrugged. "I have not thoroughly tested the limits. Perhaps a kilometer? Or two? Christian's abilities exceed mine in this, however, such that he would be likely to notice me first."

I frowned. Sir Walter's son, who was hanging somewhere with Sam, had me beat everywhere I looked. I kept the thought to myself.

"We shall visit your home in case Sam and Christian thought to hide there," Sir Walter said. "Unless you have a better idea?"

Mickie shook her head.

"I got nada," I said. I was starting to think about how big the planet was. How Sam could be anywhere. How Bridget Li better have something for us.

"I miss driving," said my sister, tapping the window to indicate her Jeep as we pulled beside our old home. I thought of all the other things she must be missing: her garden, her collection of books, her safety.

Sir Walter was the only one of us who got out to investigate, but the cabin was empty. I felt strange, staring at its familiar shape, and I had to turn away. Nothing about Las Abs was right without Sam here.

Sir Walter returned to the car and asked Mickie if she'd mind hiding. "Perhaps your cabin would be comfortable?"

"I don't want to stay here," she said. Turning to me, she smiled. "Put me in that wall you like. The Bakery rock wall. Bridget plays good music, so I won't get bored."

Bridget Li's café was slammed for business when we arrived. Well, when *Sir Walter* arrived: he had made me ripple invisible with Mickie back at our old cabin.

We exited the rental car, and while Sir Walter went to speak with Bridget, I drifted to the bakery kitchen at the back of the café and placed Mick in the rock wall, trying hard not to think about when I'd first showed Sam how to ghost through solid things. Then I glided into the café, brushing through Sir Walter so he'd know I was back.

Your sister is safe? he asked from inside my head.

Yup, I wrote back.

Madame Li has agreed to speak with me as soon as her daughter arrives for lunch and can confirm my identity, he said, taking a seat in the booth closest to the front door after placing a generous tip in the Cat Fund jar.

Why don't we just go upstairs and talk to Gwyn now? I wrote, as Sir Walter placed a generous tip in the Cat Fund jar.

Madame Li's daughter is, unfortunately, in school at the moment.

Oh, right. I'd totally forgotten. School had continued without me. It made me feel strange. Adrift.

The café clock inched past 12:15 PM, and students began milling around campus, a few crossing Main Street to eat at Las ABC.

Ten minutes passed and Gwyn didn't show.

Bridget looked uncomfortably at Sir Walter a few times, but she didn't make any moves to come talk to him in the midst of the lunch rush. end

After a couple of minutes, I saw him startle.

I wrote, *What?*

He didn't respond; instead he looked super-alert.

What? I wrote again.

I thought I heard something, he said.

Chrétien? I wrote.

No, I thought I heard Hans, said Sir Walter. *Very near. And very angry.*

At this moment, Bridget crossed over to us.

"Listen," she said. "I don't know where Gwyn is, so how about you give me a good reason why I should trust you."

I'm checking the kitchen! I wrote, tearing off to maybe catch Hans off-guard behind the door.

Sir Walter rose and dashed towards the back of the café as well, with Bridget following and heads turning.

The kitchen was empty when I solidified. Seconds later, Sir Walter and Bridget entered.

"Will?" She sounded pretty shocked and not sure where to put her attention: on me or Sir Walter.

"This truly *is* Sir Walter," I said to Bridget. To the Frenchman, I said, "Go check upstairs. I'll try outside."

Sir Walter shook his head. "I hear him no more. It would be of no use to search. He could have fled in any direction."

"What's going on?" demanded Bridget. "Is this about Sam?" She lowered her voice. "She was fine last night. In fact, she was on her way to France to see you."

My heart felt the wrong size and weight.

A loud knock sounded on the door leading from the café to the kitchen. "Bridget? Everything okay?"

"I'll be right back," Bridget said to us before exiting to reassure her customers.

"Retrieve your sister," said Sir Walter. "It appears we shall be returning to France."

I rippled invisible, feeling a moment's doubt that I could find the edges of Mickie's insubstantial body, but it wasn't that hard. Invisible sister felt quite distinct from rock wall. I eased us out of the wall and into the center of the kitchen.

We came solid just as Gwyn's mom returned.

The moment my sister had lungs and vocal chords again, she turned to me in panic. "Gwyn's been kidnapped!"

Chapter Thirty-Three

MESSAGES

• SAM •

Christian and I located a non-stop flight out of San Francisco, but we had to pass six long hours in the airport before it departed. It was still faster than the connecting flights, so we waited. I thought about Sylvia and my dad, wondering how safe they'd be from Hans. Dad said they were going to New Mexico, far from family, and therefore, hopefully less traceable.

Traveling on a trans-Atlantic flight while invisible was far, far nicer than traveling coach. Although, knowing that each mile brought me closer to Will, I think I would have been grinning from ear-to-ear even if I'd sat on one of those little flight attendant seats that flip down from the wall.

When we landed in France, Christian and I went into the ladies washroom so that I could ripple solid for the phone call to Sir Walter, to figure out where to meet up. When I powered up my cell, I saw I had two messages. Both were from Gwyn's number. Which was weird because she'd agreed we shouldn't call each other except for really important stuff.

"Hello, Miss Ruiz," said a voice that made my spine tingle with fear. "As you may have surmised, Gwyn Li is no longer, ah, in control of her cell phone. Perhaps you would be so good as to check the attachment on the next message from this number? I've prepared a small video for your entertainment."

Christian came solid in the tiny bathroom stall. Luckily, European stalls had floor to ceiling doors.

"*Mademoiselle*," he said. "Do you need fresh air?"

I choked back something—a sort of hysterical laughter that resembled crying. Then I took a slow breath. "No," I said. "I need to see the next message."

It was a hostage video.

Chapter Thirty-Four

PLANE TO CATCH

• WILL •

"Hans was here," Mickie said. "Well, first Gwyn came through the back door, and then Hans rippled solid in the middle of the room and asked her where Sam was, which she wouldn't tell. I think Gwyn knew it was him. She told him she'd scream if he came any closer." Mick's face wrinkled in anxiety. "And then he said he dared her to scream because he'd have her invisible faster than she could make the noise. And then he said he hoped she liked France, because he was taking her to his Father's castle. Château something . . ."

"Château Feu-froid," said Sir Walter.

Mick turned to him. "That was it. With all the 'F's'. Do you know where that is?"

"I do, indeed," said Sir Walter.

"Take me there," said Bridget, her voice all thin like she was barely keeping it together. "She's my only child. She's all I've got."

Sir Walter frowned and began pacing.

I was dying inside, 'cause Gwyn had been kidnapped, and that was awful, but we'd come all this way to find Sam, and she'd gone to France? I grabbed my head with my hands, 'cause it honestly felt like it might explode.

Sir Walter and Bridget argued and planned and my sister twirled a chunk of her hair like she could fix everything if she got it wrapped around her finger tight enough. Then they were back to talking about Sam again.

"She must intend to discover us there," said Sir Walter. He patted his jacket like he was searching himself for a concealed weapon. After a moment he brought out his cell phone. The one he never used.

Sir Walter sighed heavily, running a hand slowly across his face. "Sam attempted to contact us."

"*And you only now thought to check your cell?*" I shouted.

"Will!" My sister addressed me in a voice that said *Chill, idiot.* "Sam is presumably safe. Gwyn is not. Priorities. Got it?"

I nodded. She was right. I needed to think straight.

"I believe we all have a plane to catch," said Sir Walter.

Chapter Thirty-Five

CHÂTEAU FEU FROID

• WILL •

As we approached the airport outside Tours, France, Sir Walter pulled his cell phone from a pocket. There weren't any messages, and he tucked the device back inside his traveling coat.

"She's safe," I kept mumbling to myself. "She's safe." The engine noise kept anyone from hearing me. I knew we had to get Gwyn to safety first, but worrying about Sam was killing me.

We rented a big, black car that turned out to have a broken heater, stuck in the "on" position. Everyone peeled off jackets, but we ended up driving with the windows down to keep the temperature bearable. Bridget, who had been unable to sleep for any of the flight, finally took a Xanax from my sister, which, combined with the heat, sent her to sleep on the drive.

Sir Walter's plan was simple. Drive to Château Feu Froid, hide the car, ripple and find Gwyn, grab her, and get out. It was pretty obvious Hans had taken Gwyn to get Sam to turn herself in. For the millionth time, I wondered what Helmann wanted with Sam.

We left our car hidden in an old tumbled-down garage about half a mile from the castle. Bridget, who was still mostly asleep, we covered with a pile of everyone's coats.

We had a little fracas there, when Mick started insisting she should be allowed to come along to the *château*. But in the end, she agreed to stay hidden in the outbuilding and keep an eye out for our return. We shifted a pile of boxes to hide her where she crouched beside a hole in the wall, facing the *château*.

I told my sister that if something went wrong, none of us would be able to ripple her and Bridget to safety. They'd be on their own.

"Well, then, you'd better make sure nothing goes wrong," she'd snapped at me.

I swallowed and hugged my prickly sister. "I love you, too, man. You know that."

The fight went out of Mick as I said this to her. Her chin got all quivery.

"You've always been my life," whispered my sister, hugging me back. She squeezed extra tight and then pushed me away. "Go on, now."

As Sir Walter and I glided invisibly to the château where Gwyn was being held, he explained that Helmann received the Château as the gift of Charles the Sixth and had lived there with Elisabeth. *When she left him, he no longer made his home at the Château.*

But he kept it, huh? I asked. *That's quite the accomplishment, keeping hold of a piece of valuable property through all the wars and stuff.*

It is more than I have done, said Sir Walter softly. *But then, my cousin's devotion to Elisabeth has always been strong.*

Feu Froid, I wrote. *That's "Cold Fire," right?*

It was a name chosen by others, descriptive of its abandoned state, explained Sir Walter. *He adopted the name some four hundred years ago.*

Every now and again, he'd drop something like that, all casual, and it would freak me that Sir Walter was so old. I wondered if Sam wanted to live that long? All's I knew for sure was I didn't if she didn't.

Are you ready?

I thought of Angel Corps guy's strange phrase: "I stand prepared."

Yeah, dude, I wrote. *Let's go.*

Chapter Thirty-Six

ON THE SAME CONTINENT

• SAM •

If my best friend hadn't been in a life-threatening situation, the video would have been almost funny. It was severely under-produced. Hans had tried cutting away at times but hadn't quite gotten things right. He'd given Gwyn a script, but she must have repeatedly refused to read out parts of it. Once, there was an entire "I'm *NOT* saying—" before the clip cut off.

In the end, however, the message was anything but funny: *If you want to see Gwyn again in one piece, alive, meet me in San Francisco in two days.* We had less than two days, seeing as the message had been sent nearly a day ago.

It looked like I was headed back to San Francisco to rescue my friend.

"Absolutely not, *Mademoiselle*," said Christian when I told him of my plan to return to the Geneses lab. "You have established that your presence can be detected there. It would be the errand of a fool."

"I'm rescuing Gwyn," I said. "I'm going to San Francisco, and you can stay behind if you don't want to help me."

Christian frowned but didn't try to argue. Instead, he asked me to play the video once more. He watched the tiny screen with intense concentration.

"There!" he said. "Cause that section to repeat itself!"

I fiddled with my cell and found the section he wanted to see. It was the moment right after Gwyn's "I'm NOT saying—" When the recording resumed, the background showed more; you could see the edge of an elaborate fireplace behind Gwyn.

"I know this place," said Christian. Looking solemnly at me, he spoke again. "*Mademoiselle*, returning to California will not help you to rescue your friend. She is being held at the Château Feu Froid."

"Cold Fire Castle?"

"Upon my fifteenth birthday, my father presented me to my uncle L'Inferne at his *château*. It lies within an easy distance of our present location."

"Where?" I asked.

"Outside the great city of Tours," he said. "I will take you there."

"You will?" I asked in shock. "You said this was the errand of a fool just a second ago."

Christian shrugged. "To travel to the facility in San Francisco, where your very presence can be measured? That would be foolish. But no such means of detection lie within the ancient castle."

"What makes you so sure they haven't put temperature detection in *all* their buildings?"

"Forgive me, *Mademoiselle*. I thought you must have overheard what I heard the day your egg was stolen. The equipment to detect invisible intruders was designed solely for that building. It is unique in the world. Helmann meant to protect your *jumelle*—your clone. Perhaps he even expected treachery from within his own ranks. It could have been used against them."

"Okay, so what are we waiting for?"

"The phone call to Sir Walter?" said Christian.

I'd completely forgotten about him. I punched in the number. It went straight to voice mail. "No good," I said, feeling anew the ache of my distance from Will, as if we still drifted on separating continents.

"Let us leave a message," said Christian.

I passed him the phone, afraid my voice would crack if I tried to speak.

"Meet your son and granddaughter where you took him upon his fifteenth birthday," said Christian. He hit end. "You see? I learned from your clever message to your father."

Christian and I rippled and passed like ghosts out of the airport and onto the road to the *château*.

Chapter Thirty-Seven

OBSESSION WITH NEEDLES

• SAM •

We approached the castle at dawn, passing like shadows through dusk. Neglect clung to the grounds; though we were within twenty miles of Chenonceau, it felt like another country. I expected wolves at every turn and shivered even without solid form.

A single light burned on the second floor, flickering and golden. Firelight.

She is within the great hall, spoke Christian.

He'd recognized Château Feu Froid on video because of the stone fireplace behind Gwyn. Carved with griffins, gargoyles, and writhing beasts, it was horrifying and unique. We made our way up a broad staircase. The marble must have been beautiful once, but now it lay in filthy disrepair. I saw the paw prints of small animals in the dirt on one side.

Christian and I passed through a set of massive oak doors, darkened with age and abandon. I scented rot along with the rich odor of oak. On the far side of the doors, however, things looked well-maintained. Thick carpets covered much of the stone floor. An ancient table ran the length of the room, pointing the way to the fireplace, where an inferno blazed. To either side of the hearth, large couches had been placed. And upon one of them, Gwyn curled, asleep.

Dropping Christian's hand, I ghosted forward.

Mademoiselle, I beg of you, remain insubstantial still.

Which was the last thing that felt right at that moment.

Think, called Christian, *Who has prepared the fire? And by whom is it maintained? She has not, surely, been left here alone.*

I froze. Gwyn didn't know the first thing about making a huge bonfire like this one. She lived in an apartment over a bakery. Fireplace-free.

I beg of you, said Christian, *allow me to attempt her rescue.*

I could do this much for him. *Yeah, okay,* I said.

Christian rippled solid.

He leaned over Gwyn's sleeping form, placing arms around her, but when he attempted to bring her into invisibility, something went wrong. Christian disappeared, but Gwyn remained behind.

Coming solid beside Gwyn once again, he tried to get a better grasp around her. I could feel how distracted he was by his previous failure. It confused him, made him less attentive than he should have been to his surroundings.

Just then, in the wavering light of the fire, I saw someone else materialize behind Christian and jab his arm with a needle.

Christian's internal shock and offense echoed my own as he felt the shot pierce his arm. He collapsed onto the floor before the couch.

I should have warned him! I, of all people, knew about the Geneses *obsession* with needles.

"I should not bother trying to escape in the manner in which you appeared," said a voice similar to Hans'. "Do you notice the heaviness in your arms?"

"What have you done to me?" asked Christian.

"Ah, French, are you? Hmmmm. I expected an American. A girl in fact. Did Samantha send you in her stead?"

"I was paid by an American of another name," replied Christian. "It appears I was not sufficiently informed as to the difficulty of my task."

"Hmmmm. Yes, we never are, are we?" mused the man. "I'm pleased to see you retain the use of speech. I shall have to compliment my brother on his improved pharmaceutical."

Could this be Franz? I wondered.

"Why can't I disappear?" asked Christian.

"I'd rather not discuss that. Proprietary, you see. However, I'm very proud of the little invention that prevented you from stealing my brother's hostage. It's a weighted blanket which has been fashioned into a garment. She weighs in excess of two-hundred kilos at the moment."

Sam, do you hear? Attempt not to take Gwyn with you, warned Christian.

Got it, I replied.

"Will she not suffocate?" asked Christian. "There is no payment for me if she dies."

Clever, I said to Christian, impressed at how he lied and kept his cool under the circumstances.

Franz chuckled. "The weights are behind and not upon her. But, my friend, I do not think you will be collecting payment in any case." He leaned forward. "Tell me truly, though, is Samantha not here with us?"

"I was sent by Bridget Li. So, unless she lied to me as to her true name, I am unacquainted with any Samancha's," replied Christian.

"Or Samantha's?" Franz rubbed his hands together. "What I wouldn't give for one of my father's devices, to search the air temperature."

"What will you pay me to carry a message back to this girl's mother?" asked Christian.

Franz laughed. "I like you." He laughed again. "Truly, I do." His face shifted from amusement to something more business-like. "However, as I can by no means trust you, I shall not at present offer you employment."

Franz dug in various coat pockets. "Ah, here it is," he said, retrieving a revolver. "Now then, how about you start telling me the truth about your association with Samantha." He paused to aim the revolver at Gwyn. "Or I shoot her."

I screamed my distress in silence.

Christian's face remained impassive. "Neither of us will be paid, I think, if you kill her." He shrugged. "Or perhaps I am mistaken."

Franz shifted the revolver to point it at Christian. "You, my young friend, are a very shrewd man." He lowered the weapon. "Indeed, I am not authorized to kill her. And I might regret killing you so early in our acquaintance. However, I must restrain you."

Saying this, Franz removed a roll of duct tape from his coat and taped Christian's wrists and then ankles together, securing him to a leg of the couch.

"We shall see what Hans says about you," said Franz, smiling. "I should sleep, if I were you. Keep your strength up." His grin turned hideously feral and I saw the clear resemblance to his siblings.

As Franz turned to pile more wood upon the blaze, I heard Christian speak within my mind.

You must leave, Mademoiselle. I felt his fear that I might refuse.

How can I? I asked.

We were most foolish not to contact my father first. With additional assistance, perhaps we could have disabled this person.

My heart sank as I saw the truth of what Christian said.

Mademoiselle, you must call my father and continue calling until you reach him. Do you understand?

Yes, I replied. *But I'm only going far enough so that I can't be overheard talking on my cell.*

Christian paused and I could tell he wanted to tell me to run far, far away. But he must've known I wouldn't leave him *and* Gwyn in this state.

I observed a small garage, perhaps a quarter mile from the château if you travel back along the drive, said Christian. *Will you do me the great kindness of placing yourself thus far distant until our friends can assist you?*

Sure, I said. I didn't remember any garages, but if he said it was there, I'd find it.

I slithered out of the room and down the marble staircase, noticing the rotted out balustrades as I descended. Along the drive I raced, finding the building just as Christian had said. I glanced around quickly, making certain I was alone. Then, after rippling solid, I reached for my cell phone and slowly, carefully, keyed in Sir Walter's phone number.

A small car was parked in the garage and I huddled beside it. It looked empty. I heard the dialing-pips on my cell.

From inside the car, another phone rang. My call went to Sir Walter's voicemail after a few rings. Frustrated, I hit redial. I was going to get his attention no matter how many calls it took.

The phone in the car rang again.

And it all clicked into place.

I rippled to pass into the car. Coming solid, I hit redial again. From inside a man's all-weather coat, the phone in the car rang again. I fumbled and retrieved it from a pile of coats on the back seat. My number scrolled across the "incoming call" screen.

Sir Walter! I cried out with my thoughts.

To my great surprise, he replied. *Samantha?*

He heard me!

A small noise of joy escaped. I wasn't alone in this after all!

And then, in the back of the car, something shifted. Something that snored. It became something that woke up and stared at me. Then the glazed eyes closed again.

"Bridget?" I whispered in shocked amazement.

Chapter Thirty-Eight

SAM IN MY ARMS AGAIN

• WILL •

There we were, all ready to stealth our way invisibly inside Château Feu Froid when Sir Walter made this gasping noise.

What's up? I wrote on my imagined note pad.

Mademoiselle Sam has preceded us, evidently, replied Sir Walter.

Sam's HERE? I wrote.

Apparently, said Sir Walter.

This was such amazing news, I thought my old friend was maybe imagining it. But some small part of me that had been squashed down inside my sneakers for the past month started jumping up and down, ready to believe.

Your friend tells me that she is with our vehicle at present, said Sir Walter, *And that Chrétien has been captured and lies unable to ripple in a room with Gwyn and*—another of Sir Walter's little intakes of breath—*with Franz.*

Crap, I wrote.

Indeed, replied Sir Walter. *I have informed her as to our whereabouts, and she should be joining us momentarily.*

My invisible heart thumped in my invisible chest. So to speak. Sam, here with me, was too good to be true. Of course, I wouldn't exactly be able to see her and hold her.

Ah, said Sir Walter, *And she has evidently awakened Mademoiselle Mackenzie from an unintended nap. Bridget sleeps more soundly.* The French gentleman allowed himself a brief laugh.

Is Sam here for Gwyn? I wrote. *She must be, right?*

Ask her yourself, said Sir Walter.

And just like that, I felt a subtle shift in the air beside me. *Sam?* I wrote. Remembering how she'd been able to understand sign language, I spelled out her name. *Sam?*

Right here, came her words, flashed upon a tiny screen which superimposed itself over my vision.

This isn't how I imagined our next time together, I signed, *But I'll take it! I've missed you so bad, Sam.*

Me too, she typed.

The three of us made a rescue plan which would require rippling solid, and man, I was looking forward to feeling Sam in my arms again. I wondered if I could get a quick hug before we rescued Chrétien and Gwyn.

But when we got to the top of the stairs, to the room where our friends were being held, we got an unwelcome surprise.

Chapter Thirty-Nine

BLOOD OF THE DE ROCHEFORTS

• SAM •

Hans? I cried out in shock. Why hadn't I noticed his thoughts?

He leaned over the long table dominating the hall. Eyes closed, fists boring into the table, he was relaxing. His emotions weren't intense, which explained why I hadn't noticed them.

Sir Walter spoke within my mind, and Will's: *Do not blame yourself, Samantha—I felt him not, either. But this changes things. I do not believe it would be wise for Samantha to appear in Hans' sight.*

He's right, Will signed. *Sir Walter and I can take on Hans and Franz alone.*

Between them, Will and Sir Walter refused to let me help, now that Hans was here. We separated so that they could attack Hans and his brother. I could still hear Sir Walter's thoughts clearly, but Will's presence receded, becoming only a sensation that he was near.

I heard as Sir Walter called out a countdown. *Ten —Nine—Eight—*I watched anxiously the space behind the two solid men. *Seven—Six—Five—*I felt a rush of anger pass through Hans as he examined Christian, bound and seated on the floor before the couch. *Four —Three—Two—*Hans pounded the table—*One!*

Will came solid behind Hans just as Hans pushed off from where he'd rested fists against the table. The back of Hans' head caught Will's nose and Will grunted in pain as his tight-balled fist passed through air, missing Hans. The two struggled, rippling in and out of solidity. Neither could land a blow on the other.

Meanwhile, Sir Walter and Franz engaged in the same strange dance, except that Franz was slower to ripple away. Sir Walter got Franz in an arm-lock that looked both painful and secure and nearly smashed a fist into Franz' face, but Franz vanished at the last second. The forward motion of the intended blow caused Sir Walter to lose his balance, but he saved himself from harm by rippling.

I couldn't stand doing nothing, and I'd just decided Will could probably use my help more than Sir Walter when I heard a sound like a branch snapping in half. It took a moment for me to place the sound. It took a moment for Will to cry out in agony. It took a moment for me to realize I couldn't do anything now that Will's leg lay broken, twisted at a horrible angle upon the cold stone floor. I was too small to carry him to safety.

Hans delivered one final kick to Will, who moaned, and then knelt to pick him up. Will's eyes rolled backwards for one second, two seconds, and then he closed them tight, screaming in pain. Hans called loudly to Sir Walter to surrender.

Sir Walter was clearly trying to escape Franz in order to get closer to Will. But I already knew Sir Walter couldn't ripple with Will either, not without my help.

Do not attempt it, Sir Walter called out to me, recognizing what I was thinking.

"Uncle," called Hans, "How long it has been. Might this child perhaps be one of your offspring?" Hans examined Will's limp form, looking for resemblances as he placed him roughly upon the large table.

Will groaned loudly; he looked pale and his breathing sounded all wrong—too shallow, too frequent.

Hans continued. "How unfortunate for you to find the boy in my possession and without the ability to vanish. But I really must insist that you remain solid and place yourself at my mercy unless you wish to see this young man's immediate demise." Hans removed a revolver from his jacket.

Sir Walter, breathing hard, came solid opposite the table from Hans. Franz rippled solid behind him and grabbed him. Probably out of reflex, Sir Walter vanished once more.

I felt Hans' anger washing past me.

"Come now," said Hans, as he aimed the pistol at Will. "You are trying my patience, Uncle."

Please Sir Walter! Come back! I cried out in fear.

Hans looked about him, as did Franz coming solid, both looking for any sign of Sir Walter.

Then Hans seemed to notice Christian and, without any warning, Hans aimed the gun at Christian and fired a single shot at him.

In the silence that followed, Hans spoke. "Upon second thought, that one has more of your look about him. What do you say, Uncle? Shall I continue shooting the other two in the room, or will you reveal yourself?"

It felt to me as though the floor of the hall had become a swelling ocean. I stumbled to Christian's side. Was he dead? I sensed myself passing through Sir Walter's invisible form, and I felt his anguish.

Please, I cried out to Sir Walter, *Come back before Hans shoots anyone else!* I brought myself to a stop beside Christian. Gazing at the blood pooling on the floor, I heard Hans' quiet laughter.

"Good, good, uncle," said Hans. "I am glad you saw reason."

Franz must have solidified again, because Hans ordered him to take charge of the old gentleman.

"Just the red syringe," murmured Hans to his brother. "I wish to question him."

I heard Sir Walter's grunt of indignation as Franz injected him like he had Christian, but I was too alarmed watching the blood leaving Christian's side. Should I solidify?

No, Mademoiselle Samanthe! I heard Sir Walter's order as clearly as if he had shouted it.

Looking closely, I discovered that Christian's *arm* bled, not his side. I knew that had to be better. No major organs, at least.

"The boy you have so invalorously fired upon is my son," said Sir Walter, wincing as Franz taped his torso to his chair. "Please, assist him. His veins spill the blood of the family de Rochefort as we speak. I do not think your father will be pleased to hear of this."

I glanced up at Sir Walter. The "red" syringe must have contained the muscle-relaxant blended with Neuroplex. He neither moved nor rippled, and was now slumping against the oaken armchair while Franz secured him with duct tape.

"My father!" Hans made a strange noise that combined laughter and a lupine howl. He was a madman. "You think I care for my father's obsession with the blood of the de Rocheforts?" Hans walked until he stood eye to eye with Sir Walter. "I *killed* the de Rochefort clone my father planned to use to supplant me."

Sir Walter's eyes closed in anguish. He knew there would be no mercy for Christian, then.

Hans dropped his voice to a whisper. "And I *will* kill the girl as well. You are going to help me locate her, or there will be *more* de Rochefort blood spilled today."

Had I been solid, all the hairs upon my neck would have stood to attention. So confident, so cruel was Hans.

And then something completely unforeseen happened.

Chapter Forty

YOUR FATHER SEES EVERYTHING

• WILL •

I totally didn't see it coming, the next thing that went down. I even thought maybe I was hallucinating from the pain of my broken leg. Because what I saw was this: out of nowhere, Helmann rippled solid, placed a gun at Hans' temple, and whispered, "Goodbye, son." Brains and stuff went flying. But the really awful part was how Hans fell backwards onto the ginormous fire.

I fought to stay conscious to watch our arch-enemy's next move.

Helmann tilted his head and gazed at the now-flaming body of his dead son. "How fitting. You always liked to burn things."

The stench was pretty awful, but at least it helped me stay alert.

Helmann sighed once and then spoke to Sir Walter. "Greetings, cousin. How long it has been." His grin was wolfish: all teeth, no friendliness.

I'd lost track of Franz during all of this, but I saw the air shudder and figured Franz must have decided to ripple to safety while he had the chance.

"Cousin, if you will forgive me? I have another child to attend to. Franz?" Helmann called. "Perhaps there is a perfectly good reason why you are not at present assisting the Angel Corps? Come, come, my dear boy. Your father is in a very forgiving mood at present, having just lost a most treasured son."

Franz solidified near me, kneeling at Helmann's feet. "Forgive me, Father. I became frightened when I saw you punish my brother. The Angels continue their work. I came here alarmed at a report of what Hans intended—"

Helmann interrupted him. "Take care of that," he said, gesturing with his gun to Hans' body in the fireplace.

I saw Franz ripple and, a moment later, the bad burning smell disappeared. Then Franz reappeared beside me and Helmann, speaking quickly.

"Father, you must hear me out. I tried to stop Hans—"

"Yes, yes, of course you did, my son," said Helmann. He tilted his head to one side like Franz was an odd specimen at a zoo. Then he shot Franz in the leg. "I expect that hurts badly enough to keep you from vanishing, does it not?"

Speaking from my own experience at the moment, I was pretty sure Helmann had that right.

"Forgive me, Father," said Franz, his voice shaking with pain. "I am your true son."

"He lies," said Christian, his voice sounding all thin and strained.

My eyes drooped closed again as I heard Helmann respond. "This much, I knew already. Franz, I've been watching you. Do you not remember? Your father sees everything."

The loud report of a gun, close by me, brought me back to awareness. As I opened my eyes, I saw Franz fall to the floor, a revolver in his grasp. He'd shot himself rather than wait for Helmann to do it.

I slipped under, losing consciousness as I heard one last thing: Helmann, murmuring beside me.

"What a pity," he said.

297

Chapter Forty-One

FIRE IN MY BONES

• SAM •

While Helmann dealt with Franz, I watched Christian's face carefully. After he'd managed to speak those few words to Helmann, Christian's color had changed. All I could think of was how alive Christian had been this morning as we raced to the *château* and how his skin looked like Deuxième's now, just before he'd died, and how badly it would hurt Sir Walter to lose his only son. I rippled solid. I heard Sir Walter groan softly, seeing me. But I couldn't allow Christian to bleed to death.

Pulling the narrow scarf I wore from my neck, I used it to form a lumpy bandage and pressed it upon Christian's wound. Could I stop the bleeding in time?

"But, my dear Samantha," whispered Helmann, "How unexpectedly wonderful to see you."

Ignoring him, I tried to remember everything I could from First Aid class that Sylvia made me take years ago.

"Allow me to assist you," said Helmann. His voice was soft as velvet.

"Stay away," I warned. Obviously I had no way to enforce my order; I wasn't the one with the gun.

"I am a licensed physician, my dear," continued Helmann. "Or I was, at one time. How the centuries rush past. Will you not allow me to save the life of my nephew?"

"Allow him to help," said Sir Walter.

I caught another *unspoken* message loud and clear: *Remove yourself from Helmann's reach!* I stood, backing away.

Ree-pill now! called Sir Walter.

I shook my head slowly. *Hans thought shooting people was a good way to make ripplers reappear,* I said to Sir Walter. *Helmann would think of it, too.* I had to work this out some other way.

Helmann stood, having created a tourniquet from my scarf. Christian's color actually looked better.

"Well, well, well," said Helmann. "What an excellent thing it is to gather one's family together." He brought the corners of his mouth up in a self-satisfied smile.

"I know what you want, and I'm not discussing it with you until you let my friends go," I said. I really wasn't sure how that was going to happen, seeing as how Christian had been shot, Gwyn was so full of drugs she'd slept through gunfire, and neither Will nor Sir Walter could ripple.

At that moment, bringing a bound and gagged Mickie with him, another person rippled into the room. Someone I'd never seen before, with graying blond hair and eyes like dark spots on his pale face.

"Pfeffer!" called Sir Walter.

I didn't understand.

Pfeffer lives, but he has betrayed us, said Sir Walter to me.

Mickie, being held forcibly by Pfeffer, looked angry enough to bite her way through the gag over her mouth.

"Ah, my dear son," said Helmann. "Hmmm, and the last of your generation as well." He then described to Pfeffer the demise of Hans and his brother. "They thought their father blind to their . . . indiscretions."

If Pfeffer felt shock, he betrayed none of it. He dipped his head slightly to Helmann, and it reminded me of one of Sir Walter's little bows.

"And it appears you have retrieved the other, ah, guest?" asked Helmann. "Place her with the sleeping one." He gestured to the couch where Gwyn lay.

Pfeffer led Mickie, snarling, to take a seat. She looked alarmed upon noticing me, solid, on the other side of the room.

"Thank you, my dear son," said Helmann. "I have two additional tasks for you. First, I must insist that you say a *final* farewell to your uncle Waldhart."

Pfeffer nodded and crossed to Sir Walter's side, injecting him with a syringe. The old gentleman slumped softly forward to rest, face down, upon the table.

I gasped, running to his side. Taking one hand, I checked for a pulse. I felt it: faint, but definitely still there.

"This is Miss Samantha Ruiz," said Helmann, indicating me to Pfeffer. "For your second task, please be so good as to *greet* her."

I didn't see the needle coming until it was too late. And then, stranger still, I didn't feel it. I must have been too full of adrenaline to feel anything.

Throwing the used needle beneath the table, Pfeffer took Sir Walter's hand from me, checking for a pulse.

"My uncle is gone," he said to Helmann.

My heart began racing double-time. "No," I moaned. I tore Sir Walter's hand from Pfeffer's. Cradling the ancient hand in both of mine, I brought it to rest against my cheek. Moisture blurred my vision. I blinked hard. I wouldn't let myself cry in front of Helmann.

Helmann cleared his throat, addressing Pfeffer. "We were just discussing Miss Ruiz's cooperation with my little plan."

"I never said I was cooperating. I said let my friends go and we'll talk."

"Let me see if I can make this clearer." Helmann reached into a pocket and pulled out the revolver again. "You really don't have a choice in the matter."

His smile as he approached me was wild, dangerous. Placing the weapon at my temple, he spoke softly. "I can obtain what I desire from you whether you live or die, my dear."

I felt his breath upon my face.

"But one way or another, I will have your obedience," he whispered.

"I think you've got me confused with someone else," I replied.

I looked into his eyes, defying him with every cell of my being.

"Kill me," I said. "There are worse things than dying."

Helmann's expression changed. The tight angry lines around his mouth relaxed, the furrow between his eyes smoothed. He smiled.

"There are indeed, my dear, worse things than death," said Helmann. "I've changed my mind." He lowered his weapon. "Let us suppose instead that your refusal spells death for your friends. Of course, I will need for you to observe their executions. You've already seen those you loved killed before your eyes, I believe? In fact—" Here he broke off, eyebrows raised. "In fact, you saw them die *in your place*, didn't you? So this should feel familiar."

To my horror, Helmann paused, pointing his revolver slowly around the room, indicating with it everyone I loved: Mickie, her eyes fierce, defiant; Gwyn, snoozing in her weighted suit, curled up like a cat; Christian, openly weeping; Sir Walter, face-down upon the cold oak table; and Will.

Will!

I wouldn't be able to say goodbye, to say *I love you.*

Despair reached with icy fingers into my lungs. No matter what I did, Helmann won. He would create his New World Order. Billions would perish. In a flash, I realized there were worse things than losing the people I loved most.

What if no one had stood up to Hitler?

What if?

The thought was like fire in my bones.

I had my answer.

"What is it to be, my dear?" asked Helmann. "Will you cooperate?"

I hated my answer.

"No," I said.

303

I felt Helmann's rage wash over me. But he contained it. Calmly passing his gun to Pfeffer, he clasped hands behind his back. His eyes traveled from Will to Sir Walter, then from Gwyn to Mickie, before finally coming to rest upon Christian.

In the cool, measured tones of a man who held all the cards and had all the time in the world, he crossed to Christian's side. To Pfeffer, Helmann said, "Let us begin with this one. Execute them all."

Chapter Forty-Two

DOUBLE AGENT

• SAM •

As Helmann pronounced the death sentence, I heard an urgent command within my mind. *Ripple!* said a voice I couldn't place.

Now! said the stranger's voice.

Was it Pfeffer's voice?

I thought of the needle, the intended injection. The odd lack of pain.

I realized what it might mean and I tried to ripple.

As I disappeared, I saw Pfeffer's gun, aimed at Christian, shift slightly. I raced towards Christian, and in that split-second, I heard Pfeffer's shot.

Coming solid, I collided into Christian.

What have I done? I heard Pfeffer's stricken cry echo within my mind. Aloud, I heard the clatter of his gun as it hit the stone floor and spun.

I twisted and I realized with shock that Pfeffer wasn't talking about what he'd done to Christian. Helmann lay face-down upon the ground, blood seeping from his torso.

"What have I done," Pfeffer moaned aloud.

Will's voice, pinched with pain, drifted to me from the table. "Is Helmann dead?"

"I think so," I said, retrieving the revolver from where it lay at Pfeffer's feet.

"Shoot Pfeffer," murmured Will. Then he appeared to slip into unconsciousness.

Training my weapon on Pfeffer, I spoke.

"Why did you fire upon Helmann?" I demanded.

Pfeffer collapsed his head into his hands. "I've doomed us all," he whispered. From inside his mind I heard a tangle of desperate thoughts. *Two years wasted . . . the Angels released . . . my doing . . . my fault.* His thoughts came so fast I couldn't unravel them.

"*Mademoiselle,*" whispered Christian. "Retrieve the weapon that lies beside Franz."

Keeping my revolver trained on Pfeffer, I quickly grabbed the other gun.

Pfeffer's head raised and his eyes rested upon Will. I felt a wash of compassion from Pfeffer's mind as he stared at Will's pale, still body.

Pfeffer spoke to me. "He needs pain relief. I have morphine." He fumbled inside his jacket. "And a mild stimulant, perhaps."

Pfeffer's concern for Will was genuine, the spoken words matching the unspoken thoughts.

"May I have your permission?" asked Pfeffer, assembling a syringe and needle.

"Go ahead," I murmured.

"Sam?" called Christian, alarmed.

"It's okay," I said. "He's not our enemy."

I caught more from Pfeffer's anguished mind. Regrets, fears, anger and self-loathing. *All the wasted years . . . my failure to sabotage Helmann.* These things he repeated again and again in different forms.

Pfeffer gave Will the medication, and I watched as his eyes fluttered open. He'd never looked so good to me, but I didn't have long to enjoy it.

During the moment it took me to tell Will that everything would be okay now, Mickie had leapt up from the couch and, running at Pfeffer, she *head-butted* him.

Chapter Forty-Three

THE SAMINATOR

• WILL •

My sister pissed off is something you don't want to be in the same room with. After she'd knocked Pfeffer to the ground using her *noggin*, she lost her balance and fell over, but that didn't stop her trying to kick his butt across the floor like he was a soccer ball.

"Mick," I groaned. "How's Sam supposed to shoot him with you going all bend-it-like-Beckham?"

She stopped kicking and commenced hurling curses through her gag. She was admirably successful getting the words out.

"Everyone, *quiet!*" ordered Sam. She turned to Pfeffer. "I want to know what is going on. Start with why you didn't shoot me full of Neuroplex. Or whatever Helmann meant for you to give me."

He shook his head. "I was trying to save your life. You're the last living descendant of Elisabeth de Rochefort, beloved by my friend Waldhart de Rochefort."

Sam looked puzzled. "How can you work for Helmann and still call yourself Sir Walter's friend?"

Pfeffer shook his head slowly and sighed. "I never served Helmann. I pretended so that I might prevent the annihilation of billions." In a voice full of anguish, he continued. "But I've failed. His secret died with him, and we are all powerless to stop him."

Sam stared at him like she was making up her mind. Then, slowly, she nodded. "I can hear the truth," she said. "I can hear your thoughts."

Mickie started in again, although it didn't sound so much like curse words anymore. More like questions. I tried to sit up, but the pain in my leg—dull, distant—wouldn't let me.

"Look," Sam said to Pfeffer, "I am *close* to trusting you right now, but you just killed Sir Walter—" Her voice choked and tears hung on the lids of her eyes. I wanted so bad to comfort her.

Pfeffer tried to interrupt, but Sam held up a hand. "No more talking from you yet. Here's what's going to happen. You are going to untie Mickie's hands, *slowly*, while I stand here with two guns aimed at your head."

He nodded and complied. As soon as my sister's hands were free, she spun around and clocked her exadvisor on the jaw. He wiped blood from his lip, but made no attempt to defend himself.

My sister reached for the gag and tore it off. "*That* was for lying to us," she said. "And this is for tying me up and rippling with me." She pulled back to nail him a second time.

"Stop!" Sam shouted.

And my sister actually listened. Maybe because Sam had a gun in each hand. It was like Sam was some avenging angel whose wings were about to unfurl. Man, I loved her.

"I did not end Waldhart's life," said Pfeffer, taking advantage of the silence. "He's only asleep, contrary to Helmann's orders."

Sam turned to him. The hope in her eyes about broke my heart in half. "Check Sir Walter's pulse," she said to my sister.

Mick nodded and walked to the old man's body. "His heart's beating," she reported.

Sam closed her eyes and took a slow breath. "Mickie, please untie him. And then Christian."

"Someone should tell Bridget everything's okay," I said. My tongue felt heavy in my mouth. "And someone should get Gwyn out of that ridiculous suit."

My sister volunteered.

Sam turned back to Pfeffer. "What was in the shot you gave Sir Walter?"

"A sedative." Pfeffer reached inside a pocket, then changed his mind, withdrawing his hands and placing them in the air, like someone surrendering. "Inside my jacket, you'll find a set of syringes. I can tell you which one will awaken Sir Walter."

"Don't trust him!" said Mickie, as she finished untying Christian.

"It's okay," said Sam. "I can hear every thought he's thinking. We can trust him."

Christian stood about as successfully as you'd expect from someone who'd been duct-taped to a couch and shot in the arm. I tried not to begrudge him the smile Sam shot his way as he approached us.

"You can really hear Pfeffer thinking?" I asked Sam in a low voice.

"She is a true de Rochefort," said Pfeffer, smiling sadly. He removed his jacket and spilled a half dozen syringes upon the table between me and Sir Walter.

"Dude," I said, shaking my head. "That's like, a whole pharmacy in there. What is it with Geneses and needles?"

"Which one will awaken Sir Walter?" Sam asked, clear and focused as I was fuzzy and slow.

"The blue-banded ones are deadly," he said. "The yellow-banded one will bring Sir Walter back to a fully alert state. The clear is the sedative."

"Franz used a red-banded one on Christian earlier," said Sam.

311

"That's Neuroplex," said Pfeffer.

"Which prevents rippling," said Sam.

Pfeffer's brows pinched together. "How did you know?"

"Do you see Christian rippling? We're not idiots," I mumbled, feeling very tired and ever so slightly happy.

Sam smiled as she seated herself on the table beside me. "Go ahead," she said to Pfeffer. "Wake Sir Walter."

"He needs to be told that you are a de Rocheforte," said Pfeffer, looking sadly from my girlfriend to Sir Walter.

"He already figured it out," said Sam. Then she made this small gasping sound. "*That* was why you sent Mickie and Will to Las Abs? To find me?"

"I hoped they might," said Pfeffer. "I told them to try."

"You might have mentioned *what* we were supposed to try," I muttered, remembering how my sister and I had argued over the meaning of his cryptic words two years earlier.

Pfeffer turned back to me, but Sam urged him on. "Wake up Sir Walter," she said again. "Can you reverse the effect of the Neuroplex as well?"

Pfeffer nodded as he chose a needle.

"You sure, Sam?" I whispered, turning my head toward her. She smelled so good it hurt to breathe for a minute.

She nodded, setting the guns down so she could place her small hand in mine. Squeezing my hand tightly, she called to Christian. "You okay?"

"I am well, *Mademoiselle*," he said. "Truly. My uncle bound my wound most admirably."

Christian smiled at Sam, and I thought maybe I liked him better all ashen-faced.

Sam reached behind me to help me sit upright. My leg didn't seem to hurt as bad as I knew it should.

"My head feels weird," I said.

"Pain meds," Sam murmured in my ear, helping me stay propped up.

We heard a stuttering intake of breath from Sir Walter as his eyes fluttered open. He looked freaked when he saw Pfeff hovering over him like a big old bird of prey.

Pfeffer backed away quickly, nearly stumbling over Helmann's dead body.

"It's okay," said Sam to Sir Walter. "Pfeffer's a friend. He's kept very busy behind enemy lines."

"Pfeffer killed Helmann," I added. That got the old dude alert real fast.

I pointed to where Helmann's body sprawled upon the stone floor. And then I saw something impossible. Helmann wasn't dead. From who-knows-where,

Helmann had retrieved another gun which he held unsteadily in his left hand. Training it on Pfeffer, he pulled the trigger.

Chapter Forty-Four

FALLEN

• SAM •

Someone screamed and I realized it was my own voice. I clapped a hand over my mouth, stunned at what had just happened. Will and I reached for the guns upon the table, but before we had a chance to fire them, Christian had launched himself upon Helmann. Pulling the dagger from his fork and knife case, he slit Helmann's throat.

The action overlapped with Pfeffer's choked cry: "No! Don't kill Helmann yet!"

But it was too late. Blood poured from Helmann's neck. He wouldn't recover this time.

I turned aside, my stomach at last beginning to revolt against the day's dreadful events.

And now Pfeffer's fallen form lay still, in apparent silence, a small red spot upon his side blossoming rapidly. I felt Pfeffer's fear, but it wasn't fear for his own life. Desperately, Pfeffer spoke to his oldest and dearest friend.

"The Angel Corps have begun a work of great destruction," he told Sir Walter, "There are pass-phrases, but only Helmann knew them . . . you must discover the phrases! Stop them!"

Sir Walter interrupted him. He cradled Pfeffer's head within strong arms. "We have the passwords, my friend."

"Impossible," said Pfeffer to Sir Walter. As he whispered the words, I saw the color draining from his face.

"Ripple!" I shouted the command to Pfeffer.

He closed his eyes, perhaps trying.

But it was too late. He had no strength now to save himself.

"No!" I cried, running to Pfeffer's side. I looked across to Sir Walter. "We have to take him together."

Sir Walter nodded. We encircled the dying man and vanished with him.

Save him! I called to Sir Walter.

I shall do my best, replied the old gentleman.

I rippled solid again.

There was nothing to do now but wait.

Chapter Forty-Five

THE WILL TO LIVE

• WILL •

We found things to do while Sir Walter remained invisible with Pfeffer. Sam covered the bodies of Helmann and Franz using carpets from the floor of the great hall. Then, with help from Sam, Mickie got me into a French ER where I got a gnarly cast up one entire leg.

Only after I was released would she take care of Gwyn and Bridget. Gwyn's mom did *not* like spending time in the old castle with all those dead bodies, especially the one that had been rippled away. Gwyn had awoken from her drugged slumber by the time we returned from the hospital.

"*Please* don't talk about the dead guys in Ma's hearing," said Gwyn. "She thinks it's not proper or something." Gwyn leaned her head on Bridget's shoulder. As she gave her mom a big squeeze, she stage-whispered, "You're *so* Chinese, Ma."

But I noticed tenderness in each of their expressions, and I figured things would be a lot better between them from now on.

I crashed for awhile, what with the pain meds and Sam at my side. Much later, after the sun had set, I awakened as Sir Walter came solid, stretching and looking tired. Just behind him, Chrétien, arm swathed in clean bandages, rippled solid. He gave his injured arm a small shrug, which made Sam laugh.

"You shrug just like your dad," she said to Chrétien.

He smiled and gave her a little half-bow.

"Does it hurt bad?" she asked.

"It is nothing," he replied.

Which kind of ticked me off, because my leg was killing me, but no way was I going to complain if Chrétien didn't. Sam didn't seem to know which of us to feel more sorry for, and that ticked me off, too.

Sir Walter had arranged for Gwyn and Bridget to take a private jet back home .

"Two journeys by private jet?" murmured Bridget to her daughter. "It's like I always tell you: investing for the long term really does pay off."

My sister drove them to the airport because Sir Walter wouldn't leave Pfeffer. Nor would he answer any questions about Pfeffer, giving me his familiar, "Later, later, dear boy," speech.

Sir Walter waited until my sister got back from her airport run. Then, before the flickering red glow of dying embers, Sir Walter told us about Pfeffer. "It would appear that my dear friend has lost the will to live."

"What?" whispered my sister.

"He has refused to allow me to either to locate or to remove the bullet lodged in his side," explained Sir Walter.

"But he can't—you can't—" Mick couldn't finish her sentence. She crinkled her face like she was trying not to cry.

"Nor does he wish to cause more pain for any of us," said Sir Walter. "You, least of all, *Mademoiselle* Mackenzie."

This made my sister lose it, and tears spilled down her face.

"It appears that we are at an impasse," said Sir Walter, pulling hard on his goatee.

Mick was a total wreck. I mean, it's not like her temper hadn't taken her places in the past that she regretted, but her attack on Pfeffer was pretty much the worst thing she'd ever done. When you beat up on a guy who's trying to save the world, you're going to feel some guilt. More than anything, she wanted the chance to apologize face-to-face.

Sam insisted this was impossible. She kept going on about what Pfeffer's color looked like just before she and Sir Walter rippled him to safety, so we were all pretty sure that bringing him back solid would be a death sentence.

"I'm sorry," I said, "But I don't get it—why he's just giving up. We've got the password, we know where the Angels are, we're all alive, and we're going to figure out a way to save the world. So what's Pfeff's problem?"

The French gentleman rose and began pacing. "He has done things in the past two years which he regrets greatly."

"He saved us all," said Mick, sniffling and twisting a ratty-looking tissue.

"He did," said Sir Walter, "But he also feels the weight of those who have perished these past three days. It is a burden from which he does not know how to release himself. Do you recall, Will, the payment entries he was making in Rome, the day we visited his office?"

"Yeah," I said.

"He made a habit of deleting zeroes from some payments, such that certain properties were *not* acquired by Helmann for the placement of the sleeping Angels."

"That's great," I said.

Sir Walter frowned. "I agree, and he did other things as well to hinder Helmann's efforts. But Pfeffer finds it difficult to let go of the guilt he feels that *some* buildings were acquired. That *some* of the sleepers were awakened and have carried out their deadly task."

I made a small noise in the back of my throat. "That's crazy."

Sam, at my side, held my hand so tightly. "It's not crazy, Will. Guilt has its own rationale." She slipped her hand from mine and stood. "I need to speak with him."

Chapter Forty-Six

SPACE OF FORGIVENESS

• SAM •

Approaching the empty space where Professor Pfeffer lay, I rippled to make sure Pfeffer could hear what I had to say. Once I was invisible, I placed myself beside him and brought an insubstantial hand to his hidden shoulder.

Professor? Can you hear me? I waited for what seemed a long time. Just as I was about to try sending written words instead, Pfeffer replied.

I am here, he said.

We all wish you would let Sir Walter heal you. Or allow us to take you to a hospital. I hesitated. *Mickie feels terrible for hitting you and for the things she said and thought about you. She's tormented, not being able to ask your forgiveness.*

Tell her she has my forgiveness, he said. *If it is of any value.*

Of course it's valuable, I said. I hesitated and then launched into the conversation I really wanted to have. *There are few things of more worth than true forgiveness. My step-mother taught me . . . she taught me forgiveness is one of the greatest acts of love we can offer to another. Or to ourselves.*

Someday you will understand that there are acts which cannot be forgiven, said Pfeffer. *Some errors are too grave.*

I don't believe that, I said.

You are young, child.

I gathered my courage in a tight bundle, pressing it to my heart as I told him how my mother and my childhood best friend had died because of something I'd done. I told him how I'd carried the weight of that guilt for years. How it had bent my soul until I didn't know how to move without it pressing upon me.

Pfeffer spoke when I had finished. *Child, the fault was not yours. You were simply in the wrong place at the wrong time.*

I know that now, I said. *But at first, I couldn't see that clearly any more than you can see things clearly at the moment.* I hesitated, but then pushed forward. *I understand now that my mother would have died regardless. I realize that there is a difference between intending a thing to happen and causing it to happen.*

I felt Pfeffer's laughter, harsh. *So you think that I was simply in the wrong place at the wrong time.*

No, I said. *You were in the right place. Pfeffer, everything you have done for two years and more has cleared the way for saving billions of lives.*

Samantha, my actions—my direct actions—have cost thousands their lives, he said.

I felt the weight of his guilt. *And that is where you and I have lived the same tale. Those thousands would have died regardless. Just as my mother would have died regardless. In both cases, the deaths would have happened because Helmann intended them. If you had not caused them, he would have made certain that someone else did. Can you not find a space within yourself, a space where forgiveness is possible?*

We sat in silence. I sensed the conflict within him.

Words fell away and I experienced instead the emotions he felt. Anguish. Grief. Blame.

His thoughts came to me in the merest whisper: *This space . . . perhaps it exists.*

Then let us go seek it out, I said. And it was as if I took his hand and walked forward with him. Together we leaned into the imagined space of forgiveness, wondering how much of a load it would support. Like children pushing into a strong wind, we angled and canted and found it each time strong enough to bear the weight of all we had been and all we had done and all we had become.

Pfeffer wept. And I wept. And we clung to one another until at last, he let go of blame, of guilt, of loathing and there was just Pfeffer and he just . . . was.

I rose and returned to Sir Walter and the others, solidifying.

"He'll let you heal him, now," I said to the French gentleman.

Chapter Forty-Seven

SAVING THE WORLD

• SAM •

Sir Walter was able to work the bullet free and Pfeffer rested through the night, recovering from wounds physical and mental. I stayed at his side, invisible, in case he needed someone.

At some point in the dark hours before dawn, Pfeffer rippled invisible.

Samantha? he called.

I'm here, I replied. *Um, I hate to mention it, because you're probably in a lot of pain, but Sir Walter did recommend staying solid so that you could heal.*

The pain is unimportant, said Pfeffer. *I can bear that well enough. But if I am invisible, I can show Sir Walter more quickly what must be done to stop Helmann's mad apocalypse. It preys upon my mind, each hour that is lost while I lay here.*

I hesitated. I knew he'd heal faster if he could complete this penance, this act of reparation. *Okay*, I said.

I awoke Sir Walter and together we watched and listened invisibly as Pfeffer unveiled Helmann's plan.

Pfeffer described how his father had placed cadres of five upon the top floor of buildings throughout the world, in areas where he wished to decimate populations quickly. We heard the insanity of it all: how Helmann would first leak information to news agencies of supposed victims of a rare and deadly disease; how Geneses' Angel Corps would then offer vaccinations to the population; how the inoculations themselves would accomplish the millions of deaths; how Geneses "wouldn't give up, even in the face of such ravaging disease"; how the world would praise Geneses and the Angel Corps for their dedication.

The operation was to last eighteen months and accomplish the deaths of five billion souls. Supposed cures would be discovered along the way, but the cures would only work on the so-called "racially-pure," by which means Helmann intended to demonstrate the superiority of some races over others, as well as to spread fear of those races that didn't respond to the "cure." As governments faced economic and social disaster of unprecedented proportion, Helmann would be ready to step in, setting up puppet dictatorships and maintaining order through force.

An especially cruel twist in all this was that the members of the Angel Corps would actually believe they were doing good. None of them had been informed as to the deadly nature of the supposed-vaccines. In fact, in order to calm detractors—people like my dad who leapt to the true conclusion—several Angels had recently inoculated themselves. When they died, the imaginary plague was blamed, not the vaccinations. Because who would knowingly inoculate themselves with something deadly?

All this, and more, Pfeffer swiftly passed to us. What would have taken hours to describe aloud, he accomplished in mere minutes. He then shared an idea for halting the deadly Angels. After that, he slipped back inside his body, grimacing, and he rested.

As dawn approached, Sir Walter woke Christian, Will, and Mickie and laid out Pfeffer's plan.

"Pfeffer believes that the black book which he stole should be used as a means of persuasion," said Sir Walter. "But not for the government officials whom I sought to influence. No, the black book will mean most to those other children of Helmann—the Angel Corps —who will recognize both the man and his methodologies in the journal. When they see what monstrosities he was capable of, it is Pfeffer's belief that they will cease their attempts at inoculating populations.

"They have been raised to value compassion without making distinction among races, as it would not have served Helmann's purposes for them to share his prejudices before his planned apocalypse."

"The Angels will be left rudderless," said Mickie. "This will challenge all they've believed, to learn they were meant to kill and not save lives."

"Indeed," said Sir Walter.

"Pfeffer can help them learn to forgive themselves," I said. "I'm sure he could."

Sir Walter nodded. "Your idea has great merit," he said. "When I rescued him from Helmann's abandoned complex at the close of World War II, it took years for him to readjust to his new picture of the world."

"I will do it," said Pfeffer's soft voice, startling all of us with his appearance. "But first, you must allow me to come with you and speak with the Angels you awaken today."

We turned, startled by his sudden appearance.

"My friend," began Sir Walter, "You must heal."

"I'm well enough," said Pfeffer. "I can stay invisible for much of the time. But I must be allowed to speak to the first cadres you approach."

"If you're invisible for long stretches," said Mickie, "You won't have a chance to heal." Tentatively, she placed a gentle hand on his shoulder.

"My dear," he said, shaking his head slightly, "The type of healing which I require can be accomplished best if I accompany you."

Mickie's eyes drifted to Will. "I don't get to go," she said, her voice low. "Someone has to stay with Will, and I can't ripple like the rest of you."

"I'll stay," I said.

I didn't need to be invisible to feel the emotions rolling off of Mickie. She was in anguish, torn between the need to care for her little brother and an incredible desire to get out there and undo Helmann's work.

"I don't even want to go," I said. "I've spent enough time with Helmann's sons and daughters to last me several lifetimes."

"I want Sam," said Will to his sister, "Not you." He smiled at Mickie as he said it.

And she smiled back.

By late that morning, plans were agreed upon and Pfeffer, Mickie, Christian, and Sir Walter departed for one of Helmann's Angel Corps buildings in a Jewish neighborhood of Rouen. I wanted to spend every minute talking to Will, but Pfeffer had said Will needed rest and gave him a mild sedative before they left. Will fell asleep in minutes, and I must have needed sleep as well. I drifted off and only awoke when Sir Walter's party returned, marching noisily up the marble staircase.

330

As they entered the great hall, I shuddered. Someone who looked very much like Hans had replaced Christian at Sir Walter's side.

"Allow me to present Günter," said Sir Walter. "He's agreed to speak to officials in the French government about the imminent threat to public health."

"Where's Christian?" I asked, panic slipping into my voice.

"Where's Pfeffer?" asked Will, waking beside me.

"They are quite well, quite well," said Sir Walter, smiling broadly. "They've chosen to travel with the others—ah, let me see if I can remember—with Georg, Hansel, Martina, and Friedrich, that is, in order to inform cadres in Clichy-sous-Bois and Lyons as to the true nature of Dr. Girard's intentions."

"It's working, then," murmured Will.

"Thank God," I said.

"Quite so," said Sir Walter. "And we must depart for Paris. *Mademoiselle* Mackenzie, I wonder if you would accompany me, and Günter, as an expert witness?"

"Expert?" she asked.

"We will be explaining certain technicalities as to the unique abilities of Helmann's children," said Sir Walter. "I believe you were Pfeffer's best pupil?"

"*Only* pupil," said Will, punching his sister's shoulder.

Mickie flushed bright pink. "Of course I'll help," she said.

Mickie hugged her brother and then turned to me, telling me to keep him in line.

"Absolutely," I said.

Chapter Forty-Eight

YOU'RE MY AFRICA

• SAM •

I felt remarkably awake and well as they departed, leaving us alone before a roaring fire.

"I don't think I'll need to sleep again for a long time," said Will, yawning.

I smiled. "That's nice, considering it's just us."

I drifted closer to Will, feeling the tiniest bit shy, but mostly feeling like I needed to kiss him before another minute passed.

His mouth felt hungry against mine. I liked it. And then I liked it too much. I'd forgotten how Will's kisses made me ripple.

Will leaned back, away from the icy air that was me, sighing.

I brought myself back solid. "So, um, about the vanishing-when-we-kiss?"

Will turned his dark eyes to meet mine. "Yeah?"

"Christian gave me some hope on that one."

"Hope? Hope, how?" asked Will.

The look on his face, doubtful, confused me.

"Hope, like, 'hopeful,'" I said. "What other variety of hope is there?"

He looked down at his shirt, picking at a loose thread. "Sam, Chrétien's the one you asked about first when Sir Walter returned just now. Is Chrétien . . . is he in love with you? Did he kiss you? Do you like him?"

"No! And no, and no!" I said, trying not to laugh. "If I liked him, would I do this?" I pressed my mouth over Will's. His lips tasted good. Not food-good, just Will-good. I sighed as I felt my skin disappear.

"I don't know," said Will, to empty air. "Geez, Sam. He's taller than me. He's faster than me—" I interrupted Will, coming solid. He shook his head, continuing. "He's way politer than me and richer than me and he's a freaking *de Rochefort*. What's not to like?"

"Hmmm," I said, tracing my finger along Will's collar-bone, where it pushed out against his shirt. "He's got a lot going for him when you put it like that. Really only one major drawback." I rested my palm against Will's chest, just over his heart.

His eyes flicked down to my hand. "What's that?" he whispered, voice low and throaty.

I leaned in, resting my forehead against his chin, inhaling the scent of him: rich, warm. With my free hand, I reached for a handful of his curls, weaving them through my fingers. My voice came out a bare whisper. "He's not you."

And this time when he kissed me, I tried so hard to stay solid, but his hair tangling in my hand was soft and his mouth on mine was sweet, and after a moment, I melted away.

"Sam," he whispered to the thin air that was me.

I returned solid.

"What?"

"I missed you so bad," he said.

"Me? The Incredible Vanishing Girlfriend?" I asked, smiling. "Hey, that can be my secret super-hero identity."

Will laughed. "Sam, do you have any idea how badass you looked the other day with a gun in each hand?"

"Seriously?"

"You were like . . . the *Saminator*. Only way hot," he said, eyes wide with admiration.

"Well, I hope you enjoyed it, because that's the last time I ever plan on holding a firearm," I said. Then I punched his shoulder. "Boys."

"I'm just calling it how I saw it," Will said, shrugging. "So tell me this hopeful news about kissing. The news that doesn't involve you and Chrétien together."

"Okay, so, Christian told me this heartbreaking part of Sir Walter's life story. He and Elisabeth were madly in love."

"Like, Elisabeth de Rochefort? Mrs. Helmann?" asked Will.

"Yeah," I said. "But Elisabeth and Sir Walter thought they couldn't ever have kids if they got married, because, well, because she always rippled when they kissed. And having heirs was a big deal in the 1300's. So she married Helmann in order to have a child and keep the family estate together."

"Sorry," said Will, "But I'm totally missing the hopeful here."

"I know!" I said. "Isn't it awful? I mean, I guess Helmann wasn't as completely Voldemort-ish back then, but she married him and not Sir Walter because of . . . well, their little problem . . ."

"Idiots," murmured Will. He tucked a hair behind my ear.

"No," I said, shaking my head, "It's tragic."

The hair slipped loose again and Will reached for it. This time his hand lingered, tracing my ear, running along my jaw line.

"Do you want to hear the rest?" I asked, my voice rasping, "Because that is seriously sexy, and I'm about to vanish."

Will dropped his hand, leaned away. "I want to hear. Absolutely. There is nothing I want more than to hear the rest of this completely ridiculous tragedy."

I frowned at him. "You're hopeless. Anyway, so a couple of hundred years later, after Elisabeth had died, Sir Walter met this husband and wife who were both ripplers and who told him if they'd just stuck it out— Sir Walter and Elisabeth—then Elisabeth would have eventually been able to . . . you know . . . stay solid. When they . . . kissed."

Will flushed and I realized my face felt hot, too.

"Well, okay," he said. "I think that sounds very hopeful."

I smiled.

"But, Sam?" His dark eyes got large and earnest. "I'd stay with you anyway. I *will* stay with you either way." He lowered his eyes and voice. "You're more than just your body to me. I love you. Invisible. Solid. Whatever."

Which led to quite a lot more kissing and equal amounts of me vanishing. Finally we lay still and solid, just grateful to be together. The fire now burned low in the enormous hearth and we murmured together about what we could see in the glowing embers.

Then Will kissed me softly and said he had something for me. He reached into his jacket pocket.

"I've kept it with me," he explained, "Ever since Christmas, which is what I bought it for, except when I showed it to Mick, she was all, *no way are you giving that to a girl*, and then I forgot about it until after you'd already gone through security at the airport."

I remembered the sick feeling in my stomach as I'd walked away from Will that day. "I'm never leaving you again," I said. "You're my Africa, Will."

He looked at me curiously. "I'm your *what?*"

"You're the shape I fit into. Like South America fit into Africa before the continental drift."

Will guffawed. "Right then. We're putting a stop to any further drift."

"Exactly," I said.

Smiling, he handed me a box. Small. Unwrapped. Made of shiny white cardboard that had been creased from sitting for months in his pocket.

"I hope you like it," he murmured.

Curious, I lifted the lid. Nestled inside, on a cottony bed, sat a twist of silver fashioned into a willow leaf that curled back around on itself. It was a ring.

I stared at its perfect replication of the leaves I knew so well from back home. From mornings spent with Will running at my side. *Swish, swish, swish* as we passed the stand of willow trees.

"Do you like it?" he asked.

I could hear the worry in his voice.

"Mick said I had no business giving a ring to a girl who was just my friend, and that's all we were on Christmas, but now, I thought—"

I stopped his mouth with mine, pulling back just before I started rippling.

"It's perfect," I murmured.

"Really? Because I could get you something else. Yesterday was Valentine's. I could get, you know, chocolate or whatever."

"Yesterday was Valentine's Day?" I asked.

"Uh-huh," he said. "We were a little busy."

"Then we have lost time to make up for," I said.

I kissed him again, a tiny hush of a kiss.

"And Will? About the ring? I love it."

"You do?"

I smiled. "I do."

THE END

Acknowledgements

Many people have contributed to make this book, and this series, a possibility. In addition to those I have acknowledged in earlier books, I am grateful to Natalie, Susan, Chelsea, Araina, and Kris, and to Sarah and the Women's Night Out Book Group in Eugene, Oregon. Your passion for my stories has been very heartwarming!

To my teen groupies, Rachael, Kate, Isabel, Toby, Misha, and Madeleine: your enthusiasm has meant more than you'll ever know. Thanks for loving Sam+Will.

I'm grateful to Chris and Jacob, who, between them, make my book readable and pretty when combined with the artistry of Claudia at phatpuppyart.com.

An additional thank you to my family members for putting up with me as I burned dinners, forgot to pick you up from events, and otherwise put mothering off to one side in order to talk with my imaginary friends. You are all way more supportive and wonderful than I deserve.

Author's Notes

Regarding Catholicism: I am not myself Catholic. When I was little, I was so jealous of the Silva kids down the street who got to go to catechism class. They explained it was like school. I loved school. It was unfair that they got EXTRA SCHOOL and I didn't! Perhaps all the research I've done this past year in regard to being Catholic has been a way of making up for missing catechism. All that to say, any errors of commission or omission regarding Catholicism are unintentional and are mine alone.

If you are interested in the grim history of the Eugenics movement in the United States during the early twentieth century, a quick internet search will provide ample returns upon the subject.

To cheer yourself up after, I recommend spending some time viewing Chagall's paintings, mosaics, and glass-work. His autobiography also makes fascinating reading.

Occitan is a real language, little spoken today, but full of pithy and droll sayings. Rippler's Syndrome, on the other hand, is not a real disease, to the best of my knowledge.

Thanks for giving *Unfurl* a read; I hope you enjoyed it! If you have a moment, you can spread the word.

Review it. Tell others why you liked this story-- even a line or two helps other people decide if it's for them or not.

Tell me about your review, too. Email me at cidneyswanson@gmail.com*

Sign up for Cidney Swanson's New Releases email list on www.cidneyswanson.blogspot.com and you will be the first to know when a new book comes out.

*I love getting notes from readers and I always respond!

Thank you!

Find Cidney Online!

www.cidneyswanson.blogspot.com
https://www.facebook.com/cidneyswanson
http://twitter.com/#!/cidneyswanson
Goodreads: http://www.goodreads.com/search?
query=cidney+swanson
Librarything:
http://www.librarything.com/author/swansoncidney
Email: cidneyswanson@gmail.com

28943719R00203

Made in the USA
Lexington, KY
09 January 2014